ICE

ICE

SARAH BETH DURST

MARGARET K. McELDERRY BOOKS

New York   London   Toronto   Sydney

MARGARET K. McELDERRY BOOKS
An imprint of Simon & Schuster Children's Publishing Division
1230 Avenue of the Americas, New York, New York 10020
MARGARET K. McELDERRY BOOKS is a trademark of Simon & Schuster, Inc.
For information about special discounts for bulk purchases, please contact
Simon & Schuster Special Sales at 1-866-506-1949
or business@simonandschuster.com.
The Simon & Schuster Speakers Bureau can bring authors to your live
event. For more information or to book an event, contact the
Simon & Schuster Speakers Bureau at 1-866-248-3049
or visit our website at www.simonspeakers.com.
Book design by Debra Sfetsios
The text for this book is set in Bauer Bodoni.
Manufactured in the United States of America
2 4 6 8 10 9 7 5 3 1
Library of Congress Cataloging-in-Publication Data
Durst, Sarah Beth.
Ice / Sarah Beth Durst.—1st ed.
p. cm.
Summary: A modern-day retelling of "East o' the Sun, West o' the Moon"
in which eighteen-year-old Cassie learns that her grandmother's fairy tale is
true when a Polar Bear King comes to claim her for his bride and she must
decide whether to go with him and save her long-lost mother, or continue
helping her father with his research.
ISBN 978-1-4169-8643-0 (hardcover : alk. paper)
ISBN 978-1-4169-9689-7 (eBook)
[1. Fairy tales. 2. Polar bears—Fiction. 3. Supernatural—Fiction.
4. Scientists—Fiction. 5. Arctic regions—Fiction.] I. East of the sun and
west of the moon. II. Title.
PZ8.D972Ice 2009
[Fic]—dc22
2009008618

❄

For my husband, Adam,

with love.

I would go east of the sun and west of the moon for you.

ACKNOWLEDGMENTS

I'D LIKE TO THANK the polar bears, arctic foxes, and caribou for their patience and kind words of encouragement during the writing of this book. I'd also like to thank my spectacular agent, Andrea Somberg, and my fabulous editor, Karen Wojtyla, as well as Sarah Payne, Emily Fabre, and all the other amazing people at Simon & Schuster. Special thanks as well to Tamora Pierce, Bruce Coville, and Thomas (Sully) Sullivan for all their advice and kindness.

Also, thanks to my friends for believing in me, especially Amy Johnson and Rick Keuler for all their encouraging e-mails, and thank you to everyone who answered my obscure research questions. Thank you as well to John Mastrobattista, Rob Harris, and my Target/Blackbaud team (past and present) for all their support.

And finally, many thanks and much love to my family. I am so lucky to have all of you in my life—the family I was born into, the family I married into, my wonderful children, and my dream-come-true husband. I love you all beyond the ends of the earth.

PROLOGUE

The North Wind's Daughter

ONCE UPON A TIME, the North Wind said to the Polar Bear King, 'Steal me a daughter, and when she grows, she will be your bride.'"

Four-year-old Cassie clutched her quilt and stared at her grandmother. Tall and straight, Gram looked like a general. She perched stiffly on the edge of Cassie's bed. She had a mahogany cane in her left hand. Tonight, Dad was away from the station, which meant Cassie would hear the story. Gram never told it when Dad was home. It was the only story she ever told.

"And so, the Polar Bear King kidnapped a human child and brought her to the North Wind, and she was raised with the North Wind as her father and the West, South, and East Winds as her uncles. She grew into a beautiful, but lonely, young woman. One day, while the Winds were gone (as they often were), she met a human man. She befriended him, and it wasn't long before they fell in love.

"When the Polar Bear King came to claim his bride, she refused him. Her heart, she said, belonged to another. 'I would not have an unwilling wife,' he told her. 'But your father has made a promise to me.'

"Knowing the power of a magic promise, the North Wind's daughter sought to counter it with her own bargain. 'Then I will make a promise to you,' the North Wind's daughter replied. 'Bring me to my love and hide us from my father, and when I have a daughter, she will be your bride.' And so, the Bear carried the North Wind's daughter to her human husband and hid them in the ice and snow.

"Angry, the North Wind tore across the land, sea, and sky. But he could not find them. For a long while, the North Wind's daughter and her husband were happy.

"In time, the woman had a child. Passing by, the West Wind heard the birth and hurried to tell the North Wind where his daughter could be found. With the strength of a thousand blizzards, the North Wind swooped down onto the house that held his daughter, her husband, and their newborn baby. He would have torn the house to shreds, but the woman ran outside. 'Take me,' she cried, 'but leave my loved ones alone!'

"The North Wind blew her as far as he could—as far as the castle beyond the ends of the world. There, she fell to the ground and was captured by trolls." Cassie heard the bed creak as Gram stood. Her rich voice was softer now. "It is said that when the wind howls from the north, it is for his lost daughter."

Cassie blinked her eyes open. "And Mommy is still there?"

Gram was a shadow in the doorway. "Yes."

PART ONE

The Land of the Midnight Sun

ONE

ONCE UPON A TIME, in a land far to the north,
there lived a lovely maiden . . .

Latitude 72° 13' 30" N
Longitude 152° 06' 52" W
Altitude 3 ft.

CASSIE KILLED THE SNOWMOBILE ENGINE.

Total silence, her favorite sound. Ice crystals spun in
the Arctic air. Sparkling in the predawn light, they looked
like diamond dust. Beneath her ice-encrusted face mask,
she smiled. She loved this: just her, the ice, and the bear.

"Don't move," she whispered at the polar bear.

Cassie felt behind her and unhooked the rifle. Placid as
a marble statue, the polar bear did not move. She loaded
the tranquilizer dart by feel, her eyes never leaving the
bear. White on white in an alcove of ice, he looked like
a king on a throne. For an instant, Cassie imagined she
could hear Gram's voice, telling the story of the Polar Bear
King. . . . Gram hadn't told that story since the day she'd
left the research station, but Cassie still remembered every

word of it. She used to believe it was true.

When she was little, Cassie used to stage practice rescue missions outside of Dad's Arctic research station. She'd pile old snowmobile parts and broken generators to make the trolls' castle, and then she'd scale the castle walls and tie up the "trolls" (old clothes stuffed with pillows) with climbing ropes. Once, Dad had caught her on the station roof with skis strapped to her feet, ready to ski beyond the ends of the earth to save her mom. He'd taken away Cassie's skis and had forbidden Gram from telling the story. Not that that had slowed Cassie at all. She'd simply begged Gram to tell the story when Dad was away, and she'd invented a new game involving a canvas sail and an unused sled. Even after she'd understood the truth—that Gram's story was merely a pretty way to say her mother had died—she'd continued to play the games.

Now I don't need games, she thought with a grin. She snapped the syringe into place and lifted the gun up to her shoulder. And this bear, she thought, didn't need any kid's bedtime story to make him magnificent. He was as perfect as a textbook illustration: cream-colored with healthy musculature and no battle scars. If her estimates were correct, he'd be the largest polar bear on record. And she was the one who had found him.

Cassie cocked the tranquilizer gun, and the polar bear turned his head to look directly at her. She held her breath and didn't move. Wind whistled, and loose snow swirled between her and the bear. Her heart thudded in her ears so loudly that she was certain he could hear it. This was it—the end of the chase. When she'd begun this chase, the aurora borealis had been dancing in the sky. She'd tracked him in its light for three miles north of the station. Loose sea ice had jostled at the shore, but she'd driven over it and then onto the pack ice. She'd followed him all the way here, to a jumble of ice blocks that looked like a minia-ture mountain range. She had no idea how he'd stayed so far ahead of her during the chase. Top speed for an adult male bear clocked at thirty miles per hour, and she'd run her snowmobile at sixty. Maybe the tracks hadn't been as fresh as they'd looked, or maybe she'd discovered some kind of superfast bear. She grinned at the ridiculousness of that idea. Regardless of the explanation, the tracks had led her here to this beautiful, majestic, perfect bear. She'd won.

A moment later, the bear looked away across the frozen sea.

"You're mine," she whispered as she sighted down the barrel.

And the polar bear stepped *into the ice*. In one fluid motion, he rose and moved backward. It looked as if he were stepping into a cloud. His hind legs vanished into whiteness, and then his torso.

Impossible.

She lowered the gun and stared. She couldn't be seeing this. The ice wall appeared to be absorbing him. Now only his shoulders and head were visible.

ICE

Cassie shook herself. He was escaping! Never mind how. Lifting the gun, she squeezed the trigger. The recoil bashed the butt of the gun into her shoulder. Reflexively, she blinked.

And the bear was gone.

"No," she said out loud. She'd had him! What had happened? Bears didn't—couldn't—walk through ice. She had to have imagined it. Some trick of the Arctic air. She whipped off her goggles. Cold squeezed her eyeballs, and the white was blinding. She scanned the frozen waves. Snow blew across the ice like fast-moving clouds. The landscape was as dead as a desert. When the cold hurt too much for her to stand it a second longer, she replaced her goggles.

Her radio crackled. She pulled it out of her parka pocket. "Cassie here," she said, trying to sound casual. She'd chased the bear onto the pack ice without backup. If she'd caught him, all would have been forgiven. But now . . . How was she going to explain this? She couldn't even explain it to herself.

"*Cassandra Elizabeth Dasent, get home NOW.*"

Dad's voice. And he was not happy.

Well, she wasn't happy either. She'd promised herself that she'd tag a bear as a birthday present to herself—she was turning eighteen in just a few hours. It seemed the ideal way for the only daughter of the head scientist at the Eastern Beaufort Sea Research Station to celebrate becoming a legal adult. When this bear had sauntered past the station while she'd been out fixing the radio antennae, it had felt like a gift. She'd never expected the chase to lead her so far out onto the ice, and she'd never expected the bear to . . . He couldn't have gone far. He had to be somewhere just beyond the ice ridges. She checked the gas gauge. She had another three hours of fuel to spare.

"Cassie? Cassie, are you there?"

"I'm going after him," she said into the radio. She revved the engine, drowning her father's response, and headed across the ice.

❄ ❄ ❄ ❄ ❄

Cassie abandoned the snowmobile in the shed. Slinging her pack over her shoulder, she trudged to the station. She ached from head to toe, inside and out. Even her fingernails ached. The sun hovered on the horizon, as it would for less and less time every day before it sank permanently for the winter. The low-angled light made her shadow look like a snow giant out of an Inuit legend.

She'd lost him.

She didn't know how, but she'd lost him. She kept replaying the search in her mind as if that would make her envision the tracks she must have missed. If she'd just searched more carefully in the first few moments instead of speeding across the sea ice . . .

Owen, the station lab technician, met her at the door. She blinked at him—a potbellied man with a pepper beard. Clearly, he'd been waiting for her.

"Cassie, the case!" Owen cried in an anguished voice.

She glanced at her pack. The syringe case dangled out

of the bag. It was encrusted in ice. Cassie winced. "He got away," she said.

Owen rescued the bag and gun from her. "Do you know how much these cost?"

Cassie followed him inside through the double door entryway. As she shut the inner door behind her, the thick, sour warmth of the station rolled over her like a smothering wave. It was the smell of home, stale and stifling and comfortingly familiar. She wished she had been coming home victorious.

Clucking over the tranquilizer gun, Owen said, "You have to be careful with this equipment. Treat it like a baby."

Her stomach sank as she watched him examine her equipment. She didn't need another strike against her. She'd taken the snowmobile out onto the pack ice alone *and* she'd been careless with equipment. Dad was not going to be pleased. Peeling off her outer layers, she asked, "Where is he? Radar room?" She'd better get it over with. There was no point in delaying.

Owen didn't respond. He was absorbed in cleaning the tranq gun. She could tell he'd already dismissed her from his mind. She almost smiled. He loved his equipment like she loved the pack ice. Both of them were a bit . . . single-minded. She could admit that about herself. "Jeremy?" she said. The new research intern looked up from his desk.

"He's not a happy camper," Jeremy confirmed. "He wants to talk to you." He nodded toward the research lab door. "You're welcome to hide here," he added helpfully, pointing under his desk.

She managed a grin. Jeremy had been blasted by Dad his first week at the station for going out on the ice without the proper gear, and now he had a healthy respect for Cassie's father's temper. Of course, in that case, he had deserved it. She didn't care if he was from UCLA—what breed of idiot went out on the ice without a face mask? You'd never catch her making that kind of newbie mistake. *No*, she thought, *I specialize in the more spectacular mistakes, such as misplacing a full-grown polar bear.*

Cassie pushed through the door to the research lab. She scooted between the boxes and equipment. She could hear Dad's voice, deep and clipped, inside the radar room. Ugh, this was not going to go well. Here in the faintly sour warmth of home, it was going to sound like she was quoting Gram's old fairy tale about the Polar Bear King. What seemed almost believable out on the sea ice seemed patently unreal here, back in the prosaic old station. Here, it seemed far more plausible that she'd imagined the bear walking through ice. She wished she'd imagined losing him.

In the radar room, Dad was in his typical position, half-perched on a stool, flanked by two other researchers. Cassie halted just inside the doorway, watching them. Her father was like the sun. People tended to orbit around him without even realizing they were. Scott and Liam were his most common satellites. She wondered if that was how she

ICE

looked next to him—overshadowed and small. Not liking that thought, Cassie stepped farther into the room.

The door swung shut behind her, and Dad looked up at the sound. He lowered his clipboard. His face was impassive, but she knew he was furious. She steeled herself. She'd deliver her report as professionally as possible. How he reacted would be his choice.

Scott flashed a smile at her. "Ah, the little workaholic."

"Could you gentlemen excuse us?" Dad said to Scott and Liam. "Family discussion." Oh, that was not a good sign. She swallowed hard.

Cassie wondered, not for the first time, if her mother hadn't died, would that have softened Dad? Would she have been able to talk to him without feeling like she was approaching a mountain? So much could have been different if her mother had lived.

The two scientists looked from father to daughter, as if suddenly noticing the tension that was thick enough to inhale. Both of them bolted.

For a long moment, Dad didn't speak. His expression was unreadable. His eyes were buried underneath thick, white eyebrows. His mouth was hidden in a mountain-man beard. Six-foot-five, he looked impervious. Cassie raised her chin and met his eyes.

Finally, he said, "You know better than to go out on the pack ice without backup. I raised you to be smarter than this."

Yes, he had. One thing he'd always made sure of was that

she knew the rules of the ice. Everything else in her childhood he may have left to others. With her mother dead soon after Cassie was born and Gram gone from the station when Cassie was five, she'd done a lot of her own raising—with only a sort of tag-team parenting from Dad, Max, Owen, and whoever else was passing through the research station. But he had made sure that she knew what to do when she stepped outside the station, and she was grateful for that. "I know," she said.

"You could have fallen into a crevasse," he said. "A pressure ridge could have collapsed. A lead could have split the ice, and you could have driven directly into ocean water."

"I know," she repeated. What else could she say? She wasn't going to make excuses. Maybe she would have a few years ago, but she wasn't a kid anymore. If she expected to be treated as a professional, she knew she had to act like one.

He continued to scowl at her.

Cassie felt her face redden, but she forced herself not to look away. She refused to be intimidated by him.

Dad sighed. "Report," he said.

"There's something unusual about this bear." Taking a deep breath, Cassie plunged into a description of how she had tracked him and how he had walked into the ice. She told Dad about searching the pressure ridge and failing to find tracks leading out of it. She told him how she had searched the surrounding area, crossing miles of pack ice, with no further sign of the bear. Finishing, she braced herself, waiting for Dad to tear apart her report.

Instead, she saw the anger drain out of her father's face. He dropped his clipboard to the table, and he hugged her. "I could have lost you," he said.

This was new. "Dad," she said, squirming. Anger she had expected, but hugs? They were not a hugging family. "Dad, please, I'm fine. I know what I'm doing. You don't have to worry."

Dad released her. He was shaking his head. "I should have known this day would come," he said. "Your grandmother was right."

Awkwardly, she patted his shoulder. "I'll bring backup next time," she promised. "I'll catch the bear. You'll see."

He didn't appear to be listening. "It's too late for application deadlines for this year, but some of my friends at the University of Alaska owe me favors. You can work in one of their labs and apply for undergrad next year."

Whoa—*what?* They'd agreed she would take courses remotely. She wasn't leaving the station. "Dad . . ."

"You can live with your grandmother in Fairbanks. She'll be thrilled to say, 'I told you so.' She's been pushing for this since you were five, but I selfishly wanted you here," he said. "I'll contact Max to fly you there."

She stared at him. "But I don't want to leave," she said. She loved it at the station! Her life was here. She wanted— no, *needed*—to be near the ice.

He focused on her, as if seeing her afresh. "You're leaving," he said, steel back in his voice. "I'm sorry, Cassie, but this is for your own good."

"You can't simply decide that—"

"If your mother were here, she would want this."

Cassie felt as if she'd been punched in her gut. He knew full well how Cassie felt about her mother, how much she wished she were here, how much she wished she'd known her. To use that as a weapon to win an argument . . . It was a low blow. Cassie shook her head as if she could shake out his words. "I'm not leaving," she said. "This is my *home.*"

Her father—who shied away from feelings so much that he had delegated her childhood to her grandmother and had left her puberty to a stack of bio textbooks—her father had tears in his eyes. "Not anymore," he said softly. "It can't be anymore."

TWO

Latitude 70° 49' 23" N
Longitude 152° 29' 25" W
Altitude 10 ft.

CASSIE BLINKED AT HER CLOCK: THREE A.M.

What were they *doing*? It sounded as if the whole station staff were stomping around outside her door. She could have sworn she'd even heard a plane engine. She tossed off her covers and raked her fingers through her hair. She knew she looked like a redheaded Medusa, and she was sure she had bags under her eyes the size of golf balls. She was wearing long johns, mismatched socks, and an oversize T-shirt that read: ALASKA—WHERE MEN ARE MEN AND WOMEN WIN THE IDITAROD. Cassie yanked on pants and a sweater over her long johns and T-shirt before she stuck her head out her door. She spotted Owen scurrying down the hallway. "Hey," she called to him. "It's three a.m." She nearly added, *And it's my birthday.*

"Max's plane is here," Owen said. "Just landed. We'd have had more warning if you had fixed the antennae instead of going off to chase trouble."

She winced. She deserved that. After all, she'd wrecked his equipment. His crankiness was justified. But what did he mean that Max's plane was here? Max wasn't scheduled for a visit. . . . Oh.

He'd come for Cassie.

Her heart sank. How had Dad convinced him to come so fast? Before the budget cuts, Max had been on the station's staff. He'd flown his Twin Otter for them when Cassie was little; he'd been her earliest babysitter, practically an uncle to her—but now he worked for a commercial runway in Fairbanks. He couldn't take off on zero notice. She hadn't imagined Dad would call for him immediately.

Cassie brushed past Owen and headed for the research lab. She had to put a stop to this right now. She had to talk sense into Dad and convince Max to return to Fairbanks without her.

Before Cassie reached the lab door, she heard boxes scrape across linoleum, and the door flew open. "Cassie-lassie!" Max bellowed. He strode down the hall and scooped her up into a bear hug. He swung her in a half circle, then thumped her shoulder blades as if he were burping her as he set her down. "Did you find the Abominable Snowman?" he asked, their old routine.

"Stuffed and mounted," she said, on cue. He grinned at her, his white teeth startlingly bright against his dark skin.

She automatically grinned back. She'd forgotten how much she'd missed seeing him.

Maybe this is a normal visit, Cassie thought as Max beamed at her. *Maybe it's unrelated to my argument with Dad. Maybe it's just a coincidence.*

And maybe there really is an Abominable Snowman. She shook her head at herself. Max wasn't here by coincidence, not within mere hours of Dad's pronouncement. She shouldn't bother trying to fool herself.

"Got a surprise for you," Max said.

"Yeah?" He hadn't said it like it was a bad surprise, but her stomach knotted as if it knew this couldn't be good.

Cassie heard a familiar tap from the doorway—a cane. Gram. Max had brought Gram. Cassie wished she could be happy. She hadn't seen her grandmother in months, and now she was here. Ordinarily, this would have been a wonderful surprise: Max and Gram, her two favorite people in the world, were here. But now she was going to have to tell her grandmother face-to-face that she didn't want to live with her in Fairbanks.

She shouldn't have told Dad about the bear walking into the ice. If she had simply left that detail out of her report . . .

Gram hit her mahogany cane sharply on the floor. "I haven't shriveled to nothing. Come hug me." She held out her arms.

Forcing herself to smile, Cassie bounded the remaining steps to the lab door. She wrapped her grandmother in her arms. It was like holding a bird. Gram was almost as tall as Cassie, but her bones were tiny. She felt breakable. Cassie released her quickly.

"You've grown," Gram said.

"You've shrunk," Cassie responded automatically.

Gram frowned and shook her head. Like Cassie, she had a fierce frown. Both of them had strong faces, but Gram's skin hung loose over hers, and her hair, once as thick and red as Cassie's, rustled like an old curtain. "Nonsense. I'm as beautiful as the day your grandfather met me. First time in the back of his pickup, do you know what he said? 'Ingrid,' he said. 'Ingrid, God himself could not have more perfect breasts than you.'"

Cassie couldn't help laughing. "I've missed you."

"Oh, my Cassandra." She hooked her arm around Cassie's waist. "Let me look at you. So grown-up. Such a fine young woman now."

Cassie swallowed a sudden lump in her throat. "Gram . . . ," she began. She stopped. How did she say this without hurting Gram's feelings? The last thing in the world she wanted to do was hurt her grandmother. "How . . . How was your flight?"

"Idiotic FCC almost didn't let us lift up," Max said. "No Fed can tell *me* how to fly safe. Thirty years flying in the bush, and I can smell ice. It's not like flying in the lower forty-eight. . . ."

Only half-listening to Max's rant, Cassie watched her grandmother's face and tried to read what she was thinking. "Gram, what did Dad tell you?"

Max fell silent.

Gram plucked lint from Cassie's wool sweater. For as long as Cassie could remember, Gram was always tidying. Gram herself was as neat as a soldier. Her white shirt was pressed with a crease down the sleeves. She looked her neatest when she was most upset. She was looking very neat now. "Ah, my Cassandra." Gram adjusted Cassie's sweater, and then she took Cassie's face in both her hands. Gram kissed her left cheek, and then her right cheek, an oddly formal gesture. Cassie pulled back. "Gram, what is it?"

"You found him," Gram said. "You found the Polar Bear King."

Cassie flinched as if she'd been slapped. Of all the things she'd been expecting Gram to say, that wasn't one of them. "That's not funny."

"I wasn't joking," Gram said.

"Did Dad tell you I also saw Elvis?" Cassie said. "Oh, yes, the King's taken up dog mushing. Saw him last week racing the Easter Bunny and the Tooth Fairy."

Gram gripped Cassie's shoulders. "Cassandra . . ."

Dad had told them . . . what? She'd been hallucinating? She was crazy? *That* was how he had convinced Max and Gram to drop everything and fly here?

Max inched backward down the hallway. "I'll just . . . let you two talk. . . . Yeah. Takeoff will be at six a.m. Um, happy birthday, by the way." He fled through the lab door.

Some birthday. Why was everyone she loved and trusted acting crazy? First Dad, and now Gram. . . . Gram steered

Cassie away from the lab door. "Come, let's go to your room," Gram said. "This isn't a public conversation."

Yes, that was a good idea. She'd talk to Gram alone—find out what was really behind all this. There had to be an explanation for Dad's uncharacteristic overreaction. Cassie managed a smile and tried for normalcy: "My room isn't exactly Gram-ready."

"I'll be the judge of that," Gram said.

Cassie banged her hip on her bedroom door, and it popped open. Socks spilled into the hall. She kicked them out of the way and switched on the bedroom light. Long johns were draped over the dresser. Her bivy sack was wound around the bed frame. On her pillow, Mr. Fluffy, her old stuffed fox with the chewed ear, sported a roll of duct tape around his neck. Gram surveyed the wreckage. "Mmm," Gram said. "You didn't make your bed."

"You can see the bed?"

Using her cane, Gram picked her way over a nest of climbing ropes. She scooted a heap of maps off the bed and onto the floor and spread the comforter. "Fix your side, dear."

Cassie really didn't want to talk about the state of her room. She was sorry she'd mentioned it. "Gram . . . ," Cassie began.

"Dear?" Gram repeated, more steel in her voice.

Cassie knew her: Gram wasn't going to talk until the bed was made. Dad had learned his implacable resolve from her. Sighing, Cassie tugged the comforter straight. "Tuck in the corner," Gram said. Cassie obeyed. "Very nice," Gram said. "Now, fetch your bag, dear. We need to get you packed."

"Gram . . . It's not that I don't want to live with you. I just don't want to live in Fairbanks. I want to stay here."

"You'll need sweaters and underwear." Gram plucked a backpack out of the mess. She laid it open on the bed.

Stay calm, Cassie told herself. *This is Gram.* Cassie continued in a reasonable tone, "It's prime season—bears are migrating back onto the sea ice. I'm needed here."

Gram poked her cane into Cassie's closet. "Clean or dirty?" She extracted a wool sweater and sniffed it. "You need to take better care of your clothes."

"Gram, talk to me," she pleaded.

Gram handed Cassie three sweaters. "Fold."

Cassie dumped the sweaters onto her bed. Gram gave her a look, and then neatly folded the sweaters and placed them inside the backpack. Cassie fished them out again and tossed them back into the closet.

"Don't be difficult," Gram said. She fetched the sweaters. "Your father worries. He has always worried, the stubborn fool." Gram refolded the sweaters. "He wanted to shield you. He thought ignorance would protect you . . . but that's an old argument, and the point is moot now. The important thing is to get you to Fairbanks. I'll explain everything once you're safely there."

Cassie felt a chill. She didn't need protection from a fairy tale. There was no Polar Bear King. What was Gram hiding behind this ridiculous lie? "Gram, what 'everything'?"

"You aren't going to make this easy, are you?" Gram said.

No, of course she wasn't. Gram was asking her to leave her life, her home, her career, and her future. "What aren't you telling me?" Cassie asked.

Gram sighed. "Oh, my Cassandra, he should have told you the truth a long time ago. He only wanted to protect you. We both only wanted to protect you. We merely disagreed on the best approach." She sounded tired. Old and tired. Cassie had never heard Gram sound like that.

"What truth?" Cassie asked.

Gram sat on the edge of Cassie's bed like she used to when she'd tuck Cassie in at night. Gram held one of Cassie's sweaters on her lap. "Your mother," Gram said gently, "was the daughter of the North Wind. She bargained with the Polar Bear King, and now, on your eighteenth birthday, he's coming for you."

Cassie heard a roaring in her ears as her pulse pounded. Her mother, the daughter of the *wind*? That was only a story.

"You know it's true," Gram said. "You've seen him."

She'd seen a bear, larger than any on record, who'd walked into solid ice. But that didn't mean . . . Cassie shook her head. Why was Gram doing this? It wasn't funny. Teasing her about the Polar Bear King, teasing her about her mother . . . It was cruel. "Don't do this," Cassie said.

"Cassandra, it is true," Gram said. "You know I left the station because your father and I had a disagreement. This was what we fought about. I believed you should have been told the truth."

Gram's expression was grave. Her eyes were kind and serious. Her hands were nervously flattening the sweater on her lap. Cassie stared at her. For a brief, marvelous, crazy instant, Cassie thought, *What if* . . .

But no, it wasn't true. Her mother had died in a blizzard shortly after Cassie was born. She wasn't at some troll castle. If she were . . . If she were, if there were even a *possibility* that Gram's story were true and her mother was a prisoner somewhere, then Dad would have rescued her. Cassie wouldn't have had to grow up feeling like she was missing a slice of herself.

"You need time to think," Gram said kindly. "I understand. It's a lot all at once." She patted Cassie's shoulder. "You rest. We'll leave in a few hours."

Before Cassie could object again, Gram left her alone.

Cassie tossed her backpack into the closet and deposited the sweaters onto her dresser. Why had Dad and Gram invented this lie? They'd never lied to her before. But they were either lying to her now or . . .

Cassie blinked fast. Her eyes felt hot as she stared at her bed. Years ago, Gram used to sit there, a profile in the dark. Her voice, telling the story, was as familiar as a heartbeat. She'd told it every time Dad had been away from the station. Cassie had always thought that was because Dad had disapproved of fairy tales. His idea of a bedtime story was Shackleton's journey to Antarctica. Now she was supposed to believe he'd objected to Gram telling her the truth?

She wished she'd caught that bear. If she had, they could've run tests on him, taken a blood sample, even tagged him with an ID and tracked his movements. She could have proved he was ordinary.

Maybe she still could. If she called their bluff, they'd have no excuse to force her to Fairbanks.

Without waiting for second thoughts, Cassie tiptoed out into the hall and then cut through the research lab. The fluorescents were off, but the computer screens glowed green. She heard hushed voices from the direction of the kitchen. If she were quick enough, no one would even notice she had left her room. She exited the lab, closing the door softly behind her, and then flicked on the light of the main room.

Someone stirred. "Whaa . . ."

Cassie froze. It was Jeremy. He'd fallen asleep at his desk again. "Go back to sleep," she whispered.

"Mmmuph," he said, closing his eyes.

She held her breath. He was the newbie—the *cheechako*, to use Max's native Inupiaq. Dad and Gram wouldn't have told him anything, she assured herself. If she acted normal, he wouldn't be alarmed, and he wouldn't fetch her father. She moved slowly to her desk and pulled on her Gore-Tex pants. The pants rustled, and Jeremy's eyes popped open again.

Jeremy peered at her blearily. "Where are you going?"

"Repair work," she lied. "Nothing to worry about." She

shoved her feet into her mukluks and secured her gaiters over them.

"Don't know how you can stand it out there," Jeremy said. "It's a wasteland. An ice desert. At least you're getting out, eh?"

Her fingers faltered as she fixed her face mask. "Who told you that?" she asked, trying to keep her voice calm and casual. She pulled the hood up over two wool hats— almost ready. She felt as if her insides were shouting, *Hurry, hurry!*

"That plane guy, Max, said you were going to under-grad."

"Max talks too much," she said. "I'm not going any-where." She Velcroed the throat gusset of her hood shut and then fetched her emergency kit. The small pack held a flashlight, her ice axe, extra flannels, and a few food rations. With this, she could search the pack ice for several days, if that's what it would take.

"Just because this is all you know, it doesn't mean this is all there is," he said. "Don't you want a normal life? You've never lived outside this station. You've been homeschooled your entire life. Don't you want to get out there, meet kids your age, do what normal people do?"

She loved the ice. She loved tracking bears. "This is home," she said shortly.

"I thought this would be my home. Coming here was my dream, you know, for years. But now . . . Hey, whatever, dreams change. Nothing wrong with that. I'm applying for a nice, cozy postdoc back at UCLA."

"Good for you," she said. Her dreams weren't changing. Nothing and no one—Dad, Gram, Max—could force her to leave her life here. "I'll just be a minute," she said as she opened the inner door and shut it behind her.

For a brief second, she debated staying inside and trying to talk sense into Dad and Gram, but words had failed to convince them before. *No*, she thought, *if I don't act now, I'll be on a plane to Fairbanks in three hours.* She couldn't let that happen. She opened the outer door and stepped out into the Arctic.

Cold seared into her, slicing her, and her face mask instantly frosted. She took a deep breath of night air. It felt brittle and sharp in her throat, as if the air were filled with shards of glass. This was exactly what she needed to clear her mind. The piercingly cold air soothed her, as it always did.

Standing within the station floodlights, she faced out toward the blue darkness. Silence surrounded her. "Polar Bear King!" she shouted into the silence. "I'm coming to find you! Do you hear me?"

She waited for a moment, listening. Snow drifted over her feet. Rubbing frost from her goggles, she scanned the darkened ice fields. Wind blew surface snow over the moonlit snowbanks and ridges. Blue shadows oscillated over the ice.

Cassie shook herself. She hadn't honestly expected the so-called Polar Bear King to answer, had she? That was crazy. *Kinnaq*, she remembered—that was the Inupiaq word for lunatic.

Just because she had let her overtiredness make her (for an instant) want to believe in a magical polar bear, that did not mean she was snow-crazed. Just because she'd wanted Gram's story to be real and her mother to be alive, it didn't make her crazy. She'd find that bear and prove to Gram, Dad, and herself that he was ordinary. Cassie marched toward the shed with the snowmobiles—

—and a shadow rose over her.

Towering over her, the bear was immense. He blotted out the stars. In the station light his fur was luminescent, his silhouette glowing as if he were some Inuit spirit-god, Mashkuapeu himself. Suddenly, the Arctic didn't feel big enough. It collapsed down to just her and the polar bear.

He opened his jaws, and she glimpsed white canines and a black tongue. A massive paw came down toward her, and she dodged. Out of the corner of her eye, she saw a glint drop from the polar bear's claws. As the glint hit the snow, the bear twisted, dropped to four paws, and retreated to the edge of the station floodlights.

Cassie looked down at her feet, at the snow where the bear had stood. Dusting snow blew into the concave curves of his tracks. In the curve of a paw-print lay a silver needle with an orange tail, the tranquilizer dart.

THREE

Latitude 70° 49' 23" N
Longitude 152° 29' 25" W
Altitude 10 ft.

SHE WAS ONLY A FEW YARDS FROM THE DOOR. If she
lunged, she could be safely inside with solid metal between
her and the bear. But she had called to him, and he had
come. The tranquilizer dart that she had shot on the sea
ice now lay in front of her. Impossibly, inexplicably, the
bear had brought it back to her. She felt light-headed, and
she knew she was shaking. She raised her eyes to look at
the bear.

He was a mass of shadows at the edge of the station
floodlights. She could make out the shape of his muzzle
and the hunch of his shoulders. "Cassandra Dasent," he
said. His voice was a soft rumble.

She felt as if her heart had stopped beating.

He spoke.

ICE

It was hard to breathe, and she felt dizzy. He'd said her name. She was certain she'd heard him say her name. But real polar bears did not speak. They couldn't. Their mouths weren't shaped for it.

"I will not hurt you," he said.

He didn't have the right vocal cords. His muzzle couldn't move like lips. His tongue couldn't form words. "Polar bears don't talk," she said flatly. "You aren't real."

"Do not be afraid," he said. He stepped into the circle of light from the station floodlights, and she automatically took a step backward. Her heart thudded faster as he came toward her. His paws were silent on the ice.

"Wake up," she whispered to herself. "Snap out of it." Cassie dug her fingernails into her palm inside her glove. It hurt, but she didn't wake, and the bear didn't disappear.

He halted directly in front of her. Up close, she could see he was huge. His shoulders were even with hers, and his muzzle . . . On four paws, he was as tall as she was. They were eye to eye. "You're a hallucination," she said. Her voice sounded thin and weak to her ears. "A mirage, a sun dog."

"No. I am not."

She flinched as she felt his breath hot on her frozen face mask. Oh, God, that felt real. That could not have been her imagination. "I don't believe in talking bears," she said—a whisper.

"You are Gail's daughter," he said. His voice was soft, gentle even.

"You're a scientific impossibility," she said. She could not be seeing this, hearing this. The universe had rules, and they did not allow for talking bears, especially talking bears who knew her mother's name. She swallowed. No one had ever referred to her like that, as her mother's daughter.

"You called to me," he said softly, inexorably. "I have watched you for a long time, waiting until you were no longer a child, waiting until you knew me. A few hours ago, you did not know me, but now you called to me. Your family told you who I am?" It was a question. She almost missed it, caught in the slow rhythm of his voice.

"They told me fairy tales," she said. She thought of Gram: *Once upon a time, the North Wind said to the Polar Bear King* . . . Fairy tales and lies. But which was the lie?

"Believe them, beloved."

Beloved?

"No," she said. No, she wouldn't listen to this. She wouldn't believe. Believing meant Dad had lied to her. Believing meant her mother had bartered her off before she'd been born.

But believing also meant her mother hadn't died in the storm that had flattened houses in Barrow, Alaska, and buried half of Prudhoe Bay.

"Doubt your family, then, but believe your own eyes and ears."

Her eyes told her he was an *Ursus maritimus;* her ears told her he was talking. Cassie squeezed her eyes shut. "You don't exist." She was deluding herself. Her senses were betraying her and making her believe something she'd given up believing more than a decade ago: that her mother was still alive. Cassie opened her eyes. The bear was still there.

"I am the polar bear," he said, "and you are my bride."

"No," she said—no to him, no to this, no to everything.

His expression was unreadable. "Your mother made a promise."

This was cruel. Simply cruel. "My mother is dead. Killed in a blizzard after I was born." She felt her heart twist as she said it.

There was silence for a moment. Snow swirled around them—around Cassie and the giant polar bear—like in a snow globe. "Is that what you want?" the bear asked.

So softly that her voice barely carried beyond her face mask, she said, "No, of course not." All her life, she'd wanted a mother. It was a hole inside her that nothing had ever filled. Not Dad. Not Gram. Not Max. Not any of the station staff who had come and gone.

"The North Wind did not kill her. He blew her to the trolls. For that, he has never forgiven himself." The polar bear's voice was a low rumble that rattled in her bones. Part of her wanted more than anything else to believe him. But she couldn't let herself. Fact was fact; gone was gone. It didn't matter how badly she wished it weren't. "And I regret that the Winds found her, despite my best efforts."

"Your best wasn't good enough," she said. She knew the

words of the story: *Bring me to my love and hide us from my father.* If the story was true, then this polar bear had failed Cassie's mother. If he'd done what he'd promised, Cassie would have had a mother.

"I did all I could."

"Your promise is invalid," she said. "You've no right to be here."

"The promise holds," he said in the same calm, impossible voice. "The North Wind would not have found her if it were not for his brother."

He talked about the winds as if they were sentient. She squeezed her eyes shut. "You should have hidden her from him, too," she said. "You failed."

"I cannot leave the Arctic. I have responsibilities that I could not neglect," he said. "I had to hide her in the ice. I am sorry." For the first time, she heard a hint of emotion. That was almost as disturbing as the speech itself. He believed what he was saying. He believed her mother was alive.

"'Sorry' doesn't help," she said. She tried to sound strong, but her voice betrayed her and cracked. Her heart beat so fast and loud that it thundered in her ears.

"If I could make it right, I would."

Would he? Could he? "Would you free her from the 'trolls'?"

His great jaws opened and shut, as if she had struck him speechless. She nearly smiled—she had flummoxed him. She'd turned the tables on the creature that was turning her world upside down. "You do not know what you are asking," he said finally.

Oh, yes, she knew very well what she was asking: an impossibility. "Bring my mother back from the dead." She felt light-headed as she said it.

"She is not dead."

"That should make it easier."

"I have responsibilities that I cannot risk."

Without stopping to think, she said, "You free her from the trolls and I will marry you."

For a long moment, he was silent. The northern lights filled the sky behind him. With his brilliant white coat and black unreadable eyes, he looked majestic and wild. Wind stirred his fur. "Is that a promise?" he asked at last.

Suddenly, it didn't seem like a dream. It didn't seem like a hallucination. It seemed real, overwhelmingly real. She put her hand on the station wall to steady herself. Her fingers were numb inside her mittens and gloves, and she felt her disbelief cracking as if her words had shattered it. Her mother . . . *My mother is alive?* And she had the opportunity to save her. Her head reeled. "Yes," she said.

"Climb onto my back," he said, kneeling in front of her.

She stared at him as the word "yes" rang in her head. Yes, she'd said. Yes, her mother was alive. Yes, Cassie would save her.

"I will carry you home," he said.

She tried to read his inscrutable black eyes and failed.

Her throat felt dry. She started to speak, swallowed, and then tried again. "Home?"

He inclined his massive head, and she shivered. "Your mother will be returned to the Arctic once our bargain is complete," he said. "I will arrange it after we arrive."

Wind whipped into her. Ice crystals pelted her parka. Gulping in burning air, she tried to nod as if she understood.

"Climb onto my back," he repeated.

If her mother was alive, then she had been a prisoner for years and no one had rescued her. Dad had not rescued her. Dad had pretended she'd died. He'd kept this all a secret from Cassie.

Suddenly, she wanted to climb onto the bear's back and ride as far away from the station as she could. She put her hand on his back and swung her leg over. She steadied herself. Oh, God, she was on a polar bear.

"Hold tight, beloved," he said.

She gripped the bear's neck fur as he carried her away from the only place she'd ever called home.

FOUR

Latitude 76° 03' 42" N
Longitude 150° 59' 11" W
Altitude 5 ft.

THE BEAR BOUNDED THROUGH THE SNOW. Cassie clutched his thick fur and clenched her teeth as the impact jarred her bones. Snow spewed out in waves.

"Are you afraid?" the bear shouted to her.

"Like hell I am."

"Keep tight hold of my fur, and then there is no danger," he said.

Impossibly, he increased speed. Blurring into white, the frozen sea rushed beneath them. She squeezed her eyes shut, and then opened them. *Don't think about the bear,* she repeated to herself. *Just focus on the ride.*

The bear raced across the ice. Shadows streaked. Stars stretched into the comet tails of time-lapse photography. Faster and faster. She felt like she was flying. She was moving faster than a snowmobile, faster than Max's Twin Otter. Wind buffeted her face mask, and she laughed out loud. She wanted to shout at the top of her lungs, *Look at me! I'm faster than wind! Than sound! Than light!* She felt as if she *were* light. She was an aurora streaking across the Arctic.

He ran on and on.

Eventually, as the stars faded and the sky lightened, she fell into a numb rhythm. Her pack bounced, bruising her shoulders rhythmically. She rode in silence, except for the harsh whistle of wind.

Several long hours later, Cassie heard ice crunch under the bear's paws. Granules crackled in the monumental Arctic silence. She straightened and thumped her muscle-sore thighs. The bear had slowed and was simply walking now, across the shimmering frozen sea. The earth was painted in white and blue streaks of ice, reflecting the sky and the low, pale sun.

Squirming inside her parka, Cassie fished her GPS out of her inner pocket. She pressed the on button, and the signal flashed. She moved it back and forth, trying to get a clear reading. The longitude fluctuated wildly: 0° to 180°, as if she were at the North Pole. Worse, the latitude said 91°. This reading didn't make sense. There couldn't be a satellite over a location that didn't exist. She shook the GPS, but the abnormal reading stayed. Cassie stared at it, and her heart started to thump faster. Either the GPS was malfunctioning or . . .

ICE

Or here was empirical proof that the impossible was real.

Cassie leaned forward and cleared her throat. "Excuse me. . . . Um, where are we?"

"One mile north of the North Pole," he said.

Obviously, the GPS was broken, and the bear was wrong. Or lying. But she didn't need either the GPS or the bear. She knew at least a half dozen low-tech ways to find south. All she needed to do was head in that direction, and she'd find the station. Everything was under control. She might be deep in the ice pack, but she was alive and well. She wasn't even cold.

She should have been cold. Her breath was condensing into crystals on the rim of her hood, but she felt hot. Her armpits were damp, and her neck itched from the many layers. It didn't make sense. The air had to be cold enough for five-minute frostbite. It was even cold enough for a fata morgana. Dead ahead was the most magnificent example of the Arctic air's mirages that Cassie had ever seen.

Cassie squinted at the castle as the bear carried her toward it. She'd never seen such a beautiful mirage. Spires soared above her. They shimmered in the bending light. At the tips of the spires, the ice curled into the semblance of banners, frozen midwave. She waited for it to shrink to its normal proportions: an ordinary ridge or an outcrop of ice that had been stretched by a trick of the light.

But it did not shrink or stretch. It shone like a jewel in the sunlight. Cassie felt her gut tighten. It had to be an iceberg frozen in the pack ice—it was as white as a moonstone, while the sea ice encircling it was a brilliant turquoise—but she had never heard of an iceberg in such old ice, except near Ellesmere, on the opposite side of Canada. She studied the GPS, which continued to display its nonsensical reading. Even at the phenomenal speed the bear had traveled, she could not have crossed the thirteen hundred miles to the North Pole. . . . Could she have?

No. It simply wasn't possible. There had to be another explanation, a rational and scientific explanation. She slid the GPS back into her parka.

Looking up again, she saw a blue wall of ice around an opalescent castle. "Oh," she said faintly. It was not a fata morgana. She tilted her head to see the banner-crowned spires that rose behind the wall.

"Welcome to my castle," the bear said.

There couldn't be a castle in the Arctic. The whole expanse had been covered by satellite photography. Someone would have seen a castle.

It was, she thought, beyond beautiful.

The polar bear brought her through an archway of blue ice into the castle grounds. Ornate turrets and overhanging arches glittered above her. Before her, a great door, a twenty-foot crystal lattice, tinkled like a thousand champagne flutes clinking in a toast as it swung open. The bear carried her inside.

Inside . . . took her breath away. She was inside a rainbow. Chandeliers of a million shards of ice danced colors over the foyer. Ice frescoes covered the walls, swirling with sapphire and emerald reflections. Frozen ruby red roses wound up columns. GPS forgotten, impossibility forgotten, Cassie lowered her face mask and pushed back her hood. Strangely, her cheeks stayed warm. Lifting her goggles, she squinted at the sparkles. She had never seen anything so magnificent. Her imagination could not have created this. She slid off the bear's back and walked over to the wall. It was too vivid, too detailed to be a hallucination. She reached toward it and stopped an inch away.

What if it *wasn't* real?

"Are you going to free my mother now?" she asked.

The bear was behind her. "Once we have made our vows, I will see to it," he said. "I cannot contact the trolls directly—they are beyond my region—but I will send word with the wind."

She couldn't tear her eyes from the rainbowed ice wall. "Vows?" she said.

"Do you, Cassandra Dasent, swear by the sun and the moon, the sea and the sky, the earth and the ice, to be my beloved wife from now until your soul leaves your body?"

Until my soul leaves my body. Until death, he meant. His beloved wife until death. Cassie swallowed hard. "Is this . . . Is this how we complete the bargain?"

"Yes," he said.

He said it so matter-of-factly. Yes, this will fulfill the bargain. Yes, this will bring your mother back to life.

Cassie took a deep breath and laid her mittened hand on

the ice wall. It felt solid and real. All at once, she couldn't help but believe: Her mother was alive and about to be rescued. All she had to do was say the word. So simple, so easy. "All right. I do."

"You must say the vows back to me now," he said.

Somehow, that seemed worse. She couldn't really marry him. Years from now, she was supposed to marry some researcher, some scientist who loved the Arctic as much as she did. She sometimes daydreamed about starting her own research station, where she and her future husband would lead expeditions together. Or maybe she wouldn't marry at all. Like Gram, she'd be an old lady with a dozen suitors. Regardless, she was *not* supposed to marry a talking bear.

But it wasn't a real wedding. It was only words. She didn't have to mean them. She just had to say them, and she would accomplish what no one else—her father, her grandmother, no one—had been able to accomplish: She'd bring her mother back! "Do you . . ." She halted. "What's your name?" She turned to look at him. His massive head was inches from her shoulder. Instinctively, she flinched. She couldn't do this. He was . . . She didn't know what he was: magic or monster, predator or rescuer.

"You may call me Bear," he said.

"Bear," she repeated. She was marrying a creature simply called Bear to save a woman she'd never known.

That was the crux of it: a woman she had never known. Cassie had never known her mother. All she had to do was say a few words, and she could change that. Her mother would live again.

Looking into his black eyes, she began. "Do you, Bear, swear by the sun and the moon . . ." After this was done, she would demand to go back. He didn't want an unwilling wife. She knew Gram's story. He'd said so himself to her mother, *I would not have an unwilling wife.* He wouldn't refuse Cassie. She'd divorce him as quickly as she'd married him. "The sea and the sky . . ." She *could* divorce him, right? Her voice faltered. She felt a roaring in her ears.

"The earth and the ice," he prompted.

"The earth and the ice," Cassie said. It was almost done. What did it mean to marry the Polar Bear King? Her eyes flicked to the door—the crystal lattice shimmered like a thousand stars in a net—and then back to the bear.

"To be my beloved husband from now until your soul leaves your body," he encouraged her.

"And you'll bring back my mother?" she said.

"Yes," he said. "Our vows are void if I fail."

Cassie closed her eyes. She had to do it for her four-year-old self, who had believed with all her heart that her mommy was in a troll castle. "Fine. Let's finish this. To be my beloved husband from now until your soul leaves your body?"

"I do," he said.

She thought she heard a sound like a bell, but she didn't hear it in her ears. She heard it inside, as if it were resonating in her rib cage. Her knees wobbled.

"Do not be afraid," he said softly. "As long as these walls are standing, nothing here will harm you."

Eyes closed, she tried to breathe. It felt as if there weren't enough oxygen.

"Come," he said.

Cassie opened her eyes to see the bear walking down the shimmering hallway. For a second, she didn't move. She looked back over her shoulder at the outside world, and then she took a deep breath and followed the bear.

The corridor widened into a golden and glowing banquet hall. The faceted walls glittered so brightly with candlelight from the chandeliers that Cassie saw sparkles when she blinked. Translucent, the cathedral ceiling glowed like stained glass. She looked around her in wonder. Carved birds and animals decorated the walls and ceilings. Buttresses arched over statues. A banquet table stretched the length of the hall with thronelike ice chairs on either end. It looked like . . . She tried to think of places to compare it to, and failed. It was as if every beautiful ray of light, every beautiful shape of ice that she had ever seen, were here all at once.

"We have had a long journey," the bear said, suddenly behind her. Startled, she spun to face him. "You must wish to eat."

When she turned back to the banquet hall, the vast table that had waited in silent splendor now overflowed with food. Fruit cascaded from ice crystal bowls. Steam rose from blue-white dishes. Breads were piled in pyramids. She

ICE

breathed in a hundred spices. "I don't understand," she said. She saw no waiter and no chefs—nothing to explain the sudden appearance of a feast.

"It is food," he said gently. "You eat it."

As if to demonstrate, the polar bear swallowed an entire loaf of bread. She shook her head. The act was so incongruous with his fierce appearance. "Bears don't eat bread," she said. "You're a carnivore."

"We all have flaws," he said.

Was that a joke? Did he have a sense of humor? She stared at him. "This can't be real," she said.

He nosed a throne. "Please. It is yours."

Backing away, he let her approach it. Her throne. Taking off her mittens and gloves, she touched the curled arms of the ice throne. "It's not cold," she said. It was an ice castle. Either she should have been cold, or the ice should have been melting. But she was as warm as she would have been inside the station. "Nothing even drips."

"It cannot melt," he said. "Not so long as I am here. I will not allow it to melt."

She jerked her hand back. "What do you mean 'allow it'?" she said. "Ice doesn't ask permission."

"It is part of being a *munaqsri*," he said.

"Moon-awk-sree," she repeated. It sounded Inupiaq.

"Yes," he said.

"Your word for 'talking bear'?" she asked.

"It means 'guardian,'" he said. "We are the caretakers of souls. Every living thing needs a soul, and everything that dies gives up a soul. Munaqsri are the ones who transfer and transport those souls."

Cassie stared at him again.

"Altering molecules. That is one of the . . . 'powers,' for lack of a better word, that nature has given us so that we can fulfill our role," he said. "On the ice, I use it to reach my bears. Here, I use it for the shape of my home, the food on the table, the warmth in your body."

She felt as if she were spinning in a centrifuge, dizzy with the sparkling light of the chandeliers, the smells of spices, and the strangeness of the bear's words. "You transfer souls," she repeated. "Others like you—other munaqsri—transfer souls."

"We are the unseen way that life continues," he said.

"Scientists should have seen you," she objected. "How can you be . . . transferring souls . . . and no one has noticed? How can you be here in a castle and no one has noticed? How can you be a talking bear—" She stopped when she heard her voice crack.

"People have seen us before," he said. "Munaqsri sightings have inspired many stories. Have you heard stories of werewolves and mermaids? Sedna and Grandmother Toad? Horus and Sekhmet?"

"Stories, not science," Cassie said. Like the story of the Polar Bear King and the North Wind's daughter.

"You are correct. The stories are not accurate," he said. "Sedna, for instance, appears in stories as a mermaid goddess, but in truth she is the senior munaqsri of the Arctic

Ocean. She oversees all of the munaqsri in that region, like the Winds oversee the munaqsri of the air." He paused. "Your family has explained none of this?"

"There's no such thing as mermaids," she said. "And I don't believe in magic." She knew as she said it that it was a ridiculous thing to say. She was talking to a bear in his magical castle in a part of the Arctic that could not exist.

"We are not magic," he said. "We are part of nature. We are . . . the mechanism by which life continues. Everything we do—transform matter, move at high speeds, sense impending births and deaths—is part of nature's design to enable us to transfer souls from the dying to the newborn."

"I don't believe in souls," she said as firmly as she could. "A brain is a collection of chemical reactions. Complex neurochemicals."

"As you wish," he said mildly.

She wished she were home where she belonged and where things made sense. Or did they make sense only because Dad and Gram had lied to her? Would the world still make sense after she met her mother?

When she didn't touch the food, the polar bear barked at the table, and the dishes melted. Pooling into colored water, they spread across the table to form a lacy tablecloth. Breads and soups disappeared like bubbles popping. Cassie backed away.

"Come," the bear said. "You must be weary after our long journey. I will show you to the bedroom. Perhaps you should rest while I arrange for your mother's release."

She couldn't imagine sleeping now, here. But she followed the bear out of the bright splendor of the banquet hall into the blue silence, deeper into the castle. She clung to his words like a lifeline: *arrange for your mother's release.*

The bear's paws were soundless on the ice. Silence wrapped around her as the hallway narrowed and the castle darkened. In the shadows, the bear loomed impossibly huge.

Candlelight danced across animal faces on golden walls. Blank, icy eyes stared at Cassie. She shrank back from them. All her instincts screamed at her to run back into the light. Deep blue, the ice surrounded her. She felt entombed. Was this how her mother felt in the troll castle? *She fell to the ground and was captured by trolls.* Cassie tried to picture her mother in a castle, and failed. What had her mother's life been like? What was *her mother* like? Cassie wished she could remember her. She would be as much a stranger as . . . as the bear. Suddenly, the idea of meeting her mother was terrifying.

The bear halted at the foot of a staircase. Amber candle-light licked his fur. His eyes were inscrutable shadows. He seemed feral in the darkness. "You will find the bedroom at the top of the stairs," he said. "You may wish to bring a candle."

She fetched a candle from a wall sconce. Even the wax was ice, and like everything else, it wasn't cold.

He rumbled, "I hope that you will be happy here."

ICE

She didn't intend to stay long enough to be happy or unhappy. Just long enough to ensure her mother was free, and then she would demand that the bear return her. But for now, she said nothing. She simply clutched the candle and stared at him.

He retreated into the blue shadows, and then she was alone. She lifted the candle higher so that the light fell shimmering onto the stairs. "Just until she's free," Cassie whispered. And then she shivered, even though it wasn't cold.

FIVE

Latitude 91° 00' 00" N
Longitude indeterminate
Altitude 15 ft.

AS THE BEAR HAD SAID, Cassie found a bedroom at the top of the stairs. She pushed open the door, a thick slab of opaque turquoise ice. She held the candle inside.

"Oh, wow," she said.

Everything looked as if it were doused in diamonds: wardrobe, washbasin, table, bed. The canopy bed arched fifteen feet into the air and was made of shimmering ice roses, interwoven like lace. Posts at each of the four corners were carved like narwhal tusks. Cassie touched one of the smooth curves. Like all the ice in the castle, it felt as warm and dry as wood. On the bed itself, feather mattresses were heaped as high as her waist, and pillows were stacked as high as her neck.

Coming inside, she put the candle on a bedside table.

She shed her pack and opened the wardrobe. A nightshirt fluttered from a single hanger. Cassie fingered the silk. Was it for her? Why would the bear want her to wear . . . She pushed the thought aside and closed the wardrobe.

She sat on the edge of the bed and thought of Gram's story, the only link to her mother that she truly had. *Once upon a time* . . . All she knew of her mother was a fairy tale.

She leaned back into the pillows and tried to imagine her mother, the daughter of the North Wind. Without intending to, she fell asleep. She dreamed of a dark-haired woman and a polar bear bargaining in the snow-swirled Arctic. When Cassie looked closer, she saw the woman had her own face.

Several minutes or hours later, Cassie woke in darkness to a scraping sound. Automatically reaching for her bedside light, she remembered in the same instant that she was not home in her bed, she had no matches for the candle, and her flashlight was in her supply pack. She shot bolt upright. "Who's there?" she asked. Her ears strained, listening.

She heard nothing.

The bear had told her that nothing within these walls would harm her. Could she trust him? "Overactive imagination," she told herself. She lay back against the pillows.

She felt the mattress sink beside her.

Yanking the sheet, she leaped out of bed. "Get out!"

"Do not be alarmed," a voice said. She didn't recognize the voice. It was male.

Dammit, she should have found her flashlight when she'd first woke! Her heart pounded as she backed to the wall. Inching along it, she crept toward her pack. She rounded the washbasin, and a hand touched her arm. She elbowed backward with all her strength. She felt him double over. "Don't touch me," she said.

"I will not hurt you," he puffed.

She kept moving toward her pack. Where was it? She had thought it was this corner. Her foot hit something solid—the pack. "One scream and you'll have a thirteen-foot predator at your throat," she warned him. Feeling for the pack, she knelt. Where was the bear? Why had he let this stranger in here? It occurred to her that she knew very little about why the bear wanted her here.

"Do not be afraid, beloved," he said. "It is our wedding night."

Oh, God. "You are not a polar bear," Cassie said. "I didn't marry you." She loosened the top flap of the pack.

"I am Bear."

"He's much furrier. Less human." Unsnapping the buckles on her pack, her hand brushed across wood. *Better than a flashlight*, she thought. She grinned wolfishly as she pulled the ice axe out of its loop. She gripped the handle and stood. "Do I look like an idiot?"

"You look beautiful, even with an axe."

He could see her in the dark? She tightened her grip. Her heart thudded, but she kept her voice steady. "Just evening the odds."

"You can trust me. I am not your enemy. In your heart, you know that."

"One step closer and I swear I'll swing."

He put his hand on her shoulder. "I do not believe you will."

Cassie swung.

She felt a rush of air—he'd leaped backward.

"Out," she said. Brandishing the axe, she advanced on him in the darkness. She heard him retreat. She heard the door open and shut. Her heart beating in her throat and her breath quick, she did not lower the axe. Her hands were sweating, and Cassie realized to her horror and embarrassment that she was crying.

SIX

Latitude 91° 00' 00" N
Longitude indeterminate
Altitude 15 ft.

CASSIE WOKE GOOSE-BUMP-COATED. "Stupid heaters," she muttered. She bet Owen was tinkering with his moth-eaten computer instead of fixing the heaters. "Owen!" she called. She flung up an arm and thumped the wall. It felt smooth and chilled, and that jolted her into alertness. She wasn't in the station, she remembered, and Owen couldn't hear her.

She snapped upright and fumbled for her flashlight. She'd left it on the nightstand after evicting her unwelcome visitor. Her heart pounded so hard that her hands shook as she turned the flashlight on.

Cassie swept the light's beam across the room. The light danced over the ice. Carvings of seabirds glistened on the wardrobe, as if the birds had frozen midflight. She'd used the wardrobe to block the door. It had worked. She was safely alone amid the crystal beauty.

She exhaled, her shoulders collapsing and her heart finally slowing down from a gallop. How could she have fallen asleep again? Outside this room was the man who'd wanted a "wedding night." Outside this room was the polar bear she'd married. Outside this castle was her mother. Cassie didn't know which of those three was more terrifying.

But I'm not going to cower here, she thought. She'd never hidden from anyone before, and she wasn't going to start now.

Leaning her back against the wardrobe, she threw her weight into it. The wardrobe grated on the ice floor. She grunted as it slid the final inch. She wondered if the man had heard it. Cassie gripped her flashlight, testing its weight as a weapon, and stepped out into the hall.

Nothing happened. She was alone.

Silent and blue and beautiful, the crystalline hallway felt peaceful. Shining her light down the hall, she saw several doors, shadows in the glistening golden walls. She wondered what was on the other side of them. How did a—what was the word? Munaqsri. Did he really transport souls? Were there stashes of souls in those rooms?

Cassie took a step toward the first door and then stopped. She wasn't here to explore. *Remember the man, the polar bear, my mother,* she thought. She had to find the bear and insist he take her home. She glanced backward over her shoulder and headed down the stairs.

She found the bear in the banquet hall. Seeing him, she halted in the archway. The Bear King had a seal on the table. His muzzle was stained red, and blood speckled the banquet table, brilliant scarlet against the white ice. He wiped his muzzle with his paw, as if embarrassed by his table manners. "Excuse me," he said. "I had thought you were resting." Gore now covered his paws as well as his muzzle. Cassie was suddenly aware of her own blood and the fragility of her skin. Those teeth and claws could tear her as easily as paper.

She focused on the caribou sculpture in an alcove behind him, instead of on his jaws. "Earlier," she said, forcing her voice to sound steady and strong, "a man entered my room."

"I know. It was I."

"You?" She felt all the blood drain out of her face. But . . . but she was sure the intruder had been human: He'd had hands.

"I did try to tell you," he said mildly. "You swung an axe at me."

She stared at him, and he licked a bit of gore off his snout. "You can be human? How . . . Why . . ."

"I wanted to surprise you," he said. "Remember, I told you that I can alter matter. We can take the shape of the species that we care for, but it is not our only shape or even necessarily our original shape. I am not always how you see me now. I thought you would be pleased."

Pleased? "You turned human, and you climbed into my bed."

"It is our bed," the Bear King said. "Husbands and wives share a bed."

Looking at his massive and bloody paws, she felt sick. Husbands and wives . . . No. She wasn't sleeping with a stranger. Especially a magic-bear stranger.

Every fiber in her wanted to run out of the banquet hall. *Stay calm,* she told herself. "I fulfilled my end of the bargain," she said. "I married you. Now I want a divorce."

"I frightened you," he said. "I am sorry. It was not my intent. Please, give me another chance. I will be charming."

She looked at him with blood matted in his fur and seal pieces clinging to his muzzle. "You can be the Casanova of polar bears," she said. "I'm not staying."

"Do not judge me so quickly," he said. "You have only just arrived."

Cassie looked down at the seal carcass. It was a mangled mess. He ate like a polar bear and spoke like a man. She couldn't judge him. He was too far outside the realm of possible for her brain to know how to judge.

"You are like nothing I have ever known," he said. "You are brightness. You are light. You are fire. I come from a world of ice."

She shivered. He sounded like he really meant that. No one had ever said anything like that to her before. She felt unbalanced. "Oh?" she said. "You know what fire and ice make?"

He looked at her with his inscrutable bear eyes. "Tell me."

"Lukewarm water," Cassie said. "I want to go home."

"I need you," he said. "I need you for my wife."

No one had ever said that to her either. She swallowed. "Why?" she said. "Why me? Why a human wife at all? Why not a bear?"

"Because I do not wish my children to be cubs," he said.

For a second, Cassie could not breathe. Children.

"Only the children of munaqsri can choose to accept the power and responsibility, and we need more munaqsri with human intelligence. We are spread too thin; our regions are too large. We lose too many souls, and species dwindle."

She didn't know what he meant by regions or losing souls, and she didn't care. "You married me to breed me?"

"Of course it is not the sole reason—I meant what I said about your brightness and light—but our children were a prime consideration." He sounded so calm. She couldn't believe how calm he sounded. *Our* children?

"You want a human incubator." Cassie felt nauseous again. She clutched the edge of the banquet table. "Count me out. Absolutely not."

"You agreed," he said.

"Not to kids." She wasn't ready to be a mother. Especially

to furry children. "You're a bear. You aren't even bipedal."

"I can be," he reminded her.

"Kids were not part of the bargain," she said. "Deal is off." Turning sharply, she walked out of the banquet hall.

She made it to the corridor before her nerve broke and she ran.

❄ ❄ ❄ ❄ ❄

Crossing through the crystal lattice archway, Cassie slowed. She couldn't run all the way home. She was thirteen hundred miles from home—thirteen hundred plus one if the bear was to be believed. She couldn't reach home on her own. She needed the bear to take her there.

Cassie looked back at the castle. Its soaring spires and elegant arches glowed as golden as dawn. A sculptor had carved delicate lines of icy leaves on the ice walls. More roses, carved to petal precision, curled around the window arches. It was so beautiful that it made her feel an ache inside that she couldn't describe.

Why did such a place have to come with a bear husband?

She walked farther, rounding the corner of the castle, and halted in her tracks. "Oh, wow," she breathed. Spread before her was a topiary garden of ice. Hundreds of sculptures sparkled in the liquid light of the low sun. Hedges, flowers, apple trees, figures of dragons and mermaids and unicorns. With her breath caught in her throat, Cassie touched a leaf on an ice rosebush. She could see veins traced on the thin folds of ice petals.

She walked down paths between ice griffins, frozen fountains, and trees with glittering glasslike fruit. She ducked under a trellis of grape leaves. She'd never seen anything like this. It was the Garden of Eden in ice. Who had created this? She turned to look back at the castle—

—and saw the Bear King standing two feet away from her, silent between the roses. She jumped backward. "Don't do that," she said.

He said nothing, and she was aware of sweat forming in her armpits. She lifted her chin and met his stare.

"I did not think you were the kind to give up without trying," the Bear King said.

"I don't give up," Cassie said automatically. She thought about it for an instant and then repeated, "I don't give up." He'd seen her stubbornness firsthand. She had tracked him until she was nearly out of fuel, despite knowing she was disobeying station rules. That chase felt like it had happened a lifetime ago.

"It is not an easy thing to have your world turned upside down," he said. "I do not blame you for not being strong enough to accept what you have seen here, or not being brave enough to want to see more."

She winced—two insults in one breath. She was not leaving because she was weak or cowardly. Was she?

He added, "I had thought that you would have the strength for this. It is not your fault that I was wrong."

That was not . . . Wait. "Are you daring me?"

He considered it. "Yes," he said.

ICE

"You think it's a joke?"

"I think you are frightened," he said.

"Like hell I am," she said.

He lumbered toward her between the crystalline shrubbery. His fur brushed ice leaves, and they tinkled like crystal. She retreated, bumping into a statue of a mermaid. "I can show you a new world," the Bear King said. "I can give you wonders that you cannot imagine, that you do not know exist, that you cannot yet comprehend."

"I comprehend enough," Cassie said, inching around the statue, away from the bear. "You want me to mother your children. Your cubs." She heard the pitch of her voice rising, and she stopped. *I'm not afraid*, she repeated like a mantra. *I'm not.*

"I will wait until you are ready," he said.

"I'll never be ready."

"I can wait beyond never."

Cassie shivered and hugged her arms, even though she wasn't cold. Her breath was condensing into miniature clouds, but she felt just as warm as she'd felt inside the castle. How long did he intend to keep her here? How long was "beyond never"?

"You have nothing to fear from me," he said gently.

"Then take me home." Home. Home to a mother she'd never met and a father who had lied to her.

"You have stepped into a larger world, Cassie," he said. "Why do you wish to throw it away so quickly? You have barely glimpsed it."

Involuntarily, she glanced again at the castle with its soaring ice turrets and crystalline ivy. If he was real, then all she knew of the world—all she knew of science and the rules of the universe—was false. Half of her wanted to explore every inch of this place. The other half wanted to turn back the clock and redo the day before.

He padded closer to her, and this time she didn't retreat. "You can return to your 'research' station and pretend all is the same as before. But it is not the same, and it will never be the same. You cannot erase what you now know. Your world has changed."

He was right. She couldn't go back to pretending none of this existed, especially with her mother there to prove that it did. His gaze burned, and she had to look away. She watched the sun dance in the topiary garden. Lemon and pink, the sculptures winked in the light.

"Do you like it?" he asked. He sounded oddly hesitant.

"It's beautiful," she admitted. "Impressive sculptor."

"The castle itself was complete before my tenure here," he said. "I have concentrated on the gardens."

A polar bear artist? Staring at his massive paws, she could not imagine him creating anything as beautiful and delicate as the ice topiaries. His paws were designed for killing seals, not shaping roses.

"I sculpt every day except in polar bear birth season," he said. "During the heart of winter, I must patrol the ice near the denning sites. My munaqsri skills—the speed, the ability to sense an impending birth or death, the ability to transform the physical world—make my work possible, but they do not ensure success. I cannot risk being late for a birth for the sake of my gardens." He hesitated, and then added, "Or even for spending time with you."

"I won't still be here then," she said as firmly as she could.

"We shall see," said the Bear King.

SEVEN

Latitude 91° 00' 00" N
Longitude indeterminate
Altitude 15 ft.

WITH ICE LEAVES TINKLING IN HIS WAKE, the Bear King walked back toward the castle. "You have questions," he said over his shoulder. "I have answers. Shall we bargain? For every question I answer, you remain one day in my castle."

"You like bargains, don't you?" she called after him. "How do I know you keep them? How do I know my mother is home?" He rounded the corner. "Hey, come back!" She hurried after him.

The Bear King waited for her by the grand entrance, flanked by shimmering pillars. "A munaqsri cannot break a promise," he said. "It is the way that nature ensures we fulfill our roles. It is the price of our power." He walked inside. She followed him and was again surrounded by iridescent sculptures. "The winds brought your mother to the ice while you slept," he said. "I carried her to your research station before you woke."

She halted. She felt as if she couldn't breathe. The ice frescoes blurred, and she blinked rapidly. Her mother was in the station, walking through the rooms Cassie had walked through, sitting in the kitchen, brushing her teeth in the bathroom, doing all the little things that Cassie couldn't imagine her mother, mythical person that she was, doing. Just thinking about it made Cassie feel as if the ice had cracked open under her feet. "Was she . . . Was she all right?"

"She was well," he said.

Cassie wanted to ask more: what he'd said and what she'd said, what she looked like, what she sounded like. But Cassie's throat clogged, and the bear was still walking away from her. "Where . . . Where are you going?" Her voice cracked.

He looked over his shoulder at her. "I wish to show you what you will leave behind if you return home. Come."

Cassie followed him. He led her up spiral blue staircases and into rooms that looked as if they were carved of diamond. She saw a music room with a translucent grand piano and an orchestra-worth of violins and cellos. The strings of the violins were impossibly delicate strands of ice. She wandered down a hall lit by iridescent chandeliers and lined with mirror-smooth ice. In a sitting room with frost-edged sofas, she marveled at a chessboard with carved ice pieces the size of her hand, each sculpted into the shape of an Arctic animal.

He was right. She had never seen a place like this. She had never imagined any of this existed. What else had she not imagined?

Her mother, home.

Maybe if I take a little time, she thought, *a couple of days maybe . . . just look at this place. Think of the secrets here, the knowledge. A bear who turns into a man, ice that doesn't melt, a hidden castle—* She could study any one of these mysteries for years. Plus, think of the progress in polar bear research she could make, the questions she could ask and he could answer.

"Your mother," she said, asking the first question that popped into her head, "is she a munaqsri like you?"

"No," he said.

Cassie turned to face him. He was sitting by a frozen fountain, images of fish midleap carved into the frozen streams of water.

"My father is a munaqsri," he said. "He is a . . . The simplest term is 'overseer.' There is a hierarchy of munaqsri. There are munaqsri who care for the souls of a particular species, as I do, and then there are senior munaqsri who care for all the munaqsri of a particular region, such as the wind munaqsri. My father is responsible for the munaqsri of a mountain range in Scandinavia. I have not seen him since I became the caretaker of the polar bears."

His face was turned away from her, as if he studied the

ICE

frozen tumbling water. She tried to imagine what he'd been before he'd become the Bear King. "You weren't always a bear?"

"A child of a munaqsri must choose to accept the power and the responsibilities," he said. "He or she is then assigned to a species by an overseer."

"So you chose to become a munaqsri? You had a choice?" She didn't know why that question was important to her, but it was.

"I was needed," he said. "Everything in the world—bears, birds, insects, rivers, seas—requires its own munaqsri to facilitate its existence. Most species require several. Humans, for instance, have hundreds. Beetles, even more. Polar bears need only one, due to the small population size. But still, there is a shortage of munaqsri. Children of munaqsri are rare, and the world desperately needs all of us."

That didn't sound like much of a choice.

In a quiet voice, the Bear King said, "I did resent my father for my non-choice. Being a munaqsri . . . We keep the world functioning, but we are not truly a part of it."

Life at the station wasn't exactly ordinary either. Cassie shook her head. She couldn't believe she was empathizing with him. Could they actually have things in common?

"You must be hungry," he said abruptly, as if he'd said too much.

The Bear King led her down another spiral staircase, back into the banquet hall. At his command, the table sprouted another feast. It opened like a flower, bowls of fruit unfolding like petals. A stalk shot into the air and bloomed into a tray of breads. It detached and floated toward Cassie. Staring at it, she retreated.

"Do not be alarmed," he said. He sounded amused.

The tray shook as if impatient, jostling rolls. She stiffened and took a croissant. She wasn't "alarmed." She just had never eaten levitating food before. He took a muffin with his massive paw.

Gingerly, Cassie sat on the ice throne. The throne dwarfed her. Her toes brushed the floor. She was suddenly aware of how small and powerless she was inside this pristine perfection.

Steam rose from the dishes, and her stomach rumbled. She licked her lips, her mouth watering. She'd never seen so much food before. And it all looked good. She shook her head at herself. The impossible had happened, *was* currently happening, and her reaction was hunger. Maybe she was adjusting to all the strangeness. Or at least her stomach was. She reached for a steaming dish of carrots in a white sauce.

The silence stretched, broken only by the tinkle and clink of the serving dishes as they jostled across the table. Cassie tried to picture her mother at the station, sitting down to a meal. She imagined her with Cassie's favorite mug, as Owen flipped pancakes, and she pictured herself at age four at the table beside her. Again, Cassie's eyes felt hot.

She tried to think of a question, an innocuous question,

that would let her get some modicum of control back. Making her voice as cheerful as she could manage, she said, "So . . . what were you like as a young cub?"

"Very humanoid," he said dryly.

She almost smiled. He really did have a sense of humor.

"My childhood . . ." He paused and regarded her as if weighing how he should answer. "My childhood was many years ago," he said finally. "I am older than I appear, several centuries older."

Several centuries? She tried to digest it. "You don't seem so old."

"Thank you," he said.

Several *centuries*?

"I had a good childhood, a human one," he continued. As Cassie filled her plate, he told her about growing up straddled between his father's mountains and his mother's Norway. His mother, he said, had been an ordinary human, and she had raised him as a human. He had played with the other village children and had gone to lessons with a tutor. His mother had had hopes he would pursue law. Weekends he'd spent with his father learning about all the things not in his tutor's books—learning about magic and the responsibilities of the munaqsri, learning how a munaqsri used his power to fulfill his responsibilities.

"Your turn," he said when he'd finished.

"What?" she said, startled.

"You tell me about your childhood," he said.

She hesitated, but she couldn't think of any excuse why

not to. Besides, for some reason that she didn't explore too closely, she wanted to talk about it.

She told him about Max and his planes, Gram and her story, and Owen and his gadgets. She told him about how different things were for her compared to, say, Owen's niece in Fairbanks, whose life consisted of makeup and movies. "First time I ever saw a movie," Cassie said, "I was four— my first trip to Fairbanks. I was terrified."

"I find nothing so strange about that."

"It wasn't a horror movie. It was *Mary Poppins.*" When she had first seen Julie Andrews float through the air with her umbrella, she had screamed, and Dad had shoved popcorn at her to quiet her. "I managed to calm myself until the scene where the children jump into a chalk painting." She had thought the sidewalk had swallowed them, and she had proceeded to scream herself hoarse.

They swapped stories as Cassie devoured honeyed breads, delicately spiced fish, a raspberry tart. Eventually, they fell silent.

She shifted on the ice throne. She hadn't meant to talk so much. He was just so easy to talk to. She didn't like how . . . comfortable she'd felt. He was supposed to be the Polar Bear King, and now when she looked at him, he looked like an overgrown stuffed animal or the Coca-Cola polar bear. Abruptly, she stood up. "Is there more to the castle?" she asked.

"You do not need to rush," he said. "You have a full week."

She frowned. "What do you mean?"

"You asked at least seven questions; you owe me at least seven days," he said. "It is not a lifetime, but it is a beginning."

"I never agreed to your bargain," she objected.

He blinked at her. "You are correct," he said, surprise in his voice. "You did not."

They looked at each other for a moment. Then the Bear King focused on the table, and the dishes began to disappear. She jumped as her plate popped like a bubble. Her silverware dissolved into the ice. The frost tablecloth withered. "Stay one week," he said, "and then decide. Only one week. You waited eighteen years for your mother. Wait one week more."

She thought of all the memories she'd just spilled, all the moments she'd lived believing her mother was dead and gone. And now . . . Cassie looked away from the Bear King's brilliant black eyes. She didn't want to think about this. "Show me more of the castle," she said.

He led her to a grand ballroom with pillars reaching up into arches and the roof open to a pale, cloudless sky. The northern lights wafted over and the deep blue floor mirrored the ribbons of light with shimmering perfection. Staring up at the sky, Cassie walked into the ballroom and slipped. She landed smack on her butt.

The Bear King bounded over to her. "Are you all right?"

"Fine, fine, fine." Her tailbone felt bruised. He bent his

neck down to help her, and she automatically shied away. She stood on her own.

"I never noticed it was slippery," he said, an apology in his voice.

"You have bear paws," she said. "I need crampons on this floor. Or ice skates." She shuffled over to a pillar. Outside the ballroom, through the arches, she could see the sculptures of the topiary garden glittering with reflections of the night aurora. It was so beautiful her breath caught in her throat.

She had an idea. She didn't stop to think about whether or not it was a *good* idea. Sitting down fast, she unstrapped her mukluks. She wiggled her toes within three layers of socks.

The Bear King hovered near her. "Are you hurt?"

Cassie used the pillar to stand. "Not yet." She pushed off. In socks, she skated across the ballroom. It made a perfect ice rink. Whooping, she crashed into the opposite pillar. Clutching it, she called to the Bear King, "Your turn."

He looked aghast.

She laughed out loud. She felt better already. "Too undignified for you, Your Royal Ursine Highness?"

"Munaqsri are not royalty. I am merely Bear." Spreading all four paws wide, Bear skidded across the ballroom on his stomach. With his legs splayed out, he spun a hundred eighty degrees to a stop. Laughing, Cassie shoved away from the pillar and slipped to the center of the room. She smashed into Bear.

"Yikes, sorry," she said, disentangling herself. What was she doing? He wasn't her friend; he was a magical soul-transferring polar bear.

"Stand still," he told her.

She tensed but obeyed. She shouldn't have started this. She was supposed to be on her way home, not— Before she could complete the thought, Bear pushed. She careened across the ballroom.

Laughing, she caught herself on a pillar.

She looked back at the polar bear, sobering. One week, he'd asked for. Was that such an awful price for all the wonders she'd seen? "One week," she said. "I'll stay for one week."

EIGHT

Latitude 91° 00' 00" N
Longitude indeterminate
Altitude 15 ft.

ONE WEEK SLID INTO TWO and then three and then four,
and so on. As the days passed, it became easier and easier
for Cassie to find excuses to delay returning to the station
and facing whatever (or, more accurately, whoever) waited
for her there. She hadn't forgiven Dad for the heavy-handed
way he'd tried to ship her off to Fairbanks, or for the way
he'd lied to her for her entire life. As for her mother . . .
Cassie wanted to see her, but every morning, she woke up
and said, "Just one more day, and then I'll go home." And
every night, she went to bed alone and dreamed of bears
and ice.

As the weeks went by, she stopped thinking about home
at all. One afternoon when they'd finished carving ice roses
into the pillars of the ballroom (Bear carving and Cassie

directing), they lay in the center of the floor admiring their handiwork.

"Why does this castle even have a ballroom?" she asked. "Did any Bear King ever hold a ball? Were there waltzing walruses? Say that ten times fast. Waltzing walruses . . ."

Beside her, Bear pushed himself up onto his hind legs. Standing, he was loosely humanoid—if one ignored that he was thirteen feet tall. He held out his paw. "May I have this dance?"

Cassie grinned at him. "Delighted, Your Royal Ursine Highness." She put her hand in his. Her hand was minuscule in his vast paw. "Don't fall on me," she ordered. She could not reach his shoulder so she settled for putting her other hand on his forearm. Her fingers sank deep into creamy white fur.

Gently, he guided her across the ballroom. His paw covered half her back. They danced in silence. Across the topiary garden, deep amber sunlight filled the horizon. Warm orange spread across the ice. It was . . . The word that popped into her mind was "romantic." He spun her. She felt dizzy staring up at his fur.

I'm happy here, she realized. Thinking that, she felt as if she were on the edge of a sea cliff. "We need music," she said, trying to break the mood.

"I could sing for you."

"You sing?"

"No," he said.

She grinned. He dipped her backward. *I'm happy here*

because of *Bear*, she thought. She glimpsed the golden light, and a tear welled in her eye. He pulled her upright. "Sun," she said quickly to explain the tear.

"It is the last of the light," Bear said.

Startled, she stumbled over her feet. He steadied her. How could she have stayed here for so long? What did Dad think had happened to her? And Gram? And her mother. She shook her head. She didn't want to think about her mother right now, not during the end of the light. She always loved the last glimpse of the sun's rays before the long polar night.

"Come with me," Bear said. He dropped down onto all fours and trotted out of the ballroom.

"Don't you want to watch?" she called after him.

"Don't you want a better view?" he called back.

Grinning, Cassie chased after him. She had only been up in the spires a few times. Bear disliked the narrow stairs. One of his predecessors had designed them for humans, not bears, and it embarrassed him, he'd told her, to waddle up them. She'd teased him about that for days, but she didn't tease him now. Today felt different somehow. Maybe it was the loss of light. Maybe it was the dancing.

Bear squeezed into the stairwell and climbed up the spiral stairs. Emerging onto a balcony, Cassie walked to the delicate bowed railing. "Careful," Bear said.

She ignored him and leaned over the ice railing. "Look at that," she breathed.

The Arctic sprawled before her. Gold and silver, it looked

like vast riches. The sky, enormous, glowed blue. Streaks of rose clouds faded into deepening blue, staining the ice azure.

"Do not turn around," he said—it was a human voice, softer and thinner. She may have heard it only once, but still she recognized it instantly. Her back straightened, tingling. He put his arms around her waist. It felt perfectly natural to lay her hands on his. She did it without even thinking about it. Both facing the horizon, they watched the last drop of gold melt into blueness, and then he released her. When she turned around, he was a bear again.

"Bear . . . ," she began. Her back felt cold now. Wind blew her hair into her face. She brushed it away from her eyes.

"I look forward to tomorrow," he said. It was the same phrase he said every night before he left her.

Where did he sleep? She'd never asked. Maybe he went onto the ice or out into the gardens or into one of the other glittering rooms. He'd told her once that she slept in his room. "Stay with me," she said.

He looked at her. Cassie saw the twilight sky reflected in his black bear eyes. She felt her face blush. Tonight was . . . different. She just didn't want it to end. That was all. "I mean, you don't have to leave," she said. "It's okay. I trust you. You can sleep in your room again." She added quickly, "Just sleep."

He regarded her silently for a moment longer. She shifted

from foot to foot and began to wish she could swallow the words back out of the air. Maybe she should have thought first before she'd made the offer. It would change things, if he stayed. She knew that instinctively, but she shied away from thinking about how they'd change.

"As you wish," he said.

He waited for her to lead the way. She brushed past him as she left the balcony, and she laid her hand on his back, intertwining her fingers in his fur. She'd touched his fur a thousand times before, but this time she pulled her hand away. He wasn't just a bear. She remembered his human arms around her waist and his breath on her neck. This was the first time since that first night that he'd turned human.

Outside the bedroom, she had him wait in the corridor while she changed into her flannels—and then changed again into the silken nightshirt that she'd found on her first night in the castle. She told herself she was just being polite. The nightshirt had been a gift. She climbed under the covers. "All right. I'm decent now."

The polar bear padded softly into the room.

Cassie tucked the sheets around her body as he approached the bedside table. She could still change her mind, she knew. If she asked him to leave, he would. But that felt . . . cowardly. This was Bear, after all. And she'd only invited him here as a friend. Friends could share a bed.

She wished she'd stuck with the flannel.

He breathed on the candle. It flickered and died with the scent of waxy smoke. Now the room was so black that it looked thick. Bear (now human, she guessed from the sinking of the mattress) climbed into the bed beside her. She remembered the last time he'd climbed into bed with her—on their wedding night. "Touch me and it's back to the axe," she said.

She heard him sigh. "I would never hurt you, not intentionally, not ever. You should know that by now."

"I don't taste as good as a seal."

"You do not have enough blubber," he agreed.

She felt the mattress shift as he settled into his pillows. Flat on her back, she lay as rigid as ice. "Don't snore."

"Your wish is my command."

She snorted. "Cute."

"Good night, Cassie."

"Night." Clutching the sheets to her chin, she listened to him breathe. It sounded like a gentle wave. Gradually, his breathing slowed. Could he be going to sleep? She prodded him. "You awake?"

"I am now." He rolled over, and she felt the mattress dip down toward him. He was facing her, she guessed. Her skin felt hyperaware. At least a thirteen-foot polar bear did not make a thirteen-foot man, she told herself. He was, at most, seven feet tall.

"Talk to me," she said. "Tell me a story."

"As you wish," he said. "Once upon a time, there was a little wallaby . . ."

She smiled. "Wallaby?"

"Yes, wallaby. And this wallaby lived . . ."

❄ ❄ ❄ ❄ ❄

She was smothering in sheets. Cassie kicked. Her foot contacted something solid. She heard a grunt. Bleary, she blinked awake. Walls did not grunt. "Bear, that you?"

"Hmm."

She kicked harder.

"Ow!"

Served him right. He was sleeping in the middle of the bed. She yanked the covers back and curled with them on the pillows.

"Thief," he said. He tugged on the sheets.

She grunted at him.

"Was I snoring?" he asked.

"You don't snore," she told him. It was a definite plus.

"You do," he said. "It is like a cat purring."

She kicked the covers away. "Too hot," she said. "Is it morning?" Crawling out of bed, she found her flashlight. She turned it on.

She saw a sudden flurry of sheets. Bear rolled off the bed in a tangle of white. "Stop the light!" he said.

Cassie pointed the flashlight at the white lump. "Hey, I'm the one who hates mornings," she said lightly, but he continued to conceal himself. "Bear? What's wrong?"

"You cannot see me."

She'd never seen him, she realized. The two times he'd transformed—last night and her first night here—she hadn't seen him. With the flashlight, Cassie climbed over the bed. He was buried on the floor under the covers. Not an inch of skin was visible. "Come on," she said. "I promise I won't laugh."

"You cannot!" There was a blur of sheets as he stood up. He looked like he was wearing a bad ghost costume. He knocked the flashlight out of her hands. It rolled under the bed. "You must never see my human face," he said. "Promise me you will not try."

"Why not?"

"Promise me."

He sounded serious, even desperate. She didn't think she'd ever heard that in his voice before. "You certainly have your quirks," Cassie said lightly. "Turning into a giant bear wasn't unique enough?" He didn't laugh.

Bear begged her, "Please, beloved. If you care about me at all, do not look."

He hadn't called her "beloved" since the day they'd met.

She dangled over the bed and retrieved the flashlight. She switched it off, and the room plunged into darkness again. "Happy now?" she said, but her voice shook. His pleading had unnerved her. She felt as if she had violated some sacred taboo. But she hadn't meant any harm. All she'd wanted to do was look at him.

Bear said nothing.

She waited another second. "Bear? Are you all right?"

"I must go," he said.

He couldn't be *that* angry. "I didn't . . . ," she began.

"There is a bear being born," he said. "I am needed."

"Now?" It wasn't birth season yet. The bear cub was premature. "You . . . feel it?" He'd told her about this once, how munaqsri could sense an imminent birth or death. They could also, he'd said, summon each other, but she'd never seen him do that. "Can I come with you?"

"It is a munaqsri duty."

She felt a rush of air, and then she heard the door open. She called after him, "See you at breakfast?"

The door slammed. She hugged her shoulders as the room chilled.

❄ ❄ ❄ ❄ ❄

Sometime the following night, Bear slid into bed. Automatically, Cassie curled against his warmth. She didn't think about how natural it felt to do so. She murmured, "Hello."

He said nothing, but buried his face in her hair.

Gradually waking, she remembered she was annoyed with him. He had left her alone. Her whole day had been turned upside down. She'd resorted to eating dried fruits and nuts from her pack. She couldn't work the table without him. Worse, she'd been bored for the first time ever here. It reminded her of blizzards in the station: nothing to do, nowhere to go.

His breathing sounded uneven, choked. She frowned and reached to touch his face. "Are you all right?" she asked. "Are you sick?"

His cheek was damp under her fingers. She snatched her hand back as if it had burned. "Bear, what's wrong?"

ICE

"I was late," he said. His voice shook. "It was far. I was too late."

"What do you mean 'too late'?" She wished she could see him. She peered into the darkness as if she could pierce it. "What happened?"

"I should have been patrolling the ice. If I had been nearby, I could have given that cub a soul in time. If I had been an hour closer, it would have all been well. I was miles late."

"Late?" She tried to understand. He'd missed the birth?

"The cub was stillborn," he said. "No soul, no life."

She could hear the tears in his voice. Did he want her to comfort him? Hesitantly, she put her arms around him. "It's all right," she said. "I'm here." She held him close.

NINE

Latitude 91° 00' 00" N
Longitude indeterminate
Altitude 15 ft.

THROUGH THE DARK DAYS OF WINTER, Bear "patrolled"
the ice, waiting to feel the summons of a birth, while Cassie
waited alone in the castle and grew more and more restless.
In his absence, she prowled the topiary gardens under the
perpetually starlit sky. By winter solstice, she knew them
by heart.

Carved owls stared down at her with glassy eyes reflecting a thousand stars. It was as silent as a museum. She
could hear the crunch of ice under her mukluks. It sounded
like firecrackers. She had a great urge to run through the
gardens with her arms stretched wide, shattering all the
trees in her path—but she didn't. Instead, her feet took her
through the maze of translucent hedges to the center of the
garden. Rosebushes ringed a single sculpture, the newest.

ICE

It was her: her long hair, her high cheekbones, her bony elbows, her height. *It is the heart of the garden,* Bear had told her after he'd finished carving it.

She studied the statue. The ice hair looked blown by wind. Stray pieces curved upward, twisted together. It was a perfect likeness, down to the short lashes on her eyes and the short nails on her hands. Her twin grinned upward, as if she were laughing at the castle spires, or higher at the star-choked sky. *What am I still doing here?* Cassie wondered. *I should be on a snowmobile, not a pedestal.*

Who was tracking bears now? Dad? Owen? Scott would be taking bets on the number of cubs being born. Jeremy was probably stir-crazy by now.

And what about her mother? Cassie couldn't imagine what she was doing. All she could picture was her mother's image from photos she'd seen, but even that memory lacked details, such as the color of her eyes.

Cassie snapped a perfect stem. The ice rose fell into her hands. Absently, she twirled it. Petals caught the moonlight, and tiny moon rainbows flickered in their curves. She put the rose behind her ear.

She'd never meant for this to become permanent. She was supposed to be an Arctic researcher, not the Polar Bear Queen. What had happened to all her plans? Didn't she care about them anymore? Didn't she care about her mother? Or her father? Or Gram? Or Max or Owen? When had she stopped thinking about them?

Cassie turned away and pushed past the bushes. Ice

tinkled like a thousand bells. She halted in front of an ice apple tree. Grabbing hold of the branches, she clambered up the tree. The ice creaked under her weight, and the rose fell from her ear and shattered.

From the top, she could see out onto the Arctic. Low and fat, the moon danced over the translucent ridges. Wind stirred stray snow. She watched drifts form and dissipate, deep blue in the polar night.

Silhouetted, Bear came over the lip of the ridges. He was majestic on the ice. She watched him take great strides across the floes. His fur rippled in the moonlight. He almost glowed.

He galloped to the castle and disappeared inside. Finally, he was home. She swung down from the tree and landed with a crunch on the ice. She followed him to the banquet hall. He was waiting for her at the table. Melting frost dripped from his fur.

Cassie flopped down onto her throne. "What's the news from the ice?"

"It is icy," he said solemnly.

Cassie picked up a frozen apple. "Perfect day here," she said. She tossed the apple up and caught it. "But then, it always is." She threw it higher, and caught it. "Monday: perfect." She tossed it. "Tuesday: perfect." Caught it. "Wednesday: perfect." Tossed it. "Thursday." Caught it. "Friday. What day is today?"

"I do not track human days." He cocked his head at her. "Are you all right?"

She tossed the apple back into its bowl. "Perfect."

ICE

"You are not happy," he said.

"Yes, I am," she said irritably. She was queen of the ice. She was the Polar Bear's wife. Of course she was perfectly happy, wandering around alone in an ice castle every dark day. Maybe if she could convince Bear to take her with him . . . But they'd had that discussion. Alone, he could travel unseen. With her, he ran the risk of detection. And besides, she'd serve no more purpose out there on the ice than she did here. She couldn't help him be a munaqsri.

"Cassie, talk to me."

"I don't know what color my mother's eyes are," she said.

"Green," he said. "Like yours."

"All better." She dared him to contradict her. Instead, he growled at the table. The table shot up a stem. It blossomed into a glass. Red wine filled it. Another bit of table folded up into a plate. Steam rose from it as her dinner grew. It was her favorite dish: chicken soaked in a white wine sauce. She stirred it with her fork. He treated her like a queen. How could she think about leaving?

The thought stopped her. *Was* she thinking about leaving? Truly leaving, as in never coming back, never seeing Bear again, not being his Polar Bear Queen?

Bear summoned a seal carcass and a dinner roll for himself. He held the carcass down with his paw and ripped upward with his teeth.

She didn't want to leave. She didn't want to never see him again. But did she want to stay? What about her life at the station? Why couldn't she have both? "I could do research," she offered.

Bear raised his head. Seal blood stained his muzzle a brilliant red. It looked like a child had smeared lipstick on him. "You cannot," he said.

She scowled at the red stains. "Can't you eat without dripping?".

"I have a large head."

"You're a slob."

"All polar bears eat this way."

"You're making me lose my appetite." Grabbing her linen napkin, she marched to Bear.

"I am sorry," he said contritely. She wiped the gore from his chin and then went back to her seat.

With her watching, he snipped the blubber delicately with his incisors. He let the blood drip onto the floor before gulping the fat whole. "Better," Cassie said. "You know if I had work to do, I wouldn't obsess over your table manners. Plenty of research topics out there. You could tell me how polar bears navigate so effectively on the changing ice, or I could have the final word on whether polar bears are evolving into sea mammals." She could be a station staffer on sabbatical, sort of. She'd already planned to do her college degree remotely. This would simply be more remote than anyone knew.

Gently, Bear said, "You cannot be a human scientist here. No one would believe you. What would you tell them? Your source is a talking bear? You live in an ice castle and feel no cold?"

ICE

Cassie swirled the sauce. She watched seal blood pool on the ice and thought about her future. Her path had always seemed so certain before. But she'd given it up by staying here, and she hadn't even noticed. No wonder she felt so restless. She'd abandoned her future and replaced it with what? Gourmet dinners and pretty sculptures? She had no purpose here.

The table absorbed the blood, and the red vanished as if down a drain. She looked at her chicken. "Have you ever seen a polar bear in a cage?" she asked. "It paces. Back and forth. All day long: back and forth. It wears a rut in the floor. It doesn't stop to eat. It doesn't stop to sleep. It simply paces until it wastes away and dies."

"You are unhappy?"

Unable to answer that, she looked up at him. "I want to go home," she said.

❄ ❄ ❄ ❄ ❄

It didn't take her long to prepare to leave. Bear watched her from the bedroom door as she packed her belongings. All was silent around them. There was no wind, no creak of ice, no nothing. It felt as if the castle were holding its breath.

"Do you plan to return?" Bear asked.

"I don't know," she said. She couldn't look at him.

"How can you not know?"

"I just don't." All she knew was the idea of staying made her miserable and the idea of leaving made her just as miserable.

"So I must wait like a good little puppy dog while you decide our future?"

Cassie couldn't answer that. Instead, she focused on pulling on her Gore-Tex and flannels over her clothes. She was heading back out into a world where she'd need all her layers. She had a memory of herself, age eight, being dressed by her father in so much fleece and down that she couldn't lower her arms. When she got back to the station, she'd see her father again. She tried to imagine that conversation. How was she going to explain why she hadn't returned sooner?

Bear growled, low in his throat, making the hair on the back of her neck prickle. "I have been a fool," he said. "I believed you cared about me."

Cassie frowned at him as she zipped her parka. "It has nothing to do with you. It's me." He was . . . sweet. And fun. But this wasn't about him. It was about her—who she wanted to be, what she wanted her future life to be.

"Of course it 'has to do' with me," he said. "It is my life you speak of."

"And *my* life," she snapped back. "You want me to sacrifice my career, friends, family, a mother I have never even met." Granted, after the first few weeks had passed, she hadn't missed her mother at all. Ruthlessly, she pushed that thought aside. "I can't do that." She'd worked so hard—late nights studying for Dad's pop quizzes, long treks chasing bears, weekends cleaning equipment, all so she could someday earn an official staff position, a future she'd just tossed away to do what? Be Bear's companion? Play in the topiary garden? Dance in the ballroom? It wasn't enough.

"You do not belong there anymore," he said. "It is your past. You cannot go back. This is your home now."

Cassie shook her head. This wasn't her home; this was Bear's castle. Her eyes swept over the ice rose bed and the seabird wardrobe and the shimmering walls and golden door. She did know every curl of ice now, every rainbow reflection. She loved the shimmering sheen of the ice, the soothing wind outside, and all the memories she now had of everything here. *But it's not home,* she told herself firmly. She had to remember that. Home was the station.

"You belong with me," he said. "We are one."

"No, we're not. You're out being munaqsri, and I'm . . ." She felt like . . . like a pet, kept at home until he was free to play with her.

"Should I let the polar bears be stillborn? Is that what you want me to do? Let their souls drift beyond the ends of the earth? I have responsibilities. You know that I do."

"I know!" This was hard enough, and he was making it worse. It reminded her of how she'd come here—by being blackmailed with a bargain she hadn't been able to refuse. But that wasn't fair. The bargain to save her mother had been her own idea. And after that, Cassie had *chosen* to stay. At least, she'd thought she'd had a choice. She'd believed him when he'd said she wasn't a prisoner. What if . . . He wouldn't force her to stay. He wasn't like that. "If you really cared about me, you'd let me go."

He turned away from her. "Go," he said. She exhaled a breath that she hadn't realized she'd been holding. He added, "I will stay here and pace like a bear in a zoo until you return to me."

Cassie sat down hard on the bed as the anger and frustration drained out of her. "I didn't mean . . ." Didn't mean what? To leave? But she *did* mean to leave. From the beginning, she had meant to leave. She just hadn't meant to hurt him. And she hadn't meant to care if she hurt him.

Bear sighed. "If you wish it, I will take you home."

TEN

Latitude 70° 49' 23" N
Longitude 152° 29' 25" W
Altitude 10 ft.

CASSIE HADN'T REMEMBERED the station being so ugly. She'd always thought it resembled a sideways soup can, but she'd never noticed what an old soup can it had become. Its metal walls were pockmarked with the red-brown stains of decades of rust. The shed walls were worse. The whole complex was incongruous with the pristine ice desert. After all the years she'd walked in and out of that dented, rusted door without ever looking at it, seeing it now felt . . . strange.

She dismounted from Bear, but her hand stayed on his neck. He turned his head to look at her with his soulful eyes. "It looks different, that's all," she said, in answer to his unspoken question.

"You are different," he said. "This place is not your home anymore."

"Don't be melodramatic," she said, taking her hand off his neck. "This is hard enough as it is."

"I do not want leaving me to be easy."

"Well, it's not, so stop it." He subsided, and she went back to staring across the station compound. Skidmarks from a Twin Otter crossed in front of the shed and headed behind the station. Max was here. Max. Owen. Liam. Scott. Jeremy. Dad and . . . and Mom. Cold pierced her cheeks even under her face mask now that she wasn't touching Bear. Cassie closed the gusset on her hood.

"Are you afraid?" Bear asked gently.

"Like hell I am," Cassie said. Ridiculous to be nervous about meeting her own mother. This should be the best day of her life.

But her feet wouldn't move. All she had to do was walk to the door and open it, and there she'd be—her mother. "You could come in with me," Cassie said.

Snow drifted across the doorstep in silence.

"I know you do not want that," Bear said finally.

She nodded. She didn't know what had made her say it.

"Raise the station flag and I will come for you," Bear said.

No more thinking, she told herself. It was time to do this. Shouldering her pack, Cassie marched briskly across the lit snow. Closer, she heard the generator humming—a comfortingly familiar sound, like the welcoming whine of a family dog—and she slowed to a stop in front of the door.

Behind her, she heard Bear rumble, "I love you."

Suddenly, going inside seemed easier than staying

outside. Without looking at Bear, she pushed the door open. The smell of unwashed bodies hit her in a wave, and she reeled backward from the sourness. Steeling herself, she stepped into the entryway and closed the door behind her. Breathing shallowly through her face mask, she opened the second door.

And she was home.

❄ ❄ ❄ ❄ ❄

Cassie stood in the second doorway and blinked, her eyes adjusting to the barrage of color: orange life vests, red parkas, bright blue packs, green and purple climbing ropes. Slowly, as the colors resolved into familiar shapes, she started to relax. Heaps of gear, stacks of files, rats' nests of clothes on top of and around the desks and file cabinets . . . She knew this mess. Cassie stripped off her outer gear. She could hear voices in Owen's workshop. She left her pack and gear on her desk and crossed to the half-open door.

The scene was very familiar: Max and Owen stood at the workbench. They were muttering over a chunk of engine. Leaning against the door frame, Cassie watched them. Max and Owen. Her two pseudo-uncles. She used to play in here while they muttered over some hunk of metal, exactly as they were doing now. She felt a grin tugging on her lips. "Nice toaster," she said lightly.

Owen dropped the clamp.

"You should be more careful with that equipment," she teased. "Treat it like a baby."

Max whipped off his goggles, reverse raccoon mask underneath. "Cassie? Lassie!" He leaped over a sawhorse and scooped her up into a bear hug. Max! She'd missed him! She hugged him back fiercely. "Look at you, Cassie-lassie!"

Owen was frowning at her. "Cassie?" he said.

"It's me. In the flesh. Good to see you." She meant it. It was very good to see them, surprisingly good. She'd focused so much on her parents that she hadn't thought about what it would be like to see the rest of her family. "Good to be home." She threw open her arms and inhaled the smell of home: stale winter. She coughed.

"Cassie . . . we didn't know if you were alive or dead, lassie," Max said.

"Your mother always believed you lived," Owen said.

Your mother. Cassie felt her heart stop for an instant. Bear had done it. Her mother was here. Alive and here. Cassie hadn't realized that up until this moment, there had still been doubt, lurking. But hearing it from prosaic Owen's lips, here in the unmagical, ordinary station . . . When her heartbeat resumed, it felt loud, like a timpani under her skin, and her voice sounded far away to her ears. "Where is she?"

Max grinned broadly. "Come on, Cassie-lassie." He draped his arm around her shoulder and shepherded her out the door. "I want to see the expression on their faces when they see you."

Cassie let herself be led. She didn't feel her feet touching the floor. She barely saw where she was walking. *Their* faces, plural, when *they* see you. Max propelled her through the research lab to the kitchen. He released her as they entered.

There was only one person in the kitchen.

Her father was sitting at the table with his head bent over his notebook. A pot simmered on the stove behind him. For a long moment, she stared at him, feeling her insides tumble, unable to sort out what she was thinking or feeling.

After months with Bear, her six-foot-five father looked small and fragile. Gray streaked his hair, and his neck sagged beneath his mountain-man beard. She had forgotten his gray. She stared at him, trying to match this man to her memories. How had she ever found him intimidating? She wanted to cross to him and push his hair out of his eyes. He looked so . . . human.

Max cleared his throat, and Dad glanced up from his papers.

"Hi, Dad," she said.

He looked stunned, as if she had dropped from the sky into the kitchen. Recovering, he shot out of his chair. The chair clattered backward to the floor behind him. In two large steps, he was in front of her. He crushed her in a hug. "Oh, my little girl," he said.

He hadn't called her that in years. Cassie swallowed a lump in her throat. "Where's Mom?" The word tasted strange in her mouth.

His face split into an enormous smile. Still holding her shoulders, he called, "Gail! Gail, she's home!" He squeezed her shoulders. "Gail!"

Cassie heard footsteps from the hall behind her. Her mother's footsteps, running. Cassie's back muscles tensed. The footsteps stopped at the doorway, and her father released her. But Cassie couldn't turn around. Her feet felt glued to the linoleum. She had dreamed of this too often for too long. *What are you afraid of?* she challenged herself. *Turn around.*

No, I don't want to.

Tough, she told herself. *Turn the hell around.*

Slowly, she turned—counter, cabinets, wall, Max, Owen . . . "Gail," Dad said to the woman in the doorway, "this is Cassandra. Cassie, this is your mother."

Green eyes. For a long moment, Cassie had no other coherent thought. She stared at her mother's eyes and felt as if her brain were spinning like a coronal aurora. Cassie *did* have her mother's eyes.

But the resemblance ended there, at the eyes. Gail was short compared to Cassie, maybe five-foot-five. She had black hair, not red. Instead of sharp cheekbones, she had soft baby-doll cheeks. Decked out in a red blouse and jeans, she looked nothing like Cassie, except the eyes.

"Mother," Cassie said, testing it.

Her mother swallowed and fluttered her hands as if she weren't sure what to do with them, as if she were surprised that she had hands. "You can call me Gail, if it makes you more comfortable," she said, her voice quivering.

Her mother was a stranger named Gail. "Gail," Cassie said. She had not pictured using her mother's first name. Cassie attempted a smile. "Very punny. North Wind's daughter. Gale."

Her mother sparkled at her with a smile out of a Crest commercial. "It's short for Abigail." Inanely, Cassie wondered where her mother had found lipstick up here. It was as red as Red Delicious apples, and as inappropriate as cotton jeans in fifty-below. "Oh," Cassie said, continuing to stare. Her mother seemed smaller than she'd been in her daydreams.

The smile faded, and Gail twisted her hands. "Could I . . . Would it be all right if I hugged you?"

"Maybe," Cassie said. Was it? "Yes."

Gail took a step toward her and awkwardly held out her arms. Cassie took a matching step forward. Her mother smelled like pine trees, like wild air. Her arms felt bony around Cassie's back. Cassie placed her hands on her mother's shoulder blades. She was hugging a stranger. This close, Cassie could feel the gulf of every year, of every minute.

Her mother said in a soft voice, "My baby. My little girl."

And something inside Cassie broke. She felt it give, like a sagging spruce under the weight of a winter's ice. All of a sudden, Cassie's cheeks were wet. Water filled her eyes, and she couldn't see. She buried her face in the sharp shoulder of her pine-scented mother. Her mother's arms started to shake. "My baby, my baby." Gail's voice cracked. She was crying too.

❊ ❊ ❊ ❊ ❊

Something had to happen next. Cassie had never thought beyond the first hello. But now the first moment was over and Cassie didn't know what to say to this woman, this stranger, her mother.

Owen—Owen, of all people—came to her rescue. She hadn't even realized that he and Max were still in the room. "How did . . . How did you escape?" Owen asked.

Gratefully, Cassie turned to him. "No escape. I asked to leave, and Bear brought me home."

"Just like that?" Gail said, surprise in her voice.

Cassie thought of Bear outside the station. *I love you*, he'd said. "Just like that," she lied.

"But munaqsri promises can't be broken—," her mother began.

"It doesn't matter," Dad cut her off. "She's here now. She's free."

Yes, it did matter. Munaqsri promises. Her mother—Gail, she corrected—was right. Cassie had made vows, promises, to a munaqsri. He could have made her stay if he had wanted. But he had chosen to let her go, even though he loved her—or maybe, she had the sudden thought, *because* he loved her?

"We won't ever let him take you again," her father said.

"Oh, no, it's not like that," Cassie said quickly. "He's not like that. We're . . . friends," she finished, for lack of

ICE

a better word. Until the birth season had begun, he'd been her constant companion. They'd talked and laughed and spent every second together.

"Friends? With the monster who took you from your family? With the monster who kept you from us for months? Cassie, we thought you might be dead."

Cassie flushed. She should have at least tried to send word. But she'd never even thought of it. It was her fault that they'd worried. "He's not a monster," she said. He'd said he loved her. . . . *Stop thinking about that.* She was here with her mother, her *mother*, who was alive and here.

"What you did . . . ," Gail said. "It was very brave. Thank you."

She didn't know about "brave." She'd liked it at the castle. She'd skated in the ballroom, designed new sculptures for the topiary garden, lost chess games. Her mother was waiting for her to speak. "I couldn't leave you . . . there," Cassie said. There, in a troll castle. It still sounded implausible. Gail fluttered her hands, obviously uncomfortable. She had a debutante's fingers, long and slender, with pristine nails and smooth skin. For eighteen years with trolls, she did not seem the worse for wear. "What are trolls anyway?" Cassie asked—the question came out harsher than she'd intended.

"Cassie, your mother doesn't like to talk about it," Dad said.

Gail shook her head. "It's all right, Laszlo," she said. To Cassie, she said, "There truly were trolls, and I truly was trapped in their castle."

Cassie glanced away, unable to keep looking at those familiar-yet-foreign green eyes. She hadn't meant to snap like that, not at her. At Dad, maybe, who had left his wife trapped in an impossible castle, leaving it to Cassie to save her.

"Trolls are . . . difficult to explain. It is an inadequate name," Gail said. "They have no shape, no physical bodies. Their queen is chosen from those who can hold a shape for the longest, but still . . ." Her voice faltered. "It's an island of wild spirits."

"How did Bear free you?" Cassie asked. Bear had never told her. She had never asked. She had, in fact, avoided every subject related to her mother, including trolls and the winds. Now she wished she had asked everything.

Gail shook her head. "I don't know," she said. "One night, I went to sleep, and when I woke, I was on the ice and the Polar Bear King was carrying me home."

Silence fell over the kitchen. It was impossible not to hear Gram's voice as Cassie looked at her mother, the North Wind's daughter, free from the troll castle. *And so, the Bear carried the North Wind's daughter to her human husband. . . .*

On the stove, bubbles spilled over a saucepan, and the burner hissed. "Ack, beans!" Dad swooped down on the saucepan. With a look of relief flashing over her face, clearly eager for the distraction, Gail dove away from Cassie and slid a bowl under Dad's elbow; he drained the beans into it. Gail took the saucepan, and he took the bowl—saucepan to the sink, bowl to the table. It looked like a dance, a well-rehearsed dance, one that didn't include Cassie.

She thought of dancing with Bear in the ballroom and then firmly pushed the thought away. "Where's Gram?" Cassie asked. "Is she back in Fairbanks?"

"I flew her back about a month after you left," Max said. "She waited a month, in case you returned."

Cassie had never meant to worry Gram, either. She owed a lot of apologies.

"Cassie," Dad said, "the others don't know about the . . . everything."

She blinked. "How can they not know?" Max and Owen knew. Granted, they had known Cassie's mother from before, and the others hadn't, but still. Her mother had come back from the dead. Surely, they must have noticed.

"Story was that we only *thought* she was dead," Max said with relish, "but really she was in a coma and no one knew who she was, and one day she woke up. As soon as she was released from the hospital, I flew her here to surprise your father."

Cassie gawked. That was the stupidest story she'd ever heard. "They believed that? What soap opera did you plagiarize?"

Max shrugged and looked embarrassed.

"We decided it was best," Dad said, "to attempt to preserve normalcy. For your mother's sake."

Before Cassie could respond, the two researchers Scott and Liam tumbled into the kitchen. Cassie realized with a shock that it had been such a long time since she'd even thought about them that she'd almost forgotten what they looked like.

Scott saw her first. He grinned. "Cassie?" He thumped her on the back. "Good to see you. How've you been? What's for dinner?" Scooping beans into a bowl, he straddled a chair.

Liam shook her hand. "Missed a great season," he said. "How's Fairbanks?"

She shot her father a look. If he'd claimed Gail had been in a coma, what had he said had happened to Cassie? "It's good," Cassie said. Dad nodded approvingly.

Jeremy stomped into the room. "Liquid nitrogen would freeze at this temperature." After shucking his gloves, he went for the beans. Mouth full, he nodded casually at Cassie, as if she hadn't been gone the whole migration season. "I know, I know, I'm still here," he said.

"He owes me three more months," Dad said as he handed Cassie a bowl of beans.

With beans squashed on his teeth, Jeremy said, "And then I'm outta this icebox. Beautiful, balmy L.A. Changing my concentration to Amazon jungles."

Gail teased, "You'll complain of sunburn in L.A., and you'll melt in the Amazon." She smiled at Jeremy with her full-teeth smile. Cassie felt her heart suddenly squeeze. Her mother was strangers with her daughter and friends with that newbie, that *cheechako*, who wasn't even family and couldn't track a polar bear in a zoo? Cassie stirred her beans, not hungry.

Jeremy wagged his spoon. "Mark my words: Hell is frozen. I should never have chosen Arctic research. But I'm man enough to change."

Cassie searched for something innocuous to say. "So . . . how are the bears?"

Scott's face lit up. "Earmarked a hundred twenty-six. That's thirty-two more than they got at NPI." National Polar Institute was one hundred fifty miles west, near Prudhoe Bay, and it was the closest thing to a football rival the Eastern Beaufort station could have. "Not that we're counting," added Max as he sat on his stool and helped himself to rice and beans.

"Course not," Cassie said. "You visiting, or back on staff?"

Grinning even more broadly, Max said, "We got the grant. Two years' worth."

"It's joint with NPI and the Chukchi Sea guys," Liam said. "But Max is back on staff, and Owen got his equipment—brand-new computers. Very snazzy."

Max was back! And they'd gotten the grant! And she'd missed it. "That's wonderful!" she said, as enthusiastically as she could. Really, it was wonderful news. She'd wished for Max to come back for years. Cassie grinned at her former babysitter. "What's the grant for?"

"Denning behavior," Dad answered. "All five polar bear nations are participating, but we are the ones who will be combining the data."

"Laszlo had us out poking sticks into dens till we got

Max back on staff. Scouting the ice with headlamps. Your kind of stuff, kiddo," Scott said. "Sorry you missed it." So was she.

Jeremy gave a visible shudder. "Insanely suicidal."

"You didn't get eaten," Dad said.

"Pure luck," Jeremy said. "Glad that's over with."

She'd missed all of it. Well, she was back now, and she wasn't missing anything else. Out of the corner of her eye, Cassie watched Gail perch on a stool and smooth her napkin across her lap. *I'm home now*, Cassie thought, *and I'm staying.*

❄ ❄ ❄ ❄ ❄

Cassie shot upright in her bed. What the hell was that? "Bear?" she said. A woman was screaming. It took Cassie several seconds to remember where she was, and several more seconds to remember what other woman was in the station.

Her mother was screaming.

Cassie chucked off her comforter and ran out her bedroom door. She made it to outside her dad's room as the screams subsided to sobs. "It's all right," her father was saying. "You're here. You're free. It's over. It's all right. They won't take you again."

"You don't know that." Her mother's voice, broken.

Cassie pushed through the door. "Mom? Gail?" She halted in the doorway. Her mother was curled against Dad and was weeping on his shoulder.

Dad raised his head, and the expression was so raw that

Cassie had to look away. "Nightmare," he said to Cassie. "She'll be all right. You go back to bed."

Cassie took a step toward the door. She wanted to retreat. She didn't know what to do with her mother weeping like that and her father looking so . . . so . . . stricken, so helpless. Every crease in his face was a deep shadow. His eyes looked like smudged holes. "Are you sure?" she asked.

"Go ahead," he said. He pressed his face against her mother's hair, and she could tell that to him she was already gone. Cassie backed out the door and closed it behind her. She hesitated in the hallway. She could hear her father's voice clearly through the door.

"Same dream?" he said.

Cassie couldn't hear the reply.

"Blame me," he said. "I failed you. I should have saved you. Blame me. Hate me. But don't be afraid. You don't have to be afraid. It's over. It's all over. You're home."

ELEVEN

Latitude 70° 49' 23" N
Longitude 152° 29' 25" W
Altitude 10 ft.

CASSIE THREW HERSELF INTO data processing. For five days, she transferred several thousand latitude and longitude measurements into minuscule triangles on a topographical map, one triangle per den. She finished late on day five, and then stepped back to survey her work. She wrinkled her nose. Anyone could have done this—a kid, a monkey, Jeremy.

"Good," Dad said behind her. "How many do we have?"

Cassie counted. "Forty-one on eastern Ellesmere, maximum distance twelve and a half miles from shore, twenty-eight within five miles." Bear could be there now, distributing souls. "Baffin Island, twenty-three near Cape Adair."

Her father took notes. "Foxe Basin?"

"Bear must have visited a number of these by now,"

she said. It was the height of birth season. Had any of the cubs been stillborn? Some must have been. If he were in Karaskoye More and he felt a call in the Chukchi Sea, he might not make it even at superspeeds. She thought of Bear alone in his castle, mourning the cubs he'd failed to save.

Dad's pencil paused. "Cassie, you don't need to think about him anymore. You're safe here."

Not again. She forced herself to smile and say in an even voice, "He's not dangerous. He's sweet." And fun and funny.

"It's a common psychological reaction for people to identify with their kidnappers," he said. "But you're home now. We won't let him take you again."

Dad was so stubborn. "You know what Bear did one time? I woke up with a sore throat, and he brought me breakfast in bed." More like a feast, really. Pancakes, waffles, cereals. She'd never had anyone bring her breakfast in bed. "And then the rest of the morning, he told me stories so I wouldn't have to talk and I wouldn't be bored." He'd even acted some of them out. Even with her sore throat, she had laughed a lot. "Does that sound so terrible?" She hadn't laughed like that since she'd returned to the station.

"You don't need to tell me," he said. "Whatever happened, you're safe now. You're with people who love you."

Bear loves me, she thought. "He's not a monster," she said.

Gail poked her face into the room. "It's after midnight.

Would you two workaholics come to bed?" She smiled with all her teeth.

"Do you want to call it a night?" Dad asked kindly, as if talking to a child.

Cassie sighed. One more argument wasn't going to convince him. "All right." She deposited her papers onto her desk, and she trotted after Dad and Gail.

At the door to her bedroom, Dad paused. "Good work today, Cassie."

She wasn't sure of that. Bear did more to help the polar bears in one jaunt across the ice than she could do in one year of drawing triangles on maps.

"Night," Gail said. She didn't try to hug or kiss Cassie. After the first few awkward nights, they had let that drop in a tacit acknowledgment of the gulf between them.

Managing a halfhearted wave, Cassie backed into her bedroom and closed the door behind her. She heard her parents' voices receding, and then their door shut too.

Cassie flopped down onto the bed. Yellow fluorescent light reflected on the photographs that her younger self had taped to the cement walls. She rolled onto her stomach to look at the shrunken images of snowdrifts and mountaintops. She leaned over and smoothed the crumpled corner of one photograph. She had scrawled: "Lomonosov Ridge 89° N." She remembered it: the fierce jumble of ice blocks, the expanse of sky, the burning cold. "Oh, Bear, what are you doing now?"

She threw a rolled sock at the light switch, and it bounced

off. Third sock, she got it. In the darkness, she missed Bear more. She knew she shouldn't. She was home now. She had her life back, plus her mother. So why wasn't she happy?

Tossing beneath her comforter, Cassie thought about her life in the castle, how she'd never gotten tired of the afternoons they'd spent in the garden, of the evenings they'd spent playing chess (even when he'd won three out of four games because she'd never had a backup plan), or of the late nights when they'd drunk hot chocolate in the dark and he'd made up stories just for her. She remembered how he had laughed the first time she'd slid down the banister, and how he had cried when that first cub had been stillborn. How many more stillborns had he had to face alone? If only she could find a way to be with him *and* help the polar bears.

Cassie sat up in bed—she was on the verge of an idea. She could feel it. Bear missed births because he did not know where and when they would be. But she had access to the precise denning dates for hundreds of expectant bears.

Cassie threw off her comforter and hurried to Owen's workroom. She clambered over boxes and engine bits to the new computer. After yanking the protective cover off, she hit the power button. She paced as it booted. Births were not random. She could predict them—or at least their likelihood. Cassie perched on the desk chair and clicked to the denning file.

"Let me do that," a voice said.

Cassie jumped. Owen was two feet from her elbow. How

on earth had he heard her from back in the sleeping quarters? "Do you have a baby monitor on this thing?"

"You're not exactly light-footed."

She relinquished the desk chair. "Be my guest." He sat, and she leaned over his shoulder. "I want an extra column on the denning sites spreadsheet." He inserted the column. "Mmm. Okay. Now put in a formula to add two months to each of the denning times to account for the final stage of the gestation period." He did. "Can you print a page?" she asked.

"It's going."

The printer whirred, and Cassie hovered over it. "Slow."

"Ink-jet. Leave it be."

"You think I'm going to break every piece of equipment, don't you?"

Owen shrugged.

"I am not a klutz," she said.

"Excitable," he said.

She yanked the page out before it finished, blurring the ink. Pacing, she scanned it. "Label that column 'Predicted Birth' and sort the data by date and location. Date first. Please."

He made the adjustments and printed. After grabbing the pages, Cassie perched on a stool. She chewed on her lower lip as she read. Could this work?

Owen cleared his throat. "The grant said nothing about predicting births," he said. "Up to your father, but I doubt we can change the basic premise now."

"Uh-huh." She barely heard him. Dates overlapped for disparate locations, but it was not impossible. If he had a route that took him from Hudson Bay . . . It would be a challenging project to determine the route and to update it, adjusting probabilities, on the fly. It would need someone with training and skills. . . .

Owen waited for a response. Cassie smiled at him. "Can you print a few more files for me?"

❅ ❅ ❅ ❅ ❅

Cassie rolled her sleeping bag and stormproof bivy sack into the bottom compartment of her backpack. She was packing full expedition gear this time, in preparation for trips out on the ice. She added freeze-dried food packets, oatmeal flakes, nuts, dried fruit. If her plan worked, she'd be out on the pack ice every day—just like she'd always wanted.

As she packed, Dad hovered beside her. Flushed, his face looked like angry lava. He leveled a finger at her. "You're not going. And that's final."

Cassie examined her MSR stove and tested the fuel pump. She wasn't going to fight with him.

"I won't let you ruin your life."

"It's my choice to make." She kept her voice calm. She didn't know when she'd see Dad again. She didn't want to leave angry.

He gripped her arm. "Cassie, I only want what's best for you."

Cassie yanked out of his grip. Turning her back on

him, she packed quickly with practiced skill—heavy items braced by clothing. "I know I'm not making the choices you would, but—"

Red nail polish flashing, Gail wrung her hands. "Cassandra, you don't have to go. You fulfilled my promise. He has no hold over you."

She shook her head. She wasn't going back because of promises or because of Gram's story or to save her mother. "I *want* to return to him," she said.

Owen wordlessly handed Cassie a stack of printed data. She thanked him and packed it. Scanning her desk, she found an ice screw. She added it to a side pocket.

"Cassie." Dad dropped his voice low. "He's not even human. You told me yourself you don't know what he looks like when he isn't a bear. You don't know what he is."

She was *not* going to fight with him.

Without a word, she marched through the lab to the bathroom. She slammed the door behind her and shoveled her toothbrush, deodorant, and shampoo into the bag. "I know perfectly well what he is," she said through the door. "He's Bear, and he's my husband." She rooted through the cabinets until she found one more item: birth control pills, left by an intern who'd worked at the station prior to Jeremy. She packed the pills and zipped the bag.

Flinging open the door, she added in a low voice, "And isn't all this a little hypocritical coming from the man who married the North Wind's daughter?" His jaw fell open, and she brushed past him. "Owen," she called, "do you have the rest of those maps?"

"Just a minute here, young lady . . ." Dad strode after her.

Max emerged from his bedroom. "What's going on? Cassie-lassie?" He followed Cassie and Dad back to where Gail waited. "What's she doing?" Max asked.

"Ruining her future," Dad said.

"Following my future," Cassie corrected. Owen handed her another stack of maps, and then, with a quick glance at Cassie's father, retreated across the room.

"You have a future here," Dad said. "You have family and friends here. You're giving up everything to be with this 'husband.' You're giving up college. You're giving up your goals. What about your plans to be a professional tracker? You always said that's what you wanted."

Cassie put on her hat and zipped her parka. Sweat heated in her armpits. "I shouldn't have expected you to understand. After all, you left your wife in a troll castle."

"Dammit, Cassie, I did that for you! You'd been born. I had to keep you safe! I couldn't go traipsing off to the ends of the earth. I had to be a father to you!" He thumped a desk with his fist for emphasis. Papers scattered, and Owen jumped. "Do you think it was an easy choice?"

It hadn't been a choice; it had been cowardice. Why else had he lied to her all these years, leaving it to Gram to finally tell her? Shame was a powerful motivator. She knew he wished he had rescued Gail. She'd heard the regret in his voice that first night when she'd eavesdropped on her parents. She slung her pack over her shoulder.

"I forbid it." Dad blocked the exit. "You don't know what you're doing."

Cassie turned to her mother. "You talk to him."

"But I don't . . . ," Gail began.

"History is repeating itself," Cassie said. "Your father didn't want you to leave either."

Startled, Gail looked at her husband.

"It's not the same thing at all," Dad protested. But Cassie could see her mother understood. It *was* the same. Cassie watched her mother's face as her father blustered. Every night, her mother woke screaming, afraid she would be imprisoned again. Would she let her daughter be kept somewhere against her will? Cassie didn't know her well enough to be certain, but she was betting not.

Gail touched his arm with her red fingernails. "Laszlo, let her go."

Aghast, he turned to her. "Do you know what you're saying? You want to send our only child, *our baby girl*, back to the mercy of a bear?"

Gail lifted her chin and did not back down. Max, wide-eyed, looked back and forth among the three of them like he was watching a convoluted Ping-Pong game. Owen ducked behind the doorway of his workshop. Dad broke first. Lowering his eyes, he said, "Cassie, please, don't do this. It isn't safe. It isn't smart. You're rushing in again. Wait for a while and then decide. Don't leave so soon."

ICE

Gail reached toward Cassie and then let her hand fall. "Cassandra . . . Cassie . . . I was just getting to know you." Cassie looked at her mother. What could she say? That no matter how much time she spent here, it wouldn't be enough to bridge the lost years? Cassie couldn't say that. Better just to leave.

"Stay with us," Dad said. "We're your family. This is your home. Please, think about this. Think of what you're giving up." Max's eyes were overbright, and Gail had tears in hers.

Looking at them, Cassie started to blink fast. Her eyes felt hot. "Tell Gram I'm sorry I didn't get to see her."

She went outside quickly—before she could change her mind, or have it changed for her. Silence slammed down on her as she closed the outer door. She inhaled deeply, and cold bit her throat. Feeling her way along the perimeter of the station, Cassie raised the U.S. flag in the blinding white darkness of an Arctic blizzard.

TWELVE

Latitude 79° 48' 44" N
Longitude 153° 37' 58" W
Altitude 6 ft.

AS BEAR CARRIED HER NORTH, Cassie laid her cheek against the soft fur of his neck. She breathed in his scent—sea salt and damp fur. Above, the northern lights played between the stars as Bear ran across the endless ice. She thought of the last time Bear had carried her away from the station. Same ride, but now she knew what waited at the end of it.

Or at least she hoped she did. What if Bear rejected her plan?

After many hours, they reached the castle. Cassie saw the spires, luminous in the light of the moon. Bear slowed to a walk, his paws crunching on granules of ice.

"We're home," Cassie said softly.

Bear paused, and she knew he'd heard her. She wrapped

her arms around his broad neck, and then she dismounted and walked through the shimmering castle gate with her hand resting on her Bear's back.

She led him to the banquet hall and removed her pack. She unzipped it and began to pull out maps, binders, and notebooks and pile them on the banquet table. Frost curled around a map as she unrolled it. "Can you tell the table not to eat this?"

Bear focused on the table, and the frost retreated. "What is all this?" he asked.

Cassie took a deep breath. Time to see if she truly had a future here. For all her fine words to Dad, Bear could squash everything without even knowing he was doing it. If he was unwilling . . . *I'll have to convince him*, she thought. She pointed to a section of the map. "Here's the coast. And here are this season's dens. One bear per triangle." Cassie flipped open a three-ring binder. "This is a record of the denning dates with the predicted dates of birth, which I can use to plot routes for you that will bring you closest to the most likely births at any given time for the rest of the birth season. Predictive modeling. We can use it to change the odds."

Bear furrowed his broad forehead.

She plunged on. "Eventually, with enough data points, I should be able to be precise . . . within an order of magnitude, of course." Thanks to Owen, she had printouts of all the files from all the cooperating research stations. It wasn't a complete record of the full bear population by any means, but it was a start. "Look," she said, "I've already plotted a preliminary course. We can test it out tomorrow."

She watched him, waiting for his reaction and trying to read his glass black eyes.

"You wish to come with me out onto the ice? Out to the births?"

"I have to," she said firmly. "For this to work, we need to record more data, and you can't do both jobs. Besides, you won't know what data we need." She tried a grin. "And you won't have opposable thumbs."

His laugh was a familiar and welcome soft rumble that washed over her, and then he was serious again. "All munaqsri travel alone. We must avoid detection—"

"All munaqsri miss delivering souls," she interrupted. "You've told me that yourself. I can help. Maybe we won't make all the births, but we can improve the odds."

He nodded slowly.

Cassie felt her shoulders unknot. He wanted to save the cubs badly enough. He'd agree. Together, they could save bears.

"You are certain you wish to do this?" he said. "It is not without risk. Once outside these walls, if I am not touching you, I cannot magic you. If we are separated . . ."

"I'll have my gear," she said, patting her pack. "If necessary, I can survive an entire week on the ice with this equipment." All her training, her skill, her education, had led to this. She'd be directly helping the polar bears instead of writing papers and securing grants. *If* he agreed.

ICE

Swinging his massive head over the documents, he studied the maps, the files, the lists of numbers. "If this helps . . . all polar bears will thank you. I thank you." He leaned his head against her stomach, and she wrapped her arms around his neck. In a lighter voice, he added, "It is, though, quite unnatural."

"So says the talking bear," she said.

His fur shook as he laughed again. "I had no one to mock me for days."

"Vacation's over," she said. "Cassie's home."

Softly, he said, "You have no idea how happy that makes me."

She felt her cheeks warm. She felt as if she could float to the ceiling. "Romantic," she said.

He covered his muzzle with his paw, miming embarrassment.

Cassie opened another binder. She wanted to show him everything. "Look, here are all the current tagging numbers from the Polar Bear Specialist Group of the IUCN."

"Come," he said, nudging her with his nose. "We have a long day ahead of us tomorrow."

Cassie grinned. Out on the ice, together. Leaving the IUCN binder, she walked alongside him, past the carvings in deep blue ice and up the staircase lit by candlelight. "You know I had a number all picked out for you: A505, Alaskan ID."

"A505," he repeated.

"I think you'd look nice with a tag. Just like an earring."

She tugged on his furry ear. She couldn't get enough of touching him. It reminded her that he was real. "Not to mention the green ink on your gums. Very attractive."

As always, he waited in the hall while she prepared for bed. Once she slid under the covers, she blew out the candle. Everything descended into darkness, and she heard the pad of bear paws and then the footsteps of a man. The mattress sank as he climbed into bed beside her.

For the first time in five nights, she slept well.

❄ ❄ ❄ ❄ ❄

Cassie woke first. Her cheek lay against his bare chest, smooth and human. Her arm was draped across his stomach. She lay there for a long moment, feeling him breathe. Her husband. She reached up in the darkness and lightly touched his face. Her fingers traced his chin and lingered over his lips. She'd never kissed him. She wondered what it would be like.

She felt him stir, and she pulled her hand away quickly. She rolled to her side of the bed. "Ready to patrol?" she asked him.

She felt the sheets shift and the mattress rise as he stood.

"We're going together, right?" she asked.

Cassie felt a wisp of wind in her face. When he spoke, it was with his deeper, polar bear voice. "Of course, O Intrepid Leader."

She grinned.

Cassie heard the door open. She waited until she heard

it click closed before finding her flashlight and turning it on. She dressed quickly in full expedition gear—Gore-Tex pants, mukluks, all of it—and then she met Bear at the front archway to the castle. Soon, she was riding him across the ice.

The Arctic spread before them, blue-shadowed and as broad as the Sahara. Cassie leaned over Bear's neck as the wind slapped her face. This was wonderful. This was magnificent. This was . . . far too slow. She shouted a dog sledding call into his ear: "Mush, mush, mush!"

"Very amusing," he said, but he sped into a blur. She whooped as the deep night-winter blue stretched into a single sheet of ice and sky. Yes! She was flying! The midday moon hung low and fat on the southern horizon. She waved to it.

Bear leaped over a pressure ridge. Laughing, Cassie grabbed his fur and clamped her thighs around his middle to keep from falling off. She loved this! They should have done this months ago.

She squinted into the dark whiteness. She saw the aurora borealis curling around the fringes of her vision, green and white flashes. According to Inuit legend, the northern lights were the dancing spirits of the dead. Cassie wondered if that was where the unclaimed souls went, the ones munaqsri missed, the ones that should have gone to newborns. *Don't be ridiculous*, she told herself. The aurora was caused by electrically charged particles from the sun hitting the upper atmosphere, not floating souls. The souls went . . . She had no idea where missed souls went. She supposed they could go to the aurora. Bear had said once that they were lost. Maybe eventually, she'd have enough data to map paths for deaths as well as births. Wouldn't that be something? But she shouldn't get ahead of herself. First she had to see whether her plan would work at all.

The first route Cassie had planned took them down into Lancaster Sound to Hudson Bay and then east to Davis Strait. At the opening to the sound, Bear shouted that he felt a call. Cassie hung on as Bear leaped and crashed through pressure ridges and over creaking ice pans.

Bear braked without warning, and Cassie flew into his neck. "Hold on," he told her. "We'll take it slow this first time." Gripping his neck fur, Cassie opened her mouth to ask what he meant.

He walked into a snowbank.

Snow melted like a mirage around them. Cassie shuddered as it slid through her. A few seconds later, she felt warm wet air on her face. Half her body was within the bear's den; the rest was immured in the hard-packed snow. She listened to the sow pant in the darkness. She'd never been so close to a birthing polar bear in the wild. She didn't think anyone ever had. This was amazing, she thought. This was impossible.

This was the power of a munaqsri. This was *why* he had power: to reach the bears as they were born or died. All the magic existed to make this moment possible.

"It is time. It is coming," Bear whispered.

"Can't see," she whispered back. Suddenly, she could. She saw white: fur and ice. Bear, she guessed, had altered her eyes. He'd changed her body, in the same way he did when he kept her warm on the ice.

Bear inched forward and laid his face next to the sow's stomach. Cassie wiggled closer too. "Do you have the soul?" she whispered.

"Watch," he said. Bear opened his mouth, and a shadow fell like a drop of water. It sank into vast mounds of fur. Cassie didn't breathe. A tiny wet shape, the cub, slid out of its mother and squirmed. In a soft voice, Bear said, "And that is how we make babies."

"It's . . . a miracle." She had no other word for it. Bear created miracles.

The cub mewled. Blind, it wormed through its mother's fur, and the sow licked it with a tongue that covered it in one swipe.

Silently, Bear retreated. They slid through the solid snow. Cassie felt as if she were being smothered, and she fought to stay calm. *Bear would never hurt me*, she told herself. She gasped in air as they emerged. Her muscles shook. "Are you all right?" Bear asked.

"Love the night vision," she said. "Hate the walking through walls." She took a deep breath to calm her racing heart.

Hands shaking, she took out her GPS: latitude 63° 46' 05" N, longitude 80° 09' 32" W. She marked it in a notebook, then tucked pencil, notebook, and GPS back into her inner layers. "We should head toward Churchill next. There are a couple mothers overdue west of Hudson Bay."

"As you wish, O Glorious Leader."

She snorted. "Cute."

❄ ❄ ❄ ❄ ❄

That night, Cassie lay beside Bear. "You awake?"

"Don't kick me," he said into his pillow.

She smiled and reached over in the darkness to touch his human shoulder. "It's going to work," she said. "That cub's birth proved it." She had a place here, not just as Bear's wife. She had a future.

"Yes," he said. She felt him shift. He was facing her now, she guessed.

"We're a team now," she said.

"Yes," he said.

She reached out again, and her fingers touched his smooth cheek. She wondered briefly what he'd look like in the light. Not that it mattered. He was her Bear. Cassie shifted closer.

He stilled, like a polar bear by a hole in the ice, but she was hyperaware of how human he was right now. She felt him waiting. He said nothing. Cassie tilted her head up, and in the darkness, she kissed him. Not moving his body, as if afraid she'd flee, he kissed her back, soft and sweet.

THIRTEEN

Latitude 83° 35' 43" N
Longitude 123° 29' 10" E
Altitude 4 ft.

AS LIGHT RETURNED to the southern Arctic, Cassie and Bear spent more and more time out on the ice. Every day under the blue-purple-pink sky, they patrolled the snowbanks of Alaska, Canada, Siberia, Greenland, and Norway. Every evening under the eyes of Bear's ice carvings, Cassie refined her maps and plotted their route for the next day. And every night in the dark, she kissed her husband until she fell asleep, curled in his arms. She'd never been happier.

One afternoon, when they were north of the Laptev Sea, Bear said, "I feel a call."

Fumbling for her notes, Cassie opened her mouth to ask which direction.

"Hold tight," he said. "There's little time."

Flattening herself, she held on to his broad neck as he sprang into superspeed. Ahead, she saw blue blackness—ocean water. He lunged forward into the black waves. Under the waves, water soaked into her parka. It seeped through her face mask and around her hood. But instead of cold, the water was as soft as air. She grinned. She loved Bear's magic.

On Bear's back, she burst out of the water. He paddled toward shore. Head and shoulders in air, Cassie clung to his wet fur. On the other side, he scrambled onto the ice and ran.

She heard the thrum of a helicopter.

Up ahead, in the distance, on ice stirred by the wind from a helicopter, a lone bear ran toward a ridge of ice. The bear's flank was streaked in red.

"Hold on!" Bear called. "We can't be seen!"

She wrapped her arms tightly around his neck, and Bear impossibly increased speed. Around them, the world streaked into a blur of white and blue.

It slowed for only a fraction of a second. She saw a flash of red on creamy white as Bear sank his teeth into the throat of the wounded bear. Bear yanked, and Cassie saw a streak of silver—and then Bear was running again.

Behind them, the bear crumpled, and the helicopter landed, kicking snow into the air. She saw it all in a fraction of an instant before they rocketed away.

"Bear, the poacher!" Cassie yelled. "Stop him!"

Bear vanished in between ice blocks. He didn't slow until

ICE

they were miles north. When he did stop, he swallowed the streak of silver—the dead bear's soul—whole.

Cassie shouted, "That bear didn't have to die! We could have scared the poacher off, and you could have healed him, magicked his cells." It was a waste. That beautiful polar bear . . . How could Bear have done that? Let that bear, one of his bears, die!

"Yes," he said.

She choked down words she'd been going to say. Yes, he could have saved the bear. "You're the Angel of Death for polar bears."

"It is necessary. If I do not claim the soul, a munaqsri from another species will. If no munaqsri does, the soul will be lost. Without souls to give the newborns, the species will become extinct."

He had prevented her from having hypothermia; he could have healed that bear. He could heal all the bears, all the time. But then where would the souls for the newborns come from? Those bears would be stillborn. She shook her head. All the implications . . .

"You knew my responsibilities."

But it was the first time she had witnessed this part of it.

"Cassie?" he said, concern in his voice. "Does this change things?"

He had such enormous power. Did that change things? She took a breath. It was his job. He existed to transport these souls, not to choose who lived and who died. That's what she had bought into—the continuation of the species, not the saving of individuals. Really, was it so much different from what a researcher did, studying without interfering?

Leaning forward, she laid her cheek on his neck. "It doesn't change things," she said. "You're my *tuvaaqan*, my soul mate." She'd never had a chance to use that Inupiaq word before. She tasted it on her tongue as she said it. "We're a team. Right?"

He nuzzled her hand with his cold nose. "We are a team, *tuvaaqan*," he affirmed. "I love that I can share this with you. I have never shared this with anyone. Thank you."

She threw her arms around his wide, furry neck. "You know, there's something else we've never shared, husband," she said very softly, and her heart beat faster. "We never had a proper wedding night."

❄ ❄ ❄ ❄ ❄

In the dark bedroom, Cassie unzipped her parka and pulled off her gaiters and mukluks. She heard Bear slough his bear fur in the familiar rush of wind. He was a man now, she knew. She grinned in the darkness. She had expected to be nervous, but she wasn't. This was Bear.

She slid off her Gore-Tex pants and pulled off three layers of socks.

She stripped off her wool sweater.

She removed her flannel shirt.

"How many layers do you wear?" Bear asked in his human voice.

ICE

"Some of us don't have blubber," she said, and took off her wool pants, her long johns, and her silkweights.

"Do you want to call me when you are done?"

"Cute," she said. She located him by listening to his breathing. She managed not to stub her toes on the wardrobe or the washbasin. Standing in front of him, she reached her fingers up to touch the bones of his cheek. She laid her hand on the side of his face and felt his eyelashes brush her skin. He blinked, and it felt like the brush of butterfly wings. Now she felt a twinge of nerves. For the first time, she was grateful for Bear's insistence on darkness. She could be bold in the dark. She could be beautiful in the dark.

"Are you certain this is what you want?" Bear asked.

It was so like Bear to ask. She felt her nervousness dissolve like sugar in water, and she smiled at him in the darkness. "Yes," she said simply.

She slid her arms around him. Her cheek against his chest, she felt his heart beat. It was as steady and as gentle as waves in the ocean. She felt the curve of his shoulder blades as his arms surrounded her. His hands covered half her back, cradling her. She burrowed against his bare chest. Leaning down, he kissed her neck.

Her skin tingled as he kissed her, and all thoughts ran out of her head. She felt the chill of the ice room, the warmth of his breath, and the touch of his hands. It was all that existed in the world.

Around them, the ice was silent.

FOURTEEN

Latitude 91° 00' 00" N
Longitude indeterminate
Altitude 15 ft.

CASSIE CLUTCHED THE EXQUISITELY carved ice toilet. Dammit, not again. For more than three months now, she'd endured random waves of nausea. Every time she thought she was well again, it reared its ugly . . . Uh-oh. She gritted her teeth as her stomach rose into her throat, tasting like rotten peanuts. Sweat pricked her forehead.

Bear padded into the bathroom. "Cassie, are you all right?"

She spat into the toilet. Her throat burned. "Ow."

Cassie leaned her head against the rim of the crystalline bowl. It was smooth and cool. "I'm never eating again," she said. Clearly, she'd had too many magical feasts. She had a potbelly now that pressed against the elastic waist of her pants.

Bear touched her damp hair with his nose. "Breathe

deeply. Fighting it will only make it worse." She felt his hot breath on her scalp. It made her itch.

"Stop hovering." Like shooing a fly, she swatted the air in front of him.

"It will pass soon."

"It better." Oh, too much motion—her insides flopped, and she felt for the toilet. Her stomach squeezed as if it were ejecting a lung. Empty, she collapsed backward. "Can't you magic me? Transform my sick molecules?"

"I do not wish to interfere," he said. "Your body is reacting naturally."

"Reacting normally for botulism."

Bear blinked his glassy black eyes at her. "You are joking. You must know the cause of this—your daily nausea, your changing shape."

Cassie clung to the ice rim of the toilet. When he put it that way . . . But no, she'd been careful. She'd been smart. "I can't be. It's not possible."

"Because of the chemical imbalance?" Lying down, he curled around her like a giant cat and laid his head on her lap, as if to reassure her. "I know. I fixed it. All is well now."

"You fixed it?" Cassie felt dizzy. She was . . . no. She tried to remember her last period and couldn't.

"It was simple. All I needed to do was adjust the hormone levels," he said, clear pride in his voice. "It was no harder than keeping your body warm or protecting you in the Arctic water."

Cassie threw herself forward and vomited with all her

strength, as if she could expel the fetus inside her. Bile scratched her throat, and she sank backward again, diaphragm sore from pushing. She dug her fingernails into her curved stomach. She sucked in, but it would not flatten. It was as firm as a muscle.

He'd retreated from her as she'd vomited, and he now stood beside her, casting a massive shadow over her. "Are you . . . You are not happy?"

"How could you do this to me?" He had deliberately altered her molecules to impregnate her without asking her, without telling her. "That 'chemical imbalance' was deliberate. I'm on the pill."

"Deliberate? You caused . . . ? But how . . . ," he said. He swung his head low, an agitated polar bear. "You were willing. I asked if you were certain. You said you were. I thought you understood." She felt like she was drowning. His words drowned her. "You knew from the beginning: I must have children. This was the reason I sought a wife. There must be more munaqsri. This child—a future munaqsri—is desperately needed."

"I thought you . . ." She felt as if her insides were shaking so hard that they'd fly apart. "I thought you loved me. For me. Not for . . ."

"I do love you," he said. "You are my *tuvaaqan*, my wife, the mother of my—"

"You used me," she said. "You didn't even ask me. You just . . . 'fixed' me." She had trusted him. She had believed they were a team.

He padded closer to her. "We are going to have a baby," he said. "We are going to bring life into the world. Do you not see how wonderful it is?"

"Just . . . leave me alone." Cassie pushed his chest, hands sinking into fur, and he backed out of the bathroom. She shut the door in his face and locked it. Back against the door, she slid to the floor. Her nausea threatened like a tidal wave. She wanted to rip her internal organs out of her. Heart included.

Through the door, he said, "I love you."

She retched on the floor and then cried.

✵ ✵ ✵ ✵ ✵

He had to reverse what he had done. It was that simple. He could manipulate her molecules; he could fix this. Ice crunched under Cassie's mukluks as she walked through the topiary garden. If he could fix a "chemical imbalance" and keep her warm in the Arctic, he could put everything back the way it had been.

She found him between the rosebushes. Facing the permanent sun, he did not turn as she came up behind him. She swallowed a lump in her throat. He could do it, yes. But would he? She didn't know. She felt as if he had turned into a stranger, hidden behind black eyes and cream fur. Looking down, she studied the roses. Amber and violet in the low sun, each petal and leaf twinkled with Bear's reflection.

"You shot at me," he said. "Do you remember? You shot

at me with your tranquilizer gun, and I still married you. Did you ever wonder why?"

She hadn't, until now.

"Because you shot at me. Because you chased me, before you knew what I was, before I dared reveal myself to you. You were so stubborn, so single-minded, so strong. Without a second's thought, you risked your life chasing me, all for your work, for your father, for his station, and for the polar bears," Bear said. She stared at him, but he wasn't finished. "And afterward? You were so courageous that you would marry a beast to save a woman you had never met. So great-hearted that you could care about a 'freak of nature.' So intelligent that you could be my partner, my teammate, my *tuvaaqan*. These are the reasons I love you. It is not because of your ovaries or chromosomes; it is because I know, out of all the world, that you are my match."

Cassie lifted her hand toward him. She wanted to bury her fingers in his fur and press her face against his neck. But she stopped an inch short of touching him. She desperately wanted to believe him. She'd thought he was her match too. She'd thought he was her *tuvaaqan*. Maybe he still was. It could all be a misunderstanding. "If it's me you love, then take this creature out of me," she said.

He shook his heavy head. "You do not know what you are asking," he said. "It is not a 'creature.'"

Who knew what kind of thing was growing inside her? It wasn't human; it was half-munaqsri. Thanks to Bear's

ICE

"quirks," she didn't know what that meant. She hugged her arms across her chest. "How can I believe you? You won't even let me see you." For the first time in months, she wondered what the darkness hid from her.

"It is a child, and the world needs it." He turned to face her. "Once you understand how important this child is, you will be as happy as I am. You have to trust me. All will be well. Give it time. You will see."

Cassie tried to read his inscrutable bear eyes, but all she saw was her own reflection, distorted to a reverse hourglass. "How pregnant am I?"

"You are due in the fall, after the equinox."

He'd known for at least three months. *Months!* He must have "fixed" her during the polar bear birth season, maybe even the first time they'd slept together. She felt sick and dizzy all over again. He'd lied to her. He'd used her.

"You will be a mother," he said. "We will have our own miracle."

She didn't know how to be a mother. "I am too young to have a baby," she said.

"And I suppose I am too old?" He looked out across the ice fields. In a soft sad voice, he said, "I had believed this would make you as happy as it has made me. Perhaps I deluded myself. I had hoped . . . once it was real, inside you, you would be happy."

She *had* been happy. She'd been happy with everything exactly as it was, or as she'd thought it was. "You were wrong."

"I did not intentionally hurt you. You know I would never do that. I am not some monster, Cassie. You know me."

Wind rustled the ice leaves. Cassie shivered, and the sun continued to circle the horizon.

❄ ❄ ❄ ❄ ❄

You know me. Clutching the sheets to her chin, Cassie listened to him breathe. She felt a tight ache inside her chest. Did she know him? She'd thought she did. But now . . . Had he truly used her, or was it all a misunderstanding, as he'd said? Was he the man she thought he was? Was he a man at all?

Loud, her heart beat staccato as she knelt on the mattress. She cupped her hand over the flashlight. She had a right to know who he truly was and what was inside her, didn't she?

She switched on the light. Her hand, covering the beam, glowed pink. Bear was now a shape in the semi-darkness. She saw his chest rise and fall. Gathering her courage, she pointed the flashlight toward the ceiling and removed her hand. The beam hit the ice canopy, and light reflected in a thousand directions. Rainbows swirled over the bed.

And she saw Bear.

Like a polar bear, his skin was black and his hair was creamy white. The flashlight shook in her hand, and the beam danced over his muscles. He was beautiful, as perfect and as ageless as a Michelangelo statue. Looking at him, she could not breathe.

He looked like an angel, or a god.

She wanted to touch him and feel his familiar skin and know this godlike creature was her Bear. Now that she had her wish, she didn't know what it meant that he was so beautiful. Seeing him did not answer anything.

She wanted to breathe him in and swallow him whole. She wanted to wrap herself around him. She wanted to feel he was real with every inch of her skin. Leaning over him, she brushed his lips with hers. Bear opened his eyes. "Cassie, no!"

Cassie dropped the flashlight. It hit her thigh and fell to the floor. Shadows spread across Bear, the bed, and the room. "Ow! Bear, don't do that!"

From the floor, the flashlight cast giant shadows on the ice walls. Bear's shadow stretched as he pulled himself to full height. Instinctively, she flinched. He looked like an angry god. "I told you never to look at me. You should have trusted me!"

Rising to her knees, she put her hands on her hips. "Trust *you*?"

As quickly as it had come, the anger seemed to drain out of him. He sank down on the bed and put his face in his hands. "Oh, Cassie."

Disconcerted, she opened and shut her mouth. He seemed truly upset. But what was so terrible about her looking at him? He was beautiful. He was perfect.

"Cassie, my Cassie." He raised his head. He looked like he was going to cry. What was wrong? He cupped her cheek in his palm. The look in his eyes . . . Wow, she was looking into his eyes. His human eyes. His hand was warm and soft on her cheek.

"Bear?" she said uncertainly. She didn't like the look in his eyes, that lost look.

She felt mist touch her skin. She brushed her arm automatically, but it was dry. He released her face and took her hand. He ran his thumb over her fingers, pausing on her ring finger. "I have to leave you now," he said.

He had to *what*?

Clearly, she'd heard him wrong. She looked at his expression, and she felt her heart squeeze. She hadn't heard him wrong. She started to shake her head. He couldn't leave!

"Please, listen, Cassie," he said before she could speak. "It was the bargain to free your mother. You could never see my human face. Or know the reason why you could not. Cassie, it was the only way to free your mother. It was the only way to marry you."

"You and your stupid bargains." She tried to sound cold and angry but her voice betrayed her. "Did you expect me to be telepathic?" She was blinking furiously now. Oh, God, what had he promised? What had he risked? What had she done?

Bear said as if quoting something, "All ties between us are snapped, and I must marry the troll princess."

She shook his shoulders. "You are not leaving," she said. She was crying. She knew it and she couldn't stop it. This was absurd. Troll princess! "I will not let the trolls take you."

ICE

"That's my Cassie." He buried his fingers in her hair. "But you cannot fight this. I must keep my promise. It is the price of being a munaqsri." She heard rustling like wind in leaves.

"You are not leaving," she said even more fiercely.

He pressed his lips on her forehead. "Take care of our baby."

"I'm not letting you go." The false wind snapped her hair. It whooshed between them and circled around them.

"No choice," he said. "It has already begun."

Dammit, no! She was not losing him! "Then I'm coming with you!"

"You cannot."

"Then I'll follow!"

He shook his head sadly. "I will be taken to the castle that is east of the sun and west of the moon. You cannot follow me there. It is beyond the ends of the earth."

"I'll find you." Sheets fluttered around them like breaking waves.

Bear gripped her. "No! It is too dangerous."

"Not for me," she said. "I find polar bears, remember? It's what I do." She'd chased him once; she'd chase him again.

The tide of wind was a roar, and Bear had to shout, "You will die before you reach it! Promise me you will not try!"

"I will find you!" She was not losing him. Not now, not like this.

Swarming faster, the water-wind swept Bear off the bed.

He hung in the air like an angel ascending. "If you love me, let me go. Please, Cassie, keep yourself safe, keep our baby safe."

She jumped to her feet and wrapped her arms around his waist. "No!"

"Cassie, promise me! Think of the baby!"

She didn't want a baby; she wanted him! She couldn't lose him! Pulled upward, he slipped through her arms. She squeezed his knees as the wind lifted him higher. His head reached the canopy, and the ice melted around him like meringue. His shoulders passed through it, then his chest, his waist, his thighs. Cassie's head hit the canopy—solid. "No! Come back!" His knees slipped through her arms. She clutched his ankles. "No!"

He disappeared through the canopy, and Cassie fell. She bounced on the silken sheets, and her head smacked backward into the bedpost.

Everything went black.

PART TWO

East of the Sun and West of the Moon

FIFTEEN

Latitude 91° 00' 00" N
Longitude indeterminate
Altitude 15 ft.

CASSIE WOKE COLD. Shivering on the silken sheets, she massaged the lump on the back of her skull. For several seconds, she wondered why she had slept on top of the sheets, why she was cold, and why her head ached. Then she heard the dripping.

She leaned down from the bed and picked her flashlight up off the floor, then shined it on the bedpost. The post glistened with a fresh sheen of water. Droplets ran down the spiral. The canopy dripped as if it were crying. *It cannot melt. Not so long as I am here.*

Bear was gone.

The bed was melting.

"Oh, no," she said.

Cassie vaulted out of bed; her bare feet hit ice. Cold shot

up her legs, and she grabbed the bedpost. It was a wet icicle. She snatched her hand back. Cold! She ran to her pack and shed her nightshirt. Limp on the floor, the silk soaked in meltwater. Cassie bundled on flannels and wools. She could have woken with hypothermia. She could have woken with hypothermia *and* a concussion. *I could have not woken at all*, she thought.

She heard a sudden snap like a rifle shot—the snap of cracked ice. *That sounded like it came from a wall*, she thought. And then she heard a sound like a thousand windows breaking.

Oh, God, it wasn't just the bedroom that was melting. It was the castle. The castle was melting. She had to get out of here—out of the bedroom, out of the castle, out into the Arctic.

Out into the Arctic, but . . . She didn't have a choice, she told herself. She had to leave *now*. Heart thudding faster, she pulled on her full gear: parka, mukluks, gaiters. She'd kept her pack prepared for her trips with Bear, so it took only a few precious seconds to lift the pack onto her back— but with each second, the shotgun sound of cracking ice crescendoed. Securing the pack, she hurried into the hall.

In the hall, it was worse. Cracks raced through the ice walls. Meltwater ran in rivers. *Run, run, run!* her mind shouted at her. Cassie skidded down the hallway, and the flashlight's beam swept over dripping walls and ceiling. Gripping the wet banister, she sidestepped down the waterfall stairs. Rumbling shook the floor. *Please, don't let it collapse,* she thought. With the ceiling and the spires, thousands of pounds of ice were above her. Catching her balance at the bottom of the stairs, she ran through the banquet hall.

Chandeliers clanked as the banquet hall shook. Shards fell and splashed into an inch of water. A caribou sculpture toppled. Chunks of ice scattered across the banquet hall. Cassie shielded her face. A chandelier plummeted from the ceiling. When the chandelier crashed down, shards flew like shrapnel.

Cassie ran through the water. *Faster, faster!* Her pack pounded on her back. Frescoes peeled from the walls, and statues tumbled from alcoves. She dodged chunks of falling ice.

Buttresses shook. Pillars crumbled. Overhead, the vaulted ceiling fractured. Plumes of ice filled the air in a thick haze. She sprinted for the crystal lattice gate as the floor heaved. She scrambled over the cracks.

The splintered gate rained daggers of ice. Covering her head, Cassie plunged through it. Ice spikes hit her arms and her neck. Screaming, she burst out the other side. Her pack slammed her tailbone.

Outside, the topiary garden melted. Faces ran into puddles. Limbs fell. Undercut by running water, the sculptures collapsed. Cassie ran for the outer wall. Half of it had fallen.

It was as if a giant were ripping the castle apart. With deafening cracks like an iceberg calving, spires split from the walls and crashed to the ground. Cassie fell forward as the ground bucked. *Keep moving,* she thought. *Must keep moving!* She splashed in meltwater, and then she scrambled to her feet while, Jericho-like, the walls came tumbling down.

She scrambled over the remnants of the blue outer wall. Behind her, she heard gushing, like a dam released. *Run!* A mammoth waterfall crashed down from the parapets. It drowned the topiary garden.

Snow cycloned, and ice pelted her face and arms. Cassie stumbled as the ground shook. Again, she was knocked down. Ice chunks rained down on her like a meteor shower. On her knees, she crawled. She inhaled snow, and tears poured from her eyes as the ice pelted her.

And then suddenly, it was still.

Curled on the ground, Cassie panted. Her muscles were as tense as fists. She heard running water. Ice tinkled. She tried to open her eyes and could not. The tears had frozen her eyelids shut.

Dammit, she had to see! What had happened? The castle, her home . . . Was she still too close? She couldn't run if she couldn't see which direction to run.

She yanked off her gloves and spat on her fingers. She rubbed the warm saliva on her eyelids. Eyelashes broke. Her hands stiffened in the cold. She scraped until she could crack her eyes open. She blinked furiously and shoved her chilled hands back into the gloves and mitts.

She was surrounded by white. Snow hung in the air, and

it was impossible to distinguish between ground and sky. The world was devoid of color. It was as if she had fallen into a bowl of milk. Securing her goggles, she stood and squinted into the whiteout. Where was the castle? Had it fallen? What about the gardens? Slowly, the snow-choked air thinned.

And the polar bears came.

One by one, the white bears walked ghostlike out of the snow. Through the blurred air, they appeared to drift. Close by—too close—one brushed past her. She stiffened, wanting to scream, not daring to scream. Bears were all around her, emerging from the white. She was surrounded, engulfed.

As the snow settled, she saw hundreds coming from all directions. Soon she could see the gardens, now a wasteland of icy spikes. Sniffing the snow, the polar bears wandered through the wreckage, trampling the remnants. Cassie swallowed, a lump in her throat. All of Bear's beautiful sculptures . . . And then she saw what was left of her home.

The castle was gone. The buttresses were ice boulders; the walls were icebergs. She began to shake. She could have been crushed. If she had woken a few minutes later . . . if she had run a little slower . . . She could have been killed. *As long as these walls are standing, nothing here will harm you*, Bear had said once. The walls were no longer standing. Her home was destroyed.

And Bear was gone.

She'd lost him. She'd truly lost Bear.

Cassie felt icy knives twisting in her gut. Her husband

ICE

was gone, her home destroyed, she was thirteen hundred miles north of the station, and she was surrounded by polar bears.

More bears came. All around her, the ice was thick with them. Cassie was squeezed between dozens—up to her neck in bears. Fur pressed against her, and the stench of their dead-seal breath made her head pound. In every direction, all she could see was the curve of their backs like waves in a cream white ocean. She was drowning in a sea of polar bears.

Surrounded by predators, she felt short of air. Bears did not gather like this. It wasn't natural. *Run,* her instincts screamed. "Keep calm," she whispered to herself.

Inches from her, a polar bear swung his head toward her face. He poked her parka with his muzzle. She smelled his breath as he snuffled her face mask. "Don't eat me," she said. Her voice cracked.

At the sound of her voice, other bears turned to stare at her.

Shivers walked up her spine.

Cassie heard a bear huff. More bears turned their heads, and then more. Hundreds of blank, black eyes bored into her. *Don't move. Just don't move,* she thought. Her skin crawled, and her feet started moving despite her. All the bears were watching her now. She heard the crunch of her mukluks and the breathing of thousands of bears. *Don't run,* she thought, but her feet retreated faster and faster. The bears parted like the Red Sea. She backed through them, out of the press of bears and onto open ice, and then she turned and ran. Her pack slapped her back. Wind pounded her face. Leaning into the wind, she ran across the frozen waves.

In an unnatural herd, the polar bears followed.

SIXTEEN

Latitude 88° 51' 42" N
Longitude 151° 25' 50" W
Altitude 10 ft.

OVERHEAD, THE SKY WAS PALEST BLUE, almost white from the reflected ice. There was not a single bird or plane. Cassie checked the GPS: 88° 51' 42" N and 151° 25' 50" W. For five days, she had trekked across the frozen waves. She should have been rescued by now.

"C'mon, Max," she whispered as she looked again at the sky. "Save me." Low on the horizon, the permanent sun pricked the corners of her eyes.

Why hadn't he come?

The low sun rolled along the horizon as she continued on. The afternoon's white glare increased as the sun passed due south. Hundreds, maybe thousands, of polar bears still plodded behind her. She felt prickles on her spine as she thought about them, her silent white shadows. Dad and his team should have noticed the absence of so many polar bears by now. They should have sent Max in his plane to investigate. He should have followed the signals from the bears' tracking collars—any signal from any bear—and they should have led him directly to her.

By evening, the sun was to her right. Ice crystals sparkled in a halo around the sun and in gold sheets around Cassie. The powdery mist cut visibility even more. She forced herself to concentrate on the ice in front of her. But even with all her concentration, she stumbled over invisible frozen waves. She had no depth perception in the glare of infinite whiteness. Her remaining eyelashes were icicles, framing her view of the world. Her nostril hairs had also frozen. She exhaled through her nose to keep it warmer. Her Gore-Tex pants rustled as she stumbled along. It was the only sound in the emptiness besides the huffing of the bears.

Even if all the collars had malfunctioned at once, someone would have had to notice that hundreds of bears had disappeared. For miles, the ice fields were clogged with bears, yet in five days, she had not heard a single engine from the Eastern Beaufort Sea Research Station or from anywhere else.

Maybe they all thought it was an equipment malfunction. No station would risk a Twin Otter this far north on an equipment malfunction. And none of them would admit to the others that they had lost track of this many bears. It would be weeks before Dad would swallow his pride and contact NPI. But she had only one week's worth of food supplies, and she'd already used five days'. If she stretched the freeze-dried food packets and cut her rations in half . . . she might have four, at most five, days left.

Dammit, Dad should know better, she thought. He knew about munaqsri. He knew impossibilities could happen. But if Dad didn't send a plane soon . . . She sucked in air, and the air burned. She had to stay positive. Someone would come.

She hiked for two more days before she reached the Lomonosov Ridge. Still no Max. Still no plane. Still no rescue. She camped in the shadow of ice monoliths, leaning towers and half-fallen pinnacles of ice, and she ate a dinner of half rations.

In the morning, Cassie scrambled out of her sleeping bag as her stomach forced last night's dinner into her throat. She clapped her hands over her mouth. She could not lose the nutrients. Bits spurted through her fingers. Warm, the oatmeal chunks steamed on the ice. She swallowed hard and clenched her teeth. *Hold it in,* she told herself. *Come on, hold it.*

Her own body had never worked against her before. She felt as if she were being sabotaged from the inside. She swallowed back bile and patted loose snow on her forehead. With a baby growing inside her, she'd need more food, not less. She might have even less time than she'd thought. How could Bear have done this to her?

Shakily, she stood. She looked out across the wasteland of ice. Brilliant in the morning light, it made her eyes water to look at it. The sky was a startling blue, and the horizon was lemon yellow. She wiped her hands on her pants and then found her gloves. Her hands had chilled fast. Her mouth was sticky, and her head was light. Exposed to the frozen air, her cheeks had begun to stiffen. She warmed them with her mitts before putting on her solid-ice face mask. The polar bears, she noticed, had returned. Expressionless, they watched her. She told herself to keep ignoring them.

She shoved her sleeping bag into her pack. It crackled, and she could feel lumps of ice in the down. She wished she had a little of Bear's warmth magic. She remembered all the rides across the ice. She had been able to leave her hood back and her coat open, and the arctic wind had felt like a summer breeze on her face. She remembered snow-ball fights in the castle ballroom, where she'd used her bare hands without any chill—*Stop it*, she told herself. She had to concentrate on surviving. *Stay focused. Be strong. Keep moving.* The farther south she went, the better the odds that Max would find her. After that, she could think about Bear.

Cassie hefted the pack onto her sore shoulders and fastened the waist strap. She'd have to pick her route carefully today. The ice around her was shattered. She could hear the low grumble of the tides deep beneath her. Picking an ice boulder, Cassie climbed it. On top, she scanned the landscape. The ice did not improve for at least ten miles. She automatically wrinkled her face to prevent frostbite as she checked the sky. Clouds were beginning to mar the brilliant blue. The clouds reflected the patchy ice below: bright white over thick ice and gray over thin.

She checked the horizon, and her heart went cold. Wind slapped into her, but she didn't move. Squinching her eyes, she stared at a smudge darkening the distance. Was that . . . Yes, yes, it was.

The winds were bringing a storm.

Oh, no. Please, no.

Maybe it would veer. Maybe she was wrong.

She didn't think she was wrong.

She had no choice but to continue on. Fine packed snow plugged the paths between pillars of ice. At times, she had to slog through it and trust that she would hear the cracking of ice underneath fast enough to jump to safety. She tried to keep to the exposed ice, listening for the telltale crinkling sounds as the ice throbbed underneath her. She climbed over a pile of ice rubble and looked again to the south. The clouds looked like a writhing mass of bruises. The storm was coming.

She wondered, as she looked across the shattered ice, if she was looking at her own death. She remembered Gram's voice: *With the strength of a thousand blizzards, the North Wind swooped down onto the house that held his daughter, her husband, and their newborn baby.* She could be swept away by her mother's winds.

If she'd had some warning of all of this . . . Bear's bargain had stranded her alone on the Arctic ice pack. He should have known that she'd encounter a storm at some point in

her trek. If he'd found some way to hint at the truth . . .
He could have found some oblique way to warn her. Had
he tried and she'd missed it? As she hiked across the ice,
she played through her memories—and with each moment
she relived, she missed him more until it felt like an aching
wound.

Two hours later, the wind howled through the pressure
ridges, kicking snow into the air. She was pelted with ice
particles. After every other step, she wiped her goggles.
Cassie tried to calculate how far she'd hiked. The layer of
ice around her collar made it difficult to move her head.
Not far enough, she thought.

More ice particles hit her, and she staggered backward.
Arms over her face, she pushed through the wind, away from
the leaning ice towers. It was tempting to hide in the shelter
of one of the mammoth ones, but the ice around them was
weaker. She needed the thick stuff if she did not want to end
up underneath waves. Wind-driven snow stung like BBs.
Visibility was low. Cassie stumbled over the rubble.

She hit flat ice. Leaning into the wind, she forded across
it. She knelt down and dusted the surface snow away so she
could see the base ice. Green-blue-brown, it seemed like
old, thick ice. *Please, let it be old, thick ice.* "It's coming,
guys," she called to the polar bears. "Better batten down
the hatches." Her voice shook. She saw only a half-dozen
bear shapes in the swirling snow. *Please, let me survive this*,
she thought.

Fighting the wind, Cassie set up her sleeping bag. Stiff

with ice, it did not want to unroll. She swore at it and flattened it with her full body weight. Hands aching, she tied it with spare straps to her pack and anchored it all with an ice screw.

Momentarily, the wind died, and she saw the storm. It sounded and looked like a cloud of hissing bees. "Oh, Bear," she whispered, "how could you do this to me?"

The boiling mass disappeared behind a wall of white ice shards. Cassie wiggled into her sleeping bag. She secured the zippers. Coming closer, the storm roared like a 747. Cassie prayed, and the storm hit.

SEVENTEEN

Latitude 87° 58' 23" N
Longitude 150° 05' 12" W
Altitude 8 ft.

THE WORLD FELL APART.

Like an angry god, the wind punished the ice. It tore the ocean open, and it slammed it shut. Plates of ice rode over one another, jutting into the black sky. The ice screamed.

She curled inside her fragile cocoon. Black in the false night, her world had shrunk to six feet by two. The ice underneath her shook. Clenching her teeth, she hugged herself into a ball, as if that would hold the ice together.

She heard thunderous grinding as if the ground were being squeezed. Her heart beat in her throat. Sweat chilled her flesh. Any second, the ice could split and she could be dropped into the ocean. She could disappear without a trace. Dad, Gail, Gram . . . they would never know what had happened to her.

ICE

The wind slammed into her sleeping bag. She skidded in a circle around the single ice screw. Clockwise, with the screw. Cassie rolled inside the sleeping bag. She clutched at the nylon sides. Like a sail in irons, the nylon flapped. Wind whipped under her, and Cassie bounced on the ice. Slamming down hard, she hit her elbow, then her knee, then her hip.

A banshee scream, the wind shifted. She skidded again. Counterclockwise, loosening the screw. Soundless against the howling, she yelled. She pushed against the confines of the sleeping bag. "Let me out of here! Please, let me out!" Shrieking, she started to cry.

Inside a prison, Cassie was tossed back and forth, bruising with each roll. Outside, the storm boiled.

Seconds, minutes, hours later, the storm howled north, the ice fell silent, and the air was full of snow. Cassie, knotted inside her sleeping bag, whimpered.

❄ ❄ ❄ ❄ ❄

Fitfully, she slept. She dreamed she was entombed in ice. Seven-foot trolls chased Bear, and she could not move. She screamed, but her throat did not work. A troll touched Bear, and he dissolved. She screamed again, soundless, and the troll turned toward her. Its face was a grotesque mask of moving shadows. She woke screaming, in blackness and in sweat.

Out! She had to get out! Cassie fumbled for the zipper to her sleeping bag. She couldn't breathe. She couldn't think. Out, out, out! Cold streamed in as she squirmed out.

She crawled into surreal whiteness. She could see nothing: no color, no shadow, no ground, no sky. "Help me! Someone! Anyone!" she called.

Surrounded by the false white night, she was utterly alone. Cassie felt around her. She found the strap she had used to tie herself to her pack. She shook the ice off it and pulled the pack toward her. At least she had not lost it in the storm. She hugged it as if it were a teddy bear, while snow seeped into her fleece.

It was the cold drip down her neck, more than anything else, that convinced her she was still alive. Her survival instincts kicked in as she started shivering, and she crawled back inside her sleeping bag.

She lay there for several hours, imagining her joints locking and her muscles stiffening like a corpse in rigor mortis. She pictured herself turning into the sculpture that Bear had carved. . . . She closed her eyes, and she could see Bear leading her by the sleeve to the center of the garden, and her following, laughing, until she saw what it was he wanted her to see: the sculpture of her. He'd carved it for her, a late birthday present. Carved it from memory, a perfect likeness. Said it was the heart of the garden. And he'd proceeded to serenade her. Artist he was; singer he wasn't. Remembering how she'd laughed, Cassie felt like crying.

He'd loved her, hadn't he?

Did it matter anymore if he had? The sculpture was gone now. Bear was gone.

ICE

"Stop it," she said out loud. It would kill her—the cold, the hunger, the exhaustion, her own thoughts. She felt like the storm had seeped inside her and was now tearing through her brain, her heart, her everything.

With an effort, she pushed her thoughts away and lay in her silent prison and listened to her heart beating like the sound of steady footsteps that were always the same distance away.

She lost track of time. At some point, her bladder demanded that she go outside. She emerged into the white-out. Snow spat into her face. Visibility was still zero. She could not even see her feet. She felt her way to the end of the sleeping bag and squatted under her parka. She did not dare go any more than a foot from the sleeping bag. She could almost hear Dad's voice telling her it was too danger-ous to move in a whiteout. She'd heard stories of people lost in whiteouts five feet from their tent, and inside the solid whiteness, she believed it.

After crawling back into her sleeping bag, she lay lis-tening to the wind. She wondered about Bear. What was it like for him in the troll castle? What were the trolls doing to him? Gail had screaming nightmares of her time there.

He'd risked so much to marry her. He *had* to have cared about her. Cassie thought of the way they used to talk late into the night until they were both falling asleep mid-sentence. She thought of how they'd worked side by side on her maps and numbers, devising better routes for patrol-ling. She thought of how he'd held her at night, stroking her hair, and whispering to her. And now he was trapped like her mother had been because she'd turned on a single flashlight.

Hours later, she checked on the conditions again. In some ways, they were better. The snow had thinned enough for her to see the red blur that was her pack, though she still could not see her full sleeping bag. From her waist down, the bag disappeared into the white as if it were an apparition. In some ways, though, conditions were worse: Thinner snow also reflected more sun. The white glare hurt, and she blinked back tears. Her eyes felt pierced by sand—the first symptom of snow blindness.

She crawled back inside. *Admit it,* she thought, *your plan has failed.* Max had not rescued her, despite all the polar bears. He certainly wasn't coming now, when she was lost in a whiteout. He had failed her. Dad had failed her— just like he'd failed Gail. And just like Bear had failed her, abandoning her one mile north of the North Pole. Or like she had failed Bear, betraying his trust after he had pleaded with her never to look at him.

The look in his eyes . . .

She *had* to escape the ice. But there wasn't an escape.

The closest land was Ward Hunt Island at 83° N and 75° W. *Too many miles,* her mind whispered. Too many miles and too little food. All the possibilities played through her mind: starvation, dehydration, freezing, drowning. Curling into a ball, she hugged herself. "Oh, Bear," she whispered, "I'm sorry." Hours passed.

EIGHTEEN

Latitude 87° 58' 23" N
Longitude 150° 05' 12" W
Altitude 8 ft.

ENOUGH WAITING.

Enough fear.

Enough of the damn whiteout. She was *not* going to continue to lie here, obsessing over Bear, until death or insanity
claimed her. Whether he had meant to betray her or not,
staying here wouldn't help.

She was an Arctic explorer, dammit. She could survive
this. She had her goggles to prevent snow blindness and
her GPS to keep her from going in circles, for as long as the
batteries lasted. She had her own skill and Dad's training to
keep her from falling through the ice. Even with the risks,
it was still her best shot at survival. She had to get further
south for there to be any chance of Max (or any other pilot)
spotting her, and she didn't have enough food left to wait

for the whiteout to lift. *I'm going*, she thought. Joints as stiff as wood, Cassie put on her gear inside the sleeping bag, and then she crawled out.

Standing, she felt dizzy. Her knees shook and she sat down hard. She was weaker than she'd thought. The half rations and forced inactivity had taken a toll. Cassie waited until her vision cleared. Visibility was at five feet, maximum. Moving slowly, she wrapped an extra silk-weight long underwear around her goggles to cut down on glare, and then she tried to roll her sleeping bag. She had sweat into it, and it had frozen. It fought her for each bend. Finally, she forced it into a squashed polygon and secured it to her pack. She lifted the pack onto her back. The straps cut into her shoulders. Numbly, her hands tried to buckle the waist belt. The belt was encrusted in ice. It took her three tries.

Then she walked into the snow-choked air.

Within minutes, her stomach hurt and even her bone marrow felt cold. The dryness of the air sucked moisture from her mouth, and she felt frostbite prickles in her cheeks under her frozen face mask. She shouldn't be out walking in a whiteout. Only idiots went out in white-outs. *Kinnaq*, her mind whispered—lunatic. But if she stopped here, in the ice rubble, then Max would never see her even when the whiteout cleared. She needed to be on flat ice for him to rescue her. *I have to at least try to make it possible for him to find me*, she thought. *This is smart*, she told herself, *not crazy*. Giving up was for the crazy. As she'd once told Bear, she didn't give up.

Cassie kept walking, listening for the familiar crackle of breaking ice. Around her, the whiteout gradually—very gradually—dispersed. She caught glimpses of the bears— still out there, still following. *Let them,* she thought. She didn't have the strength to fear them anymore. She shuffled across the ice with her eyes only on the next step. When she finally remembered to look up, she could see fifty feet. Beyond, the world was swallowed by snow.

The storm had pulled the ice apart at the seams.

Leads, riverlike cracks, crisscrossed the ice. A dense haze rose off the open water. New pressure ridges had been born, and others had caved. She stared at the landscape. She hadn't imagined the damage would be so severe. She had been lucky to find a solid floe. Another few feet and . . . Very lucky.

It took Cassie several minutes to work up the courage to move on. She stepped across a lead onto the more fractured ice. In some leads, the water had frozen into a smooth road. She followed one, watching for mouse gray thin ice. Elastic, the ice bent under her weight. She scrambled forward as the ice fractured behind her. Plates of ice tilted like seesaws under her. The ice made faint grating sounds beneath her. It was so hard to focus. Bear wasn't here to save her from freezing or drowning, she reminded herself; she had to save herself. "Don't miss," she whispered.

Cold permeated her. Her blood felt sluggish in her veins. She placed her foot down, and a plate of ice shot up. Cassie dove forward and grabbed for the top. Her feet slid out from under her and dangled over black water.

All around her, the polar bears watched.

Squinching her legs up, she forced the plate to tilt. Cassie dove for the next pan of ice. Her legs splashed into the water as the plate leaned in the opposite direction. Ice tore her Gore-Tex pants as she, with a burst of adrenaline she did not know she had, hauled herself out of the water.

She forced herself to stand. The cold . . . It burned. It sliced. She heard her father's voice in her head yelling out instructions. Shedding her pack, she dropped into the snow and rolled as if extinguishing a fire. Snow absorbed the water on her legs. Her pants crinkled as the outer layer froze.

She had to move. *It will dry if you move*, Dad's voice told her. Shivering uncontrollably, Cassie lifted her pack and walked on across the ice. Wind pushed right through her. She wished she were at the castle. She wished this were over. No, she wished it had never begun. She would have given anything, done anything, to have everything back the way it had been. *Bear, where are you?* She missed him so much that it hurt, like a fist squeezing her stomach. Or was that the cold? Or the hunger?

She missed him with every single cell of her body. It didn't matter how he felt about her. Whether he loved her or not didn't change how she felt about him. She loved him independent and regardless of whether he loved her. She wished she had realized that sooner. If she had, she'd never have switched on that flashlight. She'd be with Bear right now.

She kept walking mile after mile, hour after hour. She became coated in snow. Her face mask molded to the shape of her face, stuck to her skin, and her parka and pants were plastered with a sheen of solid ice. A chunk of it had wormed around her hood. Rivulets of ice water ran down her neck. She had a crust of ice between her parka lining and the down. Her parka felt like a straitjacket. Hoarfrost coated her goggles. Creeping cold infused her joints. It hurt to walk. *Hell*, she thought, *has nothing to do with fire. Jeremy was right: Hell is frozen.*

She could have frostbite, she knew. She could be slowly freezing to death. Killed by the ice she loved. She kept moving, mostly from habit now rather than conscious choice. Cassie picked her way through the chaos of ice, birthed by the storm and the pull of the moon on the tides. The low sun lengthened the mounds and made the spaces between them dark blue and cold. She shivered in the shadows. She could think of nothing but how cold she was. And Bear. Always Bear. Seeing a patch of warmer gold ahead of her, she tried to hurry toward it.

Instantly, her empty stomach cramped. Clutching it, Cassie lost her balance. She fell forward. She tried to catch herself, but she felt as if her arms were moving in slow motion. She collapsed forward before her arms were half-raised.

She needed to stand. Keep moving. *Must keep moving.*

Not moving meant death—how often had Dad told her that?

She heard the familiar creaking from deep within the ice. It sounded like a ghost, a tired and sad murmur. She imagined it was speaking, but she could not understand the words. With her pack like a turtle shell weighing down on her, she crawled forward. Her elbows shook. She inched across the frozen waves.

Enough, she thought. The ice was flat enough. She could rest here. Spread full-length, she would be more visible from the air, from Max's plane, than if she were standing. It made sense to lie here. She closed her eyes. Rescue me, Max. Dad. Bear. *Bear.*

A voice inside her whispered he was not coming. She was never going to see him again. She didn't have the strength to cry.

Snow drifted over her.

❄ ❄ ❄ ❄ ❄

Cassie basked in warmth. Pillows pressed around her, and it was as dark as a womb. She cuddled the cushions. Her cheek squashed against them, pressing her face mask into her. Half-thawed, the fleece soaked her skin. She itched to tear it off, mask and skin. She wormed into the pillows. She was comfortable at long last, and no stupid face mask was going to—

A cramp squeezed her left leg.

That half-woke her. Her thigh was wedged between the pillows at an awkward angle. She shifted again and sniffed:

sour sweat. *Must not be dead yet,* she thought vaguely. Soon maybe. She turned her face so that the rim of her goggles was not digging into her cheekbones, and she drifted back to sleep.

She dreamed about Bear. She dreamed that he lay beside her in his polar bear form, warm fur pressed against her and hot breath on her cheek. Cassie woke again. Fuzzy-eyed, she blinked at the warm darkness.

She wasn't dead. The realization rushed through her, and she wanted to cry or shout. She wasn't dead! Thank you, thank you!

She tested her muscles. They still worked. Cassie pushed at the pillows, and her mittens sank four inches, but with mitts, gloves, and liners, she could not feel the texture.

The pillows breathed.

Cassie recoiled, and the sudden movement turned her empty stomach upside down. She felt the world pressing in on her as if she were again trapped in a sleeping bag in a storm. "Let me out!" she shouted. She elbowed the warm darkness and wriggled upward.

She squirmed out of the press of fur and emerged in a sea of polar bears: sleeping bears as far into the misty white as she could see. Blackness swam up over her eyes and then retreated. The bears were still there when the dizziness passed. "Oh, my," she murmured.

At the sound of her voice, a dozen bears raised their heads. She swallowed. Expressionless, another dozen bears also turned to look at her. As one, the mass of bears—bears, not pillows—shifted, freeing her. Her legs shook, and the wind bit into her.

They had kept her warm while she slept. The bears had saved her life. "Oh, my," she repeated as her knees caved. Bears rolled back to support her as she slid to the ground.

Cassie turned her head—and stared directly at the nose of a polar bear. He huffed at her. She ogled back. "You're bears," she said. "You aren't even magical bears." She didn't understand. The fog in her brain wouldn't lift. She couldn't think. Why had the bears saved her?

A bear prodded her with his muzzle.

"What? Don't eat me." Her words were slurred. She leaned backward and felt another bear behind her. This one pushed in the middle of her back. "What do you want?" Another push. Did they want her to stand? She tried to make her brain function. Was she dreaming? She didn't feel like she was dreaming. She hurt too much to still be asleep. Wincing, Cassie lurched to her feet.

Had Bear sent them to save her?

The bears parted, uncovering Cassie's pack.

"I can't," she said. Her eyes felt hot, near tears. The bears were helping too late. She didn't have the strength to go on. "I'm tired. I'm hungry." She mimed chewing. "You know, hungry?" She made sucking noises.

Obligingly, a female bear rolled, exposing four round nipples. Cassie licked her cracked lips. Lolling her head, the bear looked at her. Half-falling to her knees, Cassie knelt and crawled to the sow's stomach. She looked over at the bear's face, and the bear placidly closed her eyes.

Cassie pulled off a mitt and her face mask. Taking a deep breath, she touched the nipple. It felt as firm as a thumb. She squeezed it, and milk welled at the top: life. When the bear did not maul her—in fact, did not move—Cassie leaned in and held her tongue catlike under the milk. She squeezed hard, and the milk squirted onto her tongue. It was oily, tasted of seal. Rich and thick, it clogged her throat.

She managed three swallows, then had to rest, leaning her head against the sow. She drifted into sleep and woke a few seconds later to swallow more milk. She alternated, drinking and sleeping, until she felt human again.

I'm going to live, she thought as she lay against the mother bear. From beyond the ends of the earth, Bear had found a way to save her. *And somehow,* she thought, *I'm going to find a way to save him.*

NINETEEN

Latitude 84° 42' 08" N
Longitude 74° 23' 06" W
Altitude 3 ft.

SQUINTING INTO THE SUN'S GLARE, Cassie scanned the softening ice. In the twenty-four-hour sun, icicles dripped into melt pools. The constant drip sounded like the second hand on a clock. Heading toward Ward Hunt Island, she'd traveled with the bears for three weeks, stopping only to drink bear milk and eat the strips of seal and fish that the bears had brought her. Often the bears had carried her while she slept so she wouldn't lose time. But it hadn't been enough.

I'm not going to make it, she thought.

She tried to ignore the knot of fear that lodged inside her rib cage. Sweat pricked the back of her neck underneath the flannel and wool. Everywhere, the ice was splintering. In five-foot-wide cracks, the ice was packed mush that moved with a hollow sound. Murres and gulls wheeled overhead, diving for cod in the widening cracks. She was not going to make it to land before the ice receded from the shore. *Not going to make it*, her mind whispered over and over. *Not going to make it.*

Summer was coming.

Facing a stretch of thin ice, Cassie mounted one of the bears. With giant paws like snowshoes, he walked across the green-gray ice. It wobbled in waves. Holding her breath, she watched the frost patterns for cracks. She stayed mounted as the bears continued to plod over thin ice and alongside ice rivers.

Five days later, Cassie and the bears reached the end of the ice.

Ahead of them, ice tossed in the waves, and then crumbled into semifrozen gruel. The slush undulated. Eventually, it dispersed into open ocean. Miles and miles of open water lay between her and land.

Cassie stared at the water. It was over. She was too late. She was stranded on the pack ice. All her grand resolve to reach the ends of the earth . . . All she'd done was reach the end of the ice.

The sun sparkled like golden jewels on the ice and the water. Blinking fast, she focused on the dancing waves. She knew better than to cry in the cold. Her father had taught her that years ago. *And did he also teach you to quit?* she asked herself. Was it to be a family tradition to fail to reach the troll castle? Like father, like daughter?

"Snap out of it," she whispered. "You aren't dead yet." She had options: Max could still come, or . . . She could not think of a second option.

Hoping for inspiration or a miracle, she looked around her at the army of polar bears. An arctic fox, diminutive beside the behemoths, trotted among them. Light as a cat, he didn't have to worry about weak ice, she thought. If she were the size of the fox, maybe the bears could have swum her across any open water without drenching her. Cassie looked at the glittering black water and shuddered. As Dad would have said, it was death water: In fifteen minutes, the muscles would seize, consciousness would fade, and death would come. As things were, without a munaqsri to warm her, she'd freeze if she tried to swim.

So all she had to do was find herself another munaqsri. Problem solved.

She snorted at herself. Like it was so easy. Billions of people spent their lives without seeing a munaqsri or even knowing they existed. Of course, she *did* know they existed, even if they moved too fast to see, but unless she just happened to know of an imminent birth or death . . .

The answer came so quickly that she nearly shouted out loud. If she were present at a creature's death . . . Cassie slid off the polar bear, her eyes fixed on the arctic fox. She'd seen foxes dogging the polar bears for weeks now. Arctic foxes were scavengers, living off the remains of bear kills. But with so many bears together, every kill was thoroughly stripped—there were few remains. She felt her heart race, thudding against her rib cage.

Somewhere on the ice behind them, there had to be a starving arctic fox.

"We're going back," she said, slapping the bear's shoulder. "Come on. Back the way we came." If she could find another munaqsri, he could help her off the ice. Even better, he could take her to Bear!

Cassie trudged north through her sprawling polar bear army. The bears milled around the ice and watched her with their black, inscrutable eyes. She stroked their fur as she passed, trying to reassure them. "I'll save him," she said. "I promise I'll bring your king home."

After five hours of walking, she saw a small dusty white shadow, nearly yellow against the blue-white ice. Loose snow swirled like fast-moving clouds around it. The shadow raised its head as she approached—it was an old fox. He was so thin that she could see his ribs pressing up through his fur. *Poor thing*, she thought. If the polar bears hadn't banded together, he might have had a chance at one more season, but he hadn't been able to compete with all the bears.

Shedding her pack, she knelt on the ice beside the fox. He laid his head back down and closed his eyes. His breathing was labored. She watched his ribs jerk up and down, his breath a harsh huff against the hiss of the wind.

Behind her, Cassie heard the soft puffing of bears. She saw them out of the corners of her eyes, blurred by the frost on her goggles. "Just a little longer," she promised them.

And then she'd be off the ice and on her way to Bear . . . if this worked.

It *had* to work. The fox munaqsri had to come, didn't he?

No one would come when a polar bear died, she thought. Their souls would . . . She didn't know what would happen to their souls. And with no one to transport the souls to the newborn, then these bears, these beautiful bears, would be extinct in a generation. No soul, no life.

Bear had risked all of them to marry her. He'd trusted that she'd respect his one and only request. And she hadn't. Cassie hugged her stomach. Even through all the layers, she could feel the slight bulge. This . . . what he'd done . . . didn't excuse the damage she'd done, however unintentionally, to all these beautiful bears. She *had* to reach Bear.

The fox shuddered, and his ribs sank down, down, as if folding into his fur. They didn't rise again. "Munaqsri!" she called.

She saw nothing.

"Fox munaqsri!" Cassie said. "I need to talk to you on behalf of the bear munaqsri!" He had to be here. She had no backup plan.

"You know the polar bear?" a voice said. Suddenly, a second arctic fox perched beside the dead fox. Spiking his fur, the fox arched his back like a cat. "You tell him I blame him for the fate of my foxes. While his bears herd, my foxes are starving." His muzzle curled back, and sunlight glinted on sharp incisors. "I will bring my complaints to the Arctic overseer—" With his thick white fur and delicate snout, he looked like a cross between a Pekinese and a Persian cat, hardly anything threatening. But he was an angry fluff ball with the power of a munaqsri.

Cassie scrambled to her feet. "Wait, listen! Bear . . . the bear munaqsri . . . is in trouble. I need you to speed me to the troll castle, east of the sun and west of the moon."

The effect of her words was instantaneous. He switched from furious to distressed in an eyeblink. "He has forsaken his bears? Oh, my foxes!" The fox tilted his head back and yowled. "My foxes will starve! No one has ever returned from there. He will never return!"

The fox's cries sliced into her. She clapped her hands to her ears. "Yes, he will!" Cassie shouted. Her mother had returned. If Bear could rescue Gail, then Cassie could rescue Bear. She would bring him back. She would fix everything. "I can bring him back!"

His howl died in yet another split-second mood change. Now silent, the fox stared at her. "Who are you?" he asked finally.

"Cassie Dasent," she said. She couldn't read the expression on his fox face. He'd already gone from furious to distressed to contemplative in less than thirty seconds. Please, let him help her.

"You are not a munaqsri," he said.

"I'm the wife of the polar bear," she said.

"Interesting taste," he said.

Cassie gritted her teeth. Now he was mocking her? Her husband was missing, suffering with trolls; the polar bears and arctic foxes were in danger of extinction; and she was stuck on the ice, at least four months pregnant, with summer rapidly approaching. "I didn't trek here from beyond the North Pole to be insulted by something cuddly," she snapped. "It's your choice, Fluffy: Help me and help your foxes, or don't help me and watch them die."

Fluffy licked his nose. Cassie held her breath. She'd either reached the erratic munaqsri or utterly antagonized him.

"I cannot take you there," he said finally. "The castle is east of the sun and west of the moon. It is beyond my region. I cannot leave the ice. Another munaqsri is responsible for foxes on land."

"Then help me find another munaqsri," Cassie said. There had to be a munaqsri who could cross from the ice to the land. Quickly, she scanned the ice, the sky, and the sea.

Out in the ocean, a whale lifted its spiral tusk. Slow and stately, a second horn rose out of the water. As if in an ancient ritual, the two narwhals crossed their unicorn horns. "Call a whale," she said.

"A whale will not help you," he said. "You are not a munaqsri, and they will have no interest in the fate of the polar bears or of my foxes."

One problem at a time, she thought as she lifted her pack onto her shoulders. "Just do it. Please, Fluffy?"

❉ ❉ ❉ ❉ ❉

ICE

The ocean buckled at her feet. Screeching, seabirds recoiled from the water. For an instant, their bodies blackened the sky. "He comes," the fox said.

Cassie stumbled as waves rocked the ice. Inches from the ice edge, a dark smooth curve as large as a submarine rose out of the water. And then it kept rising, larger and larger. As Cassie stared, the bowhead whale lifted its mouth above the swirling waves. Its maw gaped open, and Cassie saw fringed plates of baleen, enormous sheaths that filled the whale's mouth. Algae, barnacles, and seaweed clung to the dripping sheaths. No ordinary whale could have been this huge.

The colossus shut its mouth, and waves swelled onto the ice. Cassie scrambled backward as freezing water splashed her mukluks. Behind her, the ice cracked. She looked over her shoulder to see a split in the ice widen from the stress of the waves. On either side of the split, her polar bears waited, shoulder to shoulder—her beautiful bears. Seeing them gave her strength.

"I need your help," she said to the whale.

"You are not a munaqsri." His voice pounded like a drum. She shuddered as each syllable hit her ears.

"My husband is," she said. "He's the polar bear munaqsri."

Rising higher in the water, as massive as a monster from a myth, the bowhead drummed, "He may be, but you are not. You have no ties to us."

The ice rocked as if in an earthquake. Spray and wind

hit her face. She spread her legs to keep her balance and held the shoulder straps of her backpack. He didn't care if he drowned her, she realized. Looking up at the leviathan, she said, "I'm tied to him. We made vows."

"We are all bound by our promises," he intoned.

Cassie pushed her hair out of her eyes and squinted up at the bowhead. He eclipsed the sun. "Please. You have to help me reach the troll castle."

"Nothing living ever goes there," the bowhead said.

"Then take me across the ocean," she pleaded. "Just to the shore. I'll find the way myself from there. But please, help me off the ice!"

"I do not help humans."

"The bears will die if I don't save their munaqsri," Cassie said. She couldn't fail. Her beloved bears would vanish from the face of the earth. "Help me for their sake."

The bowhead drifted against the crumbling ice. Cassie flailed as the ice rocked. "The bears are not my concern," he said.

He had to care about something! She cast around for another idea, and she hit on inspiration. "I'm carrying the Bear's child," she said. "One of you. A future munaqsri."

The bowhead sprayed water from his spout. Screaming, Cassie threw her gloved hands over her head and ducked as it rained ice-cold seawater. "You risk a munaqsri," the bowhead boomed. "It cannot be allowed."

Beside her, the arctic fox hissed and growled. "You hold

a species' future inside you, and you undertake this quest? You seek death."

Oh, no, she'd made it worse. "But I have to save—"

"I cannot allow you to endanger a future munaqsri," the bowhead said.

"Nor I!" Fluffy said.

"You must stay on the ice where you belong." With that pronouncement, the bowhead submerged. A vast wave of water surged in his wake.

Cassie scrambled away from the wave. "I'll die if I stay!" She would die, the bears would die, the foxes would die. Bear would be trapped in the place that had made Gail scream.

"The bears will care for you until the child is born," Fluffy said. "And when he is grown, the bears will have their new king. My foxes shall live, and all will be as it should."

She shook her head. Her throat felt choked. She had to make him help her. She couldn't lose her one chance at Bear. "Bowhead!" she shouted at the waves. Could he still hear her? Please, let him hear her. The glittering black waves still churned in his wake. Cassie called to the deep, "You want your precious child to live? Then keep its mother alive!"

She ran and dove into the Arctic Ocean.

TWENTY

Latitude 84° 10' 46" N
Longitude 74° 22' 53" W
Altitude -32 ft.

COLD SEARED HER SKIN. Knives sliced her bones. She kicked the water. Thirty feet down, she shed her pack. It sank. I'm not dying, she thought. This isn't the end. She saw the surface: golden green. Clawing the water, she swam toward it.

She could not feel her hands. She had no arms. No legs.

Numb, she burned. Her lungs screamed.

Golden green turned black.

Fifteen minutes. Death water.

It hurt to die.

And then it didn't hurt. Cassie was cocooned in currents. She swept through silver fish and translucent jellies. Cod eddied around her body, and comb jellies grazed her with their rain-bow cilia. Light—green—hung in the water like dust in air.

ICE

She looked down at a garden of brilliant orange starfish and golden sea anemones. Was this heaven? Small lobsters crawled over rocks. Crabs with spider legs scrambled over mud to hide in soft strands of algae. She looked upward. Belugas undulated through the green light. The water filled with the sounds of their chirps and whistles. She watched them swim, singing, overhead. No one's heaven had lobsters and off-pitch belugas. It would even be odd for a hell. She smiled and tasted salt. She was underwater. Alive.

But how? She'd hoped the bowhead munaqsri would save her, but she didn't see him. He would have to be touching her to save her. Oddly, no one was touching her. So who was keeping her alive? And warm? And not in pain? "Hello? Anyone?" Her words burbled in the water.

The tide carried her through strands of algae. Soft ribbons of green brushed against her. The algae coated the loose ice overhead and the floor below so that they looked like an overgrown lawn. Cassie eyed the dustlike krill. "Hello? Do any of you talk?"

No shrimp answered. At least she wouldn't have to hold a conversation with something almost microscopic. She nearly laughed at the image, but then the sea darkened. Cassie looked up; the bowhead blocked the sun. He looked as if he could swallow her entire universe. Cassie shrank from the living eclipse, acutely aware how much she didn't belong here. She was alive only by someone else's decision. What if whoever it was changed its mind? The bowhead passed over her, and in his wake, sunlight flooded the water.

She didn't want to be down here a second longer. She swam toward the sun.

Current slammed against her, sending her tumbling sideways. Her hood fell back and her hair swirled. She tried again, aiming diagonally upward.

Fish swarmed her. Cod, their silver bodies streaking in the slanted light, surrounded her. She could not move her arms without slapping them. The fish butted their heads against her, pushing her down and then propelling her through the water. She flailed like a windmill, and the fish scattered.

As the water cleared, she saw a shape—it was coral, a city of coral, rising out of the muddy sea floor. Teeming with fish, the city was an organic Manhattan. In its own way, it was as grand as Bear's castle.

She heard a laugh. Cassie spun in the water. "Who's there?" she called. Really, it could be anything from the pink crustaceans to the comb jellies.

It was a mermaid.

Perched on a salt-encrusted rock, the mermaid had cod-like scales on her tail that spread into silvery skin at her navel. Her human skin rippled in soft wrinkles, like a bloated drowned body. She laughed in streams of air bubbles.

Without thinking, Cassie said, "You're mythical."

The mermaid's laugh grew wilder and harsher. It sounded like waves breaking.

Cod nibbled at the mermaid's hair. Made of kelp, her hair drifted around her face like Medusa's snakes. Cassie noticed the mermaid had no fingers, and a memory tugged at her, one of the local stories. This was the creature who had spawned the Sedna stories, the Inuit sea woman whose father had chopped off her fingers. "You're Sedna," Cassie said. Months ago, Bear had mentioned Sedna as the overseer of the Arctic Ocean.

With a flick of her fin, the mermaid rocketed toward Cassie. Instinctively, Cassie shielded her face, but the mermaid veered around her and circled her in a jet stream of bubbles. "I have heard of you as well," Sedna said. "You are the girl who was forced to marry the polar bear to save your mother from the trolls."

"No one forced me," Cassie said. "I chose to save her." And now she was choosing to save him, whether he loved her or not. "I need to reach the castle that's east of the sun and west of the moon. Will you help me?"

"The bowhead says that you have a future munaqsri inside you," the mermaid said. She swam faster. Bubbles cycloned around Cassie.

Cassie pressed her hands to her curved stomach. It was only a fetus right now. "It's not even born yet, and it might not want to be a munaqsri. But Bear's alive now. Please, help me. If not for me, then for the polar bears."

"Land creatures," said the mermaid dismissively. She kept swimming, tail flicking through the water.

Cassie tried to watch the mermaid, but the mermaid swam in a blur now, still circling her. "They're almost sea mammals," Cassie said. It was a controversial theory, but her father had done a paper on it. Maybe the caretaker of the sea would like the theory. "Blubber. Water-resistant fur. Streamlined ears. Webbing between their toes. They're evolving into the sea." Please, let her believe!

The mermaid laughed, and the bubbles spun in waves. "I *am* helping you," she said. "You have not drowned."

The mermaid swam even faster. Cassie felt dizzy. She squeezed her eyes shut, but the vertigo stayed. She opened her eyes. "But I need to find Bear!" she shouted. Bubbles cycloned faster and faster. She was surrounded, as if in a net. Cassie swam at the bubbles. She was thrown back into the center. She could not see through the bubbles. "Wait!" The mermaid blurred into silver and green.

The cyclone lengthened. Cassie saw it stretch like a Slinky through the sea. "Hush, child," Sedna said. "Trust the munaqsri. We want what is best for our world, as all creatures do."

"Not the trolls," Cassie called through the bubbles. "The trolls don't want 'what's best.' They want the polar bears extinct!"

"No one knows what the trolls want," the mermaid said. "You must go to Father Forest. He knows best how to help you."

"Who is he?" she asked eagerly. "How do I find him?"

The cyclone collapsed around her. Bubbles hit Cassie's skin. She kicked, yelling, and the bubbles squeezed. Cassie flew. Like paint squirting from a tube, she shot down the cyclone through the water. The roar of the water drowned her screaming as she sped through a tunnel of bubbles. Just when she thought the ride would never end, she felt the sea undulate beneath her and the cyclone of bubbles thrust her into the air. She broke out of the water. Sun hit her eyes. "Whoa!" she yelled as she rushed to meet the shore.

TWENTY-ONE

Latitude 68° 32' 12" N
Longitude 89° 49' 33" W
Altitude 2 ft.

CASSIE SKIDDED ON HER TAILBONE. "Ow, ow!" Shielding her face, she slammed into a dune of snow. For an instant, she lay there, limbs tangled. She was alive. She had dived into the Arctic Ocean and lived.

Closing her eyes, Cassie inhaled. The air tasted wonderful, like salt and sun and earth. Opening her eyes, she turned her head. Her pack lay beside her. The nylon had ripped in three spots, and the frame had warped into an *S*, but it was dry and whole.

Gingerly, she untangled herself and tested her joints—no broken bones. Just a lot of bruises. She pushed herself up to sitting and looked around. Glacier-scoured rocks stretched for miles, patches of snow alternating with windswept expanses. She was on the tundra.

ICE

A brown blur scooted over her mukluks. She jerked her feet under her.

"I am here," a voice said.

"Where? Who said that?" she asked. She looked around at the rocks, the waves, the sky.

The brown blur shot past her, darting from rock to rock. Suddenly, it stopped, and she saw a roly-poly brown rodent, like a furry toy football perched on a rock—a lemming. Cassie grinned. Sedna had said she'd help. Cassie just hadn't expected that help to take the shape of a magical rodent. She pictured herself telling Bear about this. He was going to laugh for days.

"Come on," the lemming said. "Pick me up. We must be off. I have responsibilities to tend to, you know."

With the lemming cradled in her hands, Cassie sped across the tundra at munaqsri speed. The world sped by like a film on fast-forward. She saw clips and heard snippets of the landscape as it changed around her. Geese flew overhead, and unseen birds called across the grasses. In hollows, purple saxifrages and arctic white heather flourished. Poppies bloomed in snow patches. She was heading south (quickly), and summer was heading north.

Late in the sunlit night, they halted. "I feel a call," the lemming said. "Camp here. I will return for you." Before she could protest, the rodent was gone.

Her one link to Bear, gone.

Cassie swallowed hard. *He'll return*, she told herself. *He said he'd return*. And Sedna had said to trust. Ordering herself to stop worrying, she looked around. She was beyond the shrub tundra now, deep in tussock tundra.

Stretching out her legs, Cassie threaded between head-size clumps of grass. Filled with stagnant water, the tussocks would burst if she stepped on them. To walk through the minefield, she had to lift her knees high like a stork. She imagined how she'd retell this to Bear: She'd march around the banquet hall as if she were walking through tussocks, and he'd laugh in his low rumble. He'd serve that chicken in white wine sauce, and she'd tell him how she'd picked lichen from rocks for her dinner on the tundra. She'd say how much she'd missed him, and he'd say he loved her and had never meant to hurt her. . . .

But all the apologies in the world wouldn't undo anything that had happened. Cassie laid her hands on her stomach. Even if she found Bear . . . everything would be different. She swallowed hard. She didn't just want Bear back; she wanted the life they'd had.

She camped between tussocks. Overhead, the northern lights chased each other in pale ribbons as the sun continued its low roll along the horizon. She dreamed about Bear, and she woke expecting him to be beside her like he used to be. She nearly cried when she realized he wasn't.

To her relief, the lemming returned shortly after she woke, and again they raced across the tundra. The next time they stopped, she was surrounded by cottongrass. Thousands of flowers that looked like gone-to-seed dandelions covered the tundra in a fine white mist. She took out her GPS. After a dip in the Arctic Ocean, it shouldn't still have worked, but the numbers flickered. She tilted it until she could read it. Latitude 66° 58' 08", longitude 110° 02' 13". Whoa. She'd come hundreds of miles in less than two days. At this rate, she'd be in the boreal forest before she knew it. "Thank you," she said to the lemming. She'd never imagined it would be a rodent who would be her savior.

"The owl will hunt for you," the lemming said. "She enjoys it."

"What owl?" Cassie scanned the skies. She didn't see . . . Wait, she saw a white splotch to the north. Silent, the snowy owl drifted over the tundra. Her feathers were like a cloud against the sky. Cassie saw her dive—right toward the lemming. "Watch out!" Cassie yelled as the owl's talons wrapped around him.

The lemming did not flinch, and the owl released him and glided a few feet away before settling in the cotton-grass. "You invite me to play," the owl said, "and you do not even run. Where is the sportsmanship in that?"

Cassie exhaled. It was the owl munaqsri, and they obviously knew each other. Cassie wasn't going to lose her transportation.

"I did not invite you to hunt *me*," the lemming said in his piping voice. "I invited you to hunt for her. She travels to Father Forest. She is the wife of the polar bear."

The owl swiveled her head a hundred eighty degrees. "I see. And the child is his?"

Cassie threw her arms around her stomach. The sun was

warm, and she had shed her parka and wool. Her curved stomach strained her flannel. More than four months now. "I need to find Bear," she said, her voice rising. "Father Forest has to help me."

The owl studied her for another moment. "Of course he will help you," the owl said. "You may rely on him to do what is best. What do you wish to eat?"

Cassie's knees wobbled in relief. The owl wasn't going to argue, and she was going to get her dinner. Food! She wanted chocolate cake and stacks of hamburgers and Dad's beans and Max's sausage omelettes, but she tried to think of what lived in sedge meadows. Dad used to refer to lemmings as "wild fast food." Cassie glanced at the lemming munaqsri. "Rabbits?" she suggested.

In a few minutes, the owl returned, soaring low. Her feathers brushed flowers. Petals flew like confetti. Cassie saw the grass sway in front of the owl. Cassie stood on top of a hummock for a better view. With wings spread a full five feet wide, the owl herded rabbits. Lots of rabbits. Politely, the owl called to her, "Would you like to kill one, or may I?"

She felt a twinge of pity for the hares being hunted by a superowl. The owl, on the other hand, seemed to be enjoying herself. "Please, be my guest," Cassie said.

Cassie set her stove as the owl neatly killed a hare.

Seconds later, a live hare appeared beside the corpse. He hopped from paw to paw. "Filthy predator!" the new hare shouted. "Return the soul you stole immediately."

ICE

The owl ruffled her feathers. "You did not come to claim the soul. It was free for me to take. You would not have wanted it to be lost, would you? It is better for it to become an owl than for it to be lost."

"I am here now!" the hare munaqsri cried. "Return it immediately."

"As you wish," the owl said. She opened her beak. Mist, the soul, drifted across the grasses. The hare chased after it. It melted into him.

The owl dropped the carcass beside the stove. "Thank you," Cassie said. "Sorry for causing problems."

The owl shrugged, an interesting feat with wings. "The hare has no sense of humor," she said.

The hare munaqsri returned. "Disgusting predators." The irate rabbit fixed its eyes on Cassie. "You are an omnivore. Why must you eat my hares?"

"Find me some wild tofu, and I'll eat that," Cassie offered.

The owl chuckled. Sputtering, the hare disappeared into the grasses.

Cassie smiled. How strange that she could now joke with talking birds and rodents. Months ago, Bear had said he could show her a new world with wonders she didn't know existed. She certainly had never imagined she'd be out on the tundra with a magic lemming, owl, and hare.

"Are we close?" Cassie asked.

"I will bring you to the end of my region," the lemming said, "and the owl will arrange for a guide to bring you into the forest. You will be with Father Forest by tomorrow afternoon."

Cassie felt her heart leap. She could see Bear tomorrow! Finally, after the ice and the sea and the tundra . . . Cassie ran her fingers through her hair, and her fingers snagged a few inches from her scalp. She hoped he didn't mind that she smelled. Cassie laughed out loud and shook her head. Her hair flew around her in a red cloud of tangles. "I'm coming, Bear!" she said. She'd bring him home. She touched her stomach. And then? She didn't know.

TWENTY-TWO

Latitude 64° 04' 50" N
Longitude 124° 56' 02" W
Altitude 1281 ft.

SHE'D BE MET BY A GUIDE, the lemming had said before he'd left her, but Cassie didn't see anything that looked like a guide. She was alone at the foot of a hill. Spruces studded the low rise, and an aspen grove blocked her view over the top. The air crackled with birds and tasted faintly of evergreen. "Hello?" she called. She wondered what kind of creature she was supposed to meet. Rodent? Bird? Mosquito?

One of the aspen trees halfway up the hill began to shiver. Aspens, northern aspens, quiver in a breath of wind. She remembered one of Dad's lessons: *Populus tremuloides*, they were called. Quivering aspens. But this was the only tree in the grove that was moving. She walked up to it. Its trunk was as thick as her arm, with bark a peeling pale green. Thin branches jutted out at uneven intervals.

It jiggled harder, as if it were doing a belly dance.

And then suddenly it laughed. Or, more accurately, a girl perched in the branches laughed. Cassie squinted—the sun was directly behind the tree and, oddly, made the girl appear greenish.

"Hellooo!" The girl waved. She swung out of the branches and landed lightly on the ground. "I am the aspen."

Cassie blinked at her. She *was* green. Her skin looked like layered leaves, and her hair looked like twigs. "You're the aspen munaqsri?"

"Yes," the girl said. Her voice was high, whistlelike, and cheerful.

"You're a tree," Cassie said.

Again, the green girl laughed. "Yes!"

Cassie decided that she'd seen stranger things than this. Or maybe she hadn't. She tried to imagine describing this creature to Owen and Max. They'd never believe her. Gail might. If Cassie went back to the station now, maybe she and her mother would have something to talk about.

Following the aspen, Cassie climbed to the top of the hill, and the view banished all other thoughts. All Cassie could do was stare. "Wow," she whispered. It was gorgeous. Far in the distance, she could see mountains, the Mackenzies. Dark purple with streaks of glacial white, the mountains crowned the horizon. Max had always wanted to fly his Twin Otter in the Mackenzies. Now she could understand why. Rivers cut through the foothills. She saw enormous rock faces. And the green . . . oh, the green. Spruces, thick and tall, dominated the landscape for the hundreds of miles between her and those foothills. Pale green tamarack and the slender spines of aspens stood out like lights against the rich spruce green.

"Father Forest is within the boreal forest," the tree-girl said. "We will ride there."

"Ride what?" Cassie asked.

Seeming to ignore her, the aspen pointed. "I like that one," she said. She was pointing at a nearby caribou, a young buck. His back was to them. He had shed most of his winter coat, but remnants hung like rags on his broad neck and back. He lowered his head into a thicket and thrashed his antlers against the branches. It sounded like a dozen snare drums; it drowned the chirps of birds. Finishing, he lifted his head. His antlers were tinted red. Cassie could hear larks and thrushes again. The tree-girl sprinted to his side, as fast as a blur.

Grinning, Cassie followed her. This was even better than traveling by lemming. The aspen-girl sprang onto his back and beckoned to Cassie. Grasping the caribou's mane, Cassie pulled herself onto his back. The length of her pack forced her to lean toward his neck. His vertebrae stuck into her legs.

"Run!" the aspen commanded.

He broke into a gallop, and the other caribou scattered. His tendons clicked with the unique caribou sound, like rubber bands snapping. Cassie bounced on his bony back as he accelerated to munaqsri speed under the aspen's power.

She knew the moment they left the taiga and entered the boreal forest: The light changed. Shadows surrounded them as conifers blocked the sun. The caribou ran over needles that crunched, and he leaped over fallen trees. Spruces were swathes of dark green punctuated by the white flash of an aspen. Finally, she was almost to Father Forest!

The aspen shouted a command, and the caribou stopped. Cassie was tossed into his neck. "Ow!" Her stomach squished. She scooted back behind his prominent shoulder blades. "Why did . . . ," she began to ask, and then she stopped.

Ahead was a picturesque cottage nestled in spruces. It looked as if it were part of the spruces. The bark of the trees bled into the wood of the walls. The roof was made of mossy stones. Cassie smiled—the cottage defined "quaint." Wild roses curled appealingly around the door and windows. The air smelled of rosemary and mint. Smoke curled invitingly from the chimney. Ferns covered the tiny yard, and wide slate stones made a path to the door. Cassie slid off the back of the caribou, and the caribou trotted away.

Opening a wooden gate, Cassie stepped on the first stone. She heard a chime like a chorus of birds. Passing her, the tree-girl skipped, laughing, down the path. Each stone sang out under her feet. It sounded like a bird-call xylophone. Cassie tested another stone. It chimed for her. Grinning, she went down the path toward the cottage door.

ICE

She could smell bread baking. She inhaled deeply.

The tree-girl flung the door open. Cassie stooped in the doorway. She squinted, her pupils expanding. Inside, the cottage was as dark, snug, and comfortable as a bear den. It took a second for her eyes to adjust before she saw the cottage's occupant.

The old man was as bent and gnarled as a black spruce tree. Broom in hand, he scuttled around the tiny home sweeping dirt from the corners and the ceilings. Dust hung in the air like morning haze. He muttered to himself. The tree-girl threw her arms around him. He patted her absently on the shoulder. "Yes, yes, dear," he said. "But everything must be perfect for our guest."

Father Forest. She wanted to shout or sing. Bear seemed so close she could almost feel his fur under her fingers and smell his seal-tinged breath. Cassie cleared her throat.

He clapped his hands together. "Our guest!" All his wrinkles seemed to smile. "Please, come in, come." He fussed around her as she ducked inside.

The cottage kitchen was full of cabinets and drawers, all carved with pictures of rabbits and squirrels. Shelves were stacked with wooden plates, bowls, and pitchers. The sink even had a wooden faucet. The only metal was a wrought-iron stove with an old-fashioned teakettle. Corners of the kitchen receded into shadows. She saw a small, cozy living room through an open doorway, and through one of three other doorways, she glimpsed a bedroom. It was nothing like Bear's castle with the open ballroom, the buttressed halls, the spiral staircase, but she liked it. It felt warm and safe and a welcome change from ice and tundra. "You are Father Forest?"

The old man bobbed his head. "Do you like it?"

He must mean the forest, she guessed. "It's beautiful."

He beamed. "You must see the Aberdeen Lake area. Beautiful white spruces. And the Peacock Hills. Some of my finest work. Yes, you must have a tour! You should see my aspen groves. And the riverbanks with the balsam poplars. The rivers are not my region, of course, but, ah . . . the riverbanks!"

"I'm sorry, but—"

"Oh, you must see the willows! Riparian willow thickets!" Unable to restrain himself, he hopped from foot to foot. He reminded Cassie of a Christmas elf. Or Santa Claus himself.

"Next time," she promised, and she smiled at him. His enthusiasm was infectious. It was impossible not to like him. "I'm sure you do wonderful work."

"It is a noble calling." For an instant, there was something in his eyes—a seriousness. "Munaqsri make the world work." And then he was all smiles. He patted her hand. "Come, sit," he said. Guiding her to an empty corner, the old man tapped the floor with his broom. In the spot it touched, a tree root bubbled up from out of the floor. It flattened under his guidance. He molded it as easily as Bear sculpted ice. She thought of Bear's topiaries—all destroyed now. Soon they'd be home, she told herself. The forest munaqsri patted the root chair. "Please, let me get you something to eat. You must be famished."

Her stomach rumbled as he scurried to the kitchen. "Thank you, but I don't have time. You're right. About munaqsri, I mean. Without Bear, the whole polar bear species will be extinct in a generation."

On tiptoe, he peered into his cabinets. "We have all sorts of delicacies here in my forest. Fresh fronds? Pinecone hearts?" Father Forest filled a tray with out-of-season berries and odd-shaped leaves.

She was not going to be distracted, not this close, though the thought of food was tempting. She hadn't eaten since the hare yesterday. "I was told you could help me get to the troll castle."

He opened the iron oven, and the smell of bread wafted across the room. Her stomach cried. He lifted out a luscious loaf. "Rest first. Then we'll talk about your polar bear."

Fresh bread. She salivated. How could it hurt? Wouldn't it be better to rescue Bear on a full stomach? For all she knew, it was thousands of miles to the castle and she would need the energy. Urgency argued with hunger, and hunger won. Cassie took off her pack and rested it against a wall. She sat on the root chair. It felt as solid as ordinary wood, even though it had just grown. He served her the tray and the bread. She wondered why he hadn't magicked the food here the way he had the chair. Then she bit into the bread and lost interest in the question.

The bread tasted like honey. It melted in her mouth. She

devoured it in three mouthfuls. "This is wonderful." Some of the leaves tasted like lettuce, some were tinged with mint, and others were nut flavored. "Thank you."

He smiled fondly at her. "You are the wife of the bear. We take care of our own."

She smiled. The owl had been right. She'd said that Cassie could rely on him. She had nothing more to worry about. Thanks to Sedna and Fluffy and the lemming and the aspen, she and Bear would be home soon. "How far is it to the castle?" she asked as she finished her food.

"Tea?" he asked. He patted a finger on the root. Cassie moved as a green shoot sprouted out of the bark beside her. It unfurled, and its tip swelled into a bulb. It fattened until it looked ready to burst. Green sides peeled away, and it opened like a tulip. From its base, color spread up it as it darkened from a light pink to a deep red. Delighted, she laughed out loud. How magical—just like something Bear would do. The forest munaqsri snapped the blossom at the base. The green shoot withered into dust. He fetched the kettle from the stove and poured tea into the flower. He handed it to her. The petals felt soft and warm. "You will like it," he said, smiling. "It's a special blend. Extra strong for you."

Steam rose into her nose as she brought it to her lips. She took a sip. It tasted of herbs and pine. Immediately, she felt calmer. "Thank you again," she said.

"I have prepared a bed for you," he told her. "You need a good night's sleep."

Cassie shook herself. "No, no." Her tongue felt thick.

ICE

"So close." She stood, and her knees felt suddenly weak. Father Forest took the tea out of her hands and set it on the root chair. Gently, he took her elbow and guided her to one of the doors. He said, "If you need anything, you have only to call out. The trees have ears, you know."

Sitting in a corner, the tree-girl giggled—a shrill sound. It grated inside Cassie's head like metal filings. She shook her head to clear it, and felt dizzy.

He led her through the door into a green room with a downy bed. She frowned at the bed. She did not want to sleep; she wanted Bear. "No, no sleep." Her words slurred. It was hard to think. Dimly, she thought, *It was the tea.* But he was such a nice old man. "See Bear when wake?" She tried to look at him, but her eyelids felt as heavy as granite. She sank onto the bed.

He patted her arm. "Rest tonight, dear. Please, do not worry. It will be all right. You will see."

On an impulse, she hugged the gnarled man.

"Yes, yes, dear," he said. "You will see."

TWENTY-THREE

Latitude 63° 54' 53" N
Longitude 125° 24' 07" W
Altitude 1301 ft.

"OW, OW, OW." Cassie peeled the clothes from her skin—long johns plastered to her with dirt and dried sweat. It felt like pulling off a Band-Aid. She grimaced at herself. She had flecks of blood from a thousand scratches, and she was mottled with purple and yellow bruises. How lovely. She turned on the shower, and the water spilled through a crevice and then was funneled out between roots on the floor. She flinched as she ducked under the stream.

Mud dripped down Cassie's legs, and the runoff turned a Mississippi brown. Father Forest had told her she would find fresh clothes in the bathroom closet, so she rinsed all her long johns and silkweights. Even considering the knockout tea, which (she had to admit) had provided much-needed sleep, he was proving to be a generous host. She felt like a hotel guest, or what she imagined a hotel guest would feel like—she'd never been one. Cassie sanded her skin with pine-scented soap. Wow, she had missed being clean! She scrubbed her hair. Grass clumps plopped onto the shower floor. She noticed one was seaweed.

She shook her hair and splattered the walls. *Father Forest should be nominated for sainthood,* she thought. She finally felt human again. First thing she would ask Bear to do when all this was over would be to resculpt the bathroom. She imagined herself and Bear rebuilding the castle side by side.

Glorying in her daydream and in the water, Cassie stretched. And she felt a fluttering in her stomach.

Her hands flew to her curved stomach. She felt the fluttering a second time. It was like wings inside her abdomen. Cassie grabbed the shower wall as her knees caved.

Oh, no. No, no. How could she have a baby? She huddled against the bark wall of the shower. Her hair stuck to her skin as water streamed over her. She wasn't ready to be a mother!

She had so cleverly avoided thinking about it too much. But the baby wasn't waiting for her to adjust to the idea. Every day, it marched closer to birth.

She forced herself to take a deep breath. She had to keep calm. Bear would help her. She wasn't going to be alone. He'd know what to do with a baby—a munaqsri baby. Once she and Bear were together again, they could face this.

Cassie got to her feet and dried herself with a towel made

of woven ferns. It fell apart on her skin. All she had to do was find Bear in time and it would all be fine. With Father Forest's help, it would all be fine.

Cassie pulled the clothes out of the cabinet, and the clothes unfolded into a dress with a leaf green blouse and a shapeless bark brown skirt. Cotton underwear fell onto the floor. She stared at the dress. No one who was going to be trekking across a boreal forest wore a dress. Cassie searched the cabinet for other choices. She found only doll-like slippers. The slippers were worse than the dress—they would shred in the forest. What was Father Forest thinking?

Cassie glanced at her wet clothes, now hanging on a branch towel rack. She didn't have much choice. If she didn't want to be naked, she'd have to wear the dress. She put it on and scowled down at herself. "Ridiculous," she said.

She pulled on her old mukluks and found Father Forest outside, waist-deep in ferns. He raised his head as she stepped on a singing stone. He beamed at her. "Sleep well?"

"Completely rested and ready to go," she announced. "Thanks for the hospitality." She decided not to say a word about the dress. It was probably all he had. His gnome pants would have been knickers on her. She shouldn't be ungrateful after all he was doing for her and Bear.

He screwed up his face like a prune. "Not now!"

She'd felt the baby move; she didn't want to wait another minute. "Why not?"

Father Forest waved at the yard of fronds. "The ferns are ready to seed."

ICE

She was waiting for ferns? She had not crossed the entire Arctic to be delayed by ferns. "Bear is waiting for me," she said.

"Ferns cannot wait," he said.

Clenching her teeth, she reminded herself that he had fed and clothed her. A little yard work was a fair trade. "Fine," she said through her teeth. "Let me help."

He smiled with eyes crinkling like Santa Claus's. Kneeling, he demonstrated how to pluck the seeds from the undersides of the ferns, scatter the seeds around the yard, and smooth pine needles over them. He acted like a child showing off a new toy. "Gravity and wind will do that, you know," Cassie said.

"You are so innocent," he said fondly. "It's really charming."

She scowled. "After the ferns, we go to Bear." Bending over the ferns, she scraped the seeds with her short fingernails. She tossed them into open patches.

"Good, good," he said, watching her.

It was as pointless as plucking autumn leaves. Cassie scraped and tossed, scraped and tossed, as fast as she could. Bear was waiting for her. She pictured him pacing in a cage while trolls prodded him and laughed. She hated the thought of him trapped and helpless. She scraped so fast that she shredded the tender leaves.

Whistling to himself, Father Forest leisurely bent over the ferns, picked the seeds one by one, examined each one in the low angled sunlight, considered the full yard, and placed the seeds individually on the ground. Cassie wanted to shake him. She had to bite her lip to keep from shouting at him to move.

Cassie worked through lunch and dinner. Father Forest came and went, tottering off to do munaqsri business (or, she thought, scratch his elbow for an hour or two). She stretched her back, wincing, as he sniffed the roses that curled around the cottage windows. He peeled back the petals until the roses were in full bloom. The old man, she decided, was a *kinnaq*, a lunatic. But as long as he brought her to Bear, she didn't care. She finished with the ferns. "Now can we go?"

Father Forest arranged the petals like an artist. "All the seeds?"

She surveyed the yard. "Yes."

He gestured to the forest. "And those?"

Cassie looked over her shoulder at the expanse of boreal forest beyond the picket fence. "You've got to be kidding."

❋ ❋ ❋ ❋ ❋

He left her looking out at the forest.

Cassie felt the baby shift inside her again, and she automatically placed her hands over her stomach. If she cooperated, this *kinnaq* would help her find Bear. Sedna had said he'd help her. Even the owl had said she could rely on him to do what was best.

For the first time, she wondered exactly what "best" meant.

She turned back to the cottage. Silent and peaceful, it

looked like a painting. The amber light of the permanent sun warmed the roof. She didn't want to spend another night without Bear. Father Forest would simply have to understand.

She marched into the cottage and through the kitchen. She found him lounging in a wooden rocking chair in the living room. He looked up as she entered. "Finished already?"

"I want my husband back," she said.

"And I want my tea," he said. "Come, have tea with me, and we will talk." He tottered into the kitchen and fetched the kettle.

"Bear needs rescuing," she said as evenly as she could. Rescuing Bear was more important than tea or ferns or showers or sleep. Rescuing Bear was more important than anything else in the world. She followed Father Forest to the kitchen. "It's not that I don't appreciate your hospitality, but every second Bear is in that troll castle is a second too long. Please, try to understand."

He poured two cups of tea. "Won't you have some?"

She wanted to scream in frustration. Instead, she gritted her teeth and tried to smile. "If I didn't know better, I'd think you were delaying me on purpose."

He shuffled to a root chair and sat. Not looking at her, he stirred his tea. "You cannot travel with that child inside you. It risks too much."

Cassie froze. She had to have heard wrong. "Excuse me?"

"I am sorry to disappoint you."

She opened and shut her mouth twice before saying, "I don't understand. You have to help me. You were supposed to help me. The mermaid said . . . Munaqsri are supposed to be good. You're supposed to do what's best."

"I do want what is best. You cannot be allowed to risk a future caretaker." Perched on the root chair with his feet dangling above the floor, he looked like a wrinkled child.

She clenched her fists. "I don't care about the risks. I have to try!" Her father hadn't tried, and look what had happened: She'd grown up without a mother, and Gail screamed at night.

His wrinkles darkened. "It is not safe. . . ."

"Bear needs me to do this." She stalked to the guest bedroom and returned with her pack. "*I* need to do this." This wasn't open for debate.

Bones creaking, Father Forest rose. "I am sorry, but I have to insist."

"You and what army?" She marched to the door.

In a quiet, sad voice, he said, "I do not need an army." Flicking his wrist, he commanded the walls. Shoots sprouted out at her and wound around her wrists. Cassie shrieked. Vines tightened around her arms and coiled up to her armpits. Wrapping around her chest, they lifted her off the floor. She kicked, and her feet ran on empty air. She spun in the vines. "Let me go!"

"Of course, I will," he said, "as soon as you understand that you must stay until the child is born. Your child is needed." His voice was so calm that it chilled her. "The world is short of munaqsri, and munaqsri make the world work. Please, try to understand. It is for the best."

Cassie fought, but the vines held her like a scarecrow—arms out and feet dangling. Her head was between the rafters. "You can't do this! You can't keep me here!"

He fetched his tea. "As soon as you agree to behave, you can come down." He went to the door.

"Where are you going?" She twisted to see him open the door. "Come back here! Don't leave me like this!" She kicked the air.

Sipping his tea, he walked out the door and shut it behind him.

Pedaling in vain, she spun in the air. "Get back here!"

She heard the last singing stone, the creak of the gate, and he was gone into the forest. Pumping her legs, she tried to swing. She was able to stir the vines. She swayed back and forth, increasing momentum.

Sensing movement, the vines shortened. Her head bumped into the ceiling. She swore. Sedna, the lemming, the owl, the aspen . . . Had they known that Father Forest would want to imprison her? Had they deliberately misled her, or had she willfully misunderstood?

Cassie clawed at the vines. They squeezed her wrists. She had to stop as they bit off circulation. She hung in the air, panting. *Oh, Bear, I'll find a way!*

Dangling from the living ceiling, she swung in a lazy circle.

❄ ❄ ❄ ❄ ❄

Cassie heard Father Forest boil his morning tea. She did not lift her head. "You need to let me down for the bathroom," she said.

"Birds and squirrels do not use bathrooms. You will not disturb me." He poured tea from the kettle. The sound made it worse.

She clamped her legs together.

The vines twined themselves around her legs, locking them tight. "Unless," he said hopefully, "you have decided to stay?"

Straining against the vines, she swore at him until she ran out of words.

"Such language for a child," he said mildly, and then he left the cottage.

After a few minutes, Cassie had to stop struggling. It hurt too much. Her arms pulled at their sockets; she felt like she was being crucified. Tears sprang into her eyes, but she blinked them back. She would not give him the satisfaction. He could not beat her. Nothing could beat her—not ice, not sea, not tundra, not this damn forest.

She wormed her fingers through the vines. Responding, vines split and wound around her fingers, paralyzing her hand. She twisted, and the vines thickened around her. "Oh, God," she whispered. Panic started to rise—she couldn't help it. She flailed against them. But more vines piled on top of the initial vines. She was cocooned from the neck downward in bark.

ICE

Soon she would be swallowed entirely, like she had been in her sleeping bag in the storm. Panic bubbled in her throat. "I can't do it," she whispered. "I can't. I can't." She could take anything but this: trapped, helpless, not in control of her own body. She took a deep breath, forcing down the fear. Her ribs strained against the wood. She took another breath, and the vines responded, squeezing the air out of her. She couldn't help herself—she begged, "Please, don't crush me. Please. Please."

The vines loosened a centimeter, and she took mini-breaths. She reminded herself she could still think and talk. The vines could not hold her mind or tongue. She shuddered at the image of vines wrapping around her tongue. Her shudder was constricted to a tiny shiver by the cocoon. She hadn't known that Father Forest had this kind of power. She should have known—Bear had it too. But Bear had never used his power like this. When she'd wanted to go, he had let her go.

He had used his power on her only once without her consent.

For the hundredth time, she replayed their conversation in her head. He'd claimed a misunderstanding. He'd said he'd hoped that once she knew how important a munaqsri child was, she'd be as happy as he was. Now that she'd seen firsthand how all the other munaqsri reacted to her unborn baby, she finally believed he hadn't meant to deceive her or use her or betray her. He may have deluded himself, but he hadn't meant to hurt her.

Nine hours later, she heard the chime of the stones. Her cocoon, as thick as three bodies now, and immobile, positioned her so that her back was to the door. She saw sunlight spill across the floor as the door opened behind her. "Father Forest?"

"Yes, my child. How are you?"

She was aching and sweating inside her wooden shell. Her ribs hurt, her bladder pinched, and her skin itched, and he had the nerve to ask how she was? He dared call her "my child," as if he were some benevolent priest? She was not a child, and she wasn't his. "You need to let me go."

He shut the door, closed out the light. "I am sorry," he said, "but you give me little choice." She heard feet shuffle. She could not see him. Neck paralyzed, she had to face the carved cabinets.

"You're making a mistake," she said.

Father Forest hobbled into view and put a pot onto the stove. "You are reckless. The young often are. In the meantime, it is up to your elders to ensure your selfish behavior does not cause lasting harm. You risk the life of a munaqsri, and that cannot be allowed."

"Bear is a munaqsri!" Why wouldn't anyone understand that? She was on their side—trying to help one of their own! She fought to keep her voice calm and even. "If you keep me here, you condemn the polar bears."

She saw pity in his face. "The bear is gone," he said gently. "I know it is difficult for you to accept, but he is beyond the world. He is as dead."

"He is not dead!" Cassie thrashed, and the vines squeezed.

"You have the baby to think of now, and the polar bears are a dying species regardless," he said. "You must accept his loss, and—"

"I will not. He's not dead!" Never dead. She couldn't think it. It wasn't true. He was a prisoner, waiting to be freed, like her mother years ago.

"Some nice stew will make you feel better. Carrots, potatoes, onions"—he fetched vegetables from the cabinet—"tomatoes. If you truly love him, you will let him go."

"He promised me," she said. "'Until my soul leaves my body.'" A munaqsri couldn't break a promise. Right? Unless it was countered with another promise. Cassie remembered Gram's story: The North Wind's daughter had countered her father's promise with her own. Cassie felt despair tighten around her, tighter than the vines.

Father Forest peeled and sliced the vegetables and then added them to the pot. "Is that what your bear wanted? For you to seek your death and your child's? No one has ever been east of the sun and west of the moon."

"Not true," she said. Gail had gone there, blown by the North Wind. The North Wind . . . Cassie cursed herself. She should have gone to the North Wind. He could have taken her to Bear. Stupid idiot. *Now* she had a plan, now when she was trussed up like a snared hare.

"No, my child, any attempt to reach the castle is doomed to fail. It is best for you to stay here. It is what the bear would have wanted."

Promise me you will not try. "He didn't mean it!" *If you love me, let me go.* "He doesn't want to be a troll prisoner. He wants to be with me!" She was surprised at the strength of her conviction. When push came to shove, she did believe he loved her. The realization took her breath away.

"Sometimes bad things happen to good people." Father Forest ladled stew into a bowl. He carried it to Cassie and commanded the floor to raise him up until his face was even with hers. The smell of the stew filled her head. Betraying her, her stomach cried. "Everything will work out for the best," Father Forest said. "You will see." He lifted a spoonful to her lips. "Open up, now. You need to keep your strength up." Saliva flooded her tongue. "Come on," he said. "For the baby."

Cassie spat in his face.

Father Forest wiped his eyes. "Foolish child. This is for your own good."

"I hope you have a forest fire," she said. She would not let him see her fear.

"You will stay up there until you understand." At the flick of his hand, the floor lowered him down and the vines jerked her arms. She bit back a scream. He turned his back on her and emptied the stew back into the pot.

Tears pricked her eyes as her arms ached. She blinked her eyes clear.

"Someday," he said, "you will thank me."

And he left her alone.

❄ ❄ ❄ ❄ ❄

ICE

Cassie wet herself during the sunlit night. She felt the warmth run down her thighs and pool at her knees, where the vines were a tight ring. Squeezing her eyes shut, she tried to think about anything but where she was. She thought of the station. Dad, Gram, Max . . . She'd always assumed that if she had a child, they'd be there with her. She pictured herself as a little kid, surrounded by scientists and snowmobiles. She'd been so lucky.

In the morning, she watched Father Forest putter in the kitchen, fixing himself breakfast. She hoped his eggs tasted like urine. But when he brought her some, she ate it. "There's a good girl," he clucked. He poured water into her mouth. Most of it spilled down her neck and seeped in between the vines. "Are you ready to cooperate?"

"I don't want to starve before I rescue Bear," she said.

He frowned at her. "Perhaps in another day, you will feel differently."

"Don't count on it."

He left her again, and she hung from the ceiling for the rest of the day. It was hard, harder than she ever could have imagined, to not despair. She thought of her mother, prisoner of the trolls for eighteen years. No wonder Gail had nightmares. The wonder was that she had survived as sane as she was.

Father Forest returned in the evening. She heard the door open behind her. She couldn't move to see him.

"You are evil," she said flatly.

"Not true, my child. I have your interests at heart." On

his command, the vines loosened. Cassie collapsed to the floor. Her cheek pressed against the wood. She tried to remember how her muscles worked. She heard the munaqsri kneel beside her. "It hurts me to see you like this," he said. "Please, be sensible. Cooperate, and your stay here will be pleasant. You will be my guest."

Arms shaking, she pushed herself up. She reeked, and her thighs felt sticky. Blood rushed into her stiff fingers. Her eyes met Father Forest's.

He had tears in his eyes. "I am not a cruel man," he said. "All I want is what is best for you and your baby. Please, do not fight me. I am not your enemy."

In a burst, Cassie scrambled for the door. Her legs failed her. She threw herself at the doorway, and then the vines snapped her back, like a dog on a leash. She sank back to the ground.

Vines lashed her to the floor. Clucking his tongue, Father Forest said, "Another day then." He stepped over her. She heard the bedroom door open and shut.

Alone, tied to the floor, she watched the shadows from the shutters move across the floor. "Oh, Bear," she whispered. How could she rescue him now? Who would rescue her? If she were in these vines for another day, she thought she would lose her mind. Anything else she could have endured—any pain, any challenge—but not this horrible helplessness. "I'm sorry."

She had to be free of the vines.

A small voice inside her whispered that once she was

ICE

free, she could earn Father Forest's trust, lull him into complacency, and escape when he least expected it. She tried to convince herself it was a plan, not an excuse.

It felt like she was betraying her husband, betraying her father, and, most of all, betraying her mother. It made her sick to think about it. But her joints hurt, and her muscles burned.

She heard Father Forest enter the kitchen. He stepped over her to put the kettle on the stove.

"Fine," she croaked. "You win."

He beamed like a cartoon character. "Release."

The vines retracted, and this time, Cassie did not run. She lay silently on the floor, telling herself it was part of the plan, but feeling like crying.

TWENTY-FOUR

**Latitude 63° 54' 53" N
Longitude 125° 24' 07" W
Altitude 1301 ft.**

CASSIE BIT THE INSIDE OF HER CHEEK so hard that she tasted blood. *Meek*, she thought, concentrating. *Beaten.* Using sheer willpower, she lowered her eyes. She could have seared a hole in the wood floor with her stare.

Father Forest beamed. "Good girl."

How could anyone think Bear was a monster? Father Forest was a true monster.

He handed her a broom. She took it, wanting to snap it over her knee. Last night, after her surrender, he had simply fed her and let her sleep. But this morning, he'd greeted her with instructions. *Become a good mother*, he had said. Be the woman that Bear would have wanted her to be.

He was wrong. Bear loved her for who she was. She

wouldn't let this gnome poison her mind. She may have doubted Bear once, but never again.

Half her height, Father Forest could not pat her on the head, so he patted her on the elbow. She gripped the broom handle with white knuckles. *Just until he's lulled*, she told herself. After she'd fooled him into thinking he'd won, she'd escape.

"Set a good example for your little one," he said.

He went out into his garden of ferns. For an instant, sunlight flooded the kitchen. She saw dust hanging in sunbeams. Then the door shut like a cell door. Her insides screamed. She wanted Bear *now*.

Follow the plan, she told herself. Cassie swept viciously. She pounded at the floor with the broom bristles. Dust plumed around her. Cassie whacked at cobwebs. "Die, die, die!"

In the doorway, Father Forest sneezed.

Cassie froze midswing.

"Energetic," he said dryly.

The broom fell out of her hands. It clattered to the floor. Both of them looked at it. Maybe "meek" wasn't her forte. She swallowed and then plastered a smile on her face. She'd be free soon, she promised herself.

❄ ❄ ❄ ❄ ❄

Three nights later, while midnight sun leaked through the shutters, Cassie inched across the bedroom. She saw the outline of her pack. Kneeling beside it, she placed her mukluks inside and packed it all down hard. She could not afford a single sound. Slowly and silently, she lifted the pack and settled it onto her shoulders. She slipped out the bedroom door.

Listening, she stood in the shadowed kitchen like a deer on alert. Her heart thumped in her throat. To her ears, her breathing sounded like a wind tunnel. Father Forest snored.

Barefoot, Cassie crept across the kitchen. She watched for coils of vines. Like sleeping snakes under the cabinets and chairs, the vines were quiescent. She put her hand on the doorknob.

Without warning, wood encased her hand. Biting back a scream, Cassie tugged. Bark spread. It grew over her wrist. She hit it with her free hand. It spread up her forearm. She pried with her fingers. It covered her elbow. Father Forest kept snoring.

Oh, no, please, no. Bracing her feet against the door, she pulled.

She couldn't be trapped again. She reached behind her. Her ice axe was lashed to the pack's outside straps. If she could reach it . . . She yanked at the straps with her left hand as the wood oozed over her right arm.

Clasps on her pack clinked as loud as bells. She did not care—the wood was covering her right shoulder. She swung backward and hoped she had good aim.

Cassie slammed the wood with the axe.

Father Forest screamed.

Cassie lost her grip. She caught the axe handle before it

ICE

fell. He was awake! As Father Forest tore into the kitchen, Cassie hacked at the wood. *Hurry, hurry, hurry!* Wood chips flew.

Vines stirred. Father Forest shouted. She yanked at her encased arm. Not enough. She chopped as the vines snaked around her body and up her left arm, the one with the axe. She fought them and brought the axe down hard. The wood splintered. Sunlight pierced through the cracks. She wiggled her right hand free.

The vines squeezed her left elbow. Cassie yelled as her muscles spasmed. Her hand opened. The axe fell. It hit the ground. She dove for it. Vines snapped her back.

She swung in the air.

"I can feel it bleed," Father Forest said softly. Cassie shivered. Vines coiled around her legs. She hung, spinning gently, watching Father Forest stroke the axe marks. "How could you? Have you no heart?"

Hating him, she said nothing.

He ordered the vines to swallow her supplies.

❋ ❋ ❋ ❋ ❋

Through the kitchen shutters, Cassie could hear him cooing at his ferns. She wanted to claw the windows. The fact that he hadn't found it necessary to cocoon her in vines this time only underscored how thoroughly trapped she was. She paced the length of the kitchen. The wood was warm under her bare feet, as if it were reminding her it was alive, as if she were likely to forget. The vines had absorbed her pack, mukluks and all, like an amoeba. She wasn't likely to forget that. How was she supposed to escape from a living prison when a magical being was the jailer and she had no equipment and no supplies?

Searching for her pack, she tested the cabinets and drawers in the kitchen, the living room, the two bedrooms, and the bathroom. But the drawers wouldn't budge, and the cabinets behaved as if they were solid wood. The entire cottage seemed carved out of a single tree. Everything—furniture, fixtures, walls—grew out of the floor. She returned to the kitchen. There had to be *something* here that could help her.

Cassie tugged on a cabinet under the kitchen sink, and to her surprise, it popped open. She shot a quick look at the vines (the vines were sleeping like coiled ropes) and at the shutters (Father Forest was just outside, humming an Irish jig). She knelt and peered into the cabinet.

The cabinet held cleaning supplies. Her heart sank. "Subtle," she said to the shutters. He must have known she'd search the cottage. He had wanted her to find this.

Cassie weeded through the cabinet, in case it miraculously held anything useful. She emptied out Comet, Pledge, Lysol . . . until all that remained was the sink plumbing. It seemed strange to her that the cottage had ordinary plumbing and that such a powerful munaqsri owned everyday cleaning supplies. Couldn't the magic do it? Maybe he preferred it not to?

Cassie shook her head. To think she had come to a point where plumbing and Lysol surprised her more than magic.

ICE

She remembered back to when she'd first met Bear— She squeezed her eyes shut. *Don't think about it*, she told herself. *Concentrate on escaping.* She rocked back on her heels, considering the cabinet. She didn't see a single crack large enough to lose a paper clip, much less a backpack. She would have to escape as she was, barefoot and without her supplies. Dad would help her. He had prepared her for this. He'd taught her to forage—she could eat berries, bird eggs, and bark. She'd do her best to avoid giardia, dysentery, and the other joys of Mother Nature. She'd drink from running streams. But first she had to escape this cottage.

Cassie stood and looked around. The only part of the cottage that she had not explored was the vines themselves. Gathering her courage, she poked the vines. They were as inert as an ordinary plant. She picked up one end with her thumb and forefinger and held it at arm's length. It dangled, as limp as a garden hose. Braver, she uncoiled it. She traced it back to its source.

The vines had grown from the floor, walls, and ceiling. She stretched them across the room to the other side of the stove. There was no place the vines could not reach. As long as she was confined inside, she would never make it past them—or the doorknob.

She had to return to her original plan: Lull Father Forest into complacency and convince him to trust her enough to let her outside. From there . . . She peered through the shutters at the trees beyond the picket fence. If she could outdistance the vines, she could disappear between the trees.

It could be weeks, though, before he trusted her enough. Or months. She did not want to think about the possibility of never.

She could do this, she told herself. It wasn't as if she were afraid of work. She knelt again by the kitchen sink, tore open a package of sponges, and began scrubbing the kitchen floor.

After three hours, her knees, back, and shoulders ached. She was sweating, and her stomach felt like a furnace. Cassie sat up and rubbed her neck. She looked around her. For some reason, the kitchen had seemed larger while scrubbing.

She had to be patient, she told herself. She had to be more patient than she had ever been in tracking polar bears. She had to sneak up on her freedom. As she took her sponge and Spic and Span (pine-scented, of course) into the living room, she thought of her mother surviving for years in the troll castle. She wished she'd asked her mother more about it. She wished she'd talked to her more in general, about real things, "feelings" things, instead of the conversations they had had about station minutiae. She promised herself she'd rectify that someday—if she ever made it out of here. Gingerly, Cassie got back down on her hands and knees. She winced as her back twinged.

Father Forest hovered in the doorway. "Good girl," he said.

TWENTY-FIVE

Latitude 63° 54' 53" N
Longitude 125° 24' 07" W
Altitude 1301 ft.

THE LONG AFTERNOON OF SUMMER slipped away. As the autumnal equinox crept closer, the stars appeared earlier, the sun rose later, and the aurora borealis rippled like a closing theater curtain over the northern forest.

Cassie pressed her cheek against the window shutters and peered up at a sliver of sky. She wrapped her arms around her broad stomach and felt her skin roll as the baby shifted inside her. Bear had said she was due in the fall. She was nearly out of time.

As she watched the sliver of sky lighten from deep blue to rosy pink, she tried to keep from screaming. She'd lost the summer to pointless chores. She was sure that Father Forest could have commanded his cottage to do them. His reliance on man-made plumbing and Spic and Span was an odd quirk, as if he'd forgotten a munaqsri's powers could affect ordinary chores. But she had done it all without complaint. Still, she was trapped inside this wooden cage and was no closer to rescuing Bear.

Stepping back from the window, she checked around her to make sure she wasn't crushing any vines. Father Forest would feel it. Four months of worrying about what Father Forest would think or feel, and still no opportunity to escape. She thought, as she often did these days, of her mother in the troll castle. Now Cassie sometimes woke screaming at night. But no one came to comfort her.

"Hellooo, little mother!"

Cassie looked out through the shutters. Outside at the gate, the aspen waved her twig arms over her head as if she were waving in an airplane.

Oh, not again.

The aspen skipped down the singing stones. "Tell Father Forest that I am here!"

Without fail, the aspen came every morning, but today Father Forest had other visitors too. Tree-people from the southern part of the boreal forest had come to the cottage to discuss placement and exposure and color of autumn leaves, as if they were artists participating in a vast art gallery. "He said he can't see you today," Cassie said through the shutters.

Racing at the window, the tree-girl hissed at Cassie— eyes wild yellow, sharp green teeth bared. In that instant, she'd transformed from a childlike tree spirit into something feral. Cassie instinctively flinched away from the window, and then the aspen burst into wailing. "Oh, my aspens! They suffer! It's the spruces. Their roots spread—they steal soil from my aspens!"

"I'm sorry," Cassie said, eyeing her through the shutters. No matter how cute the tree-girl could look, she wasn't a child. The perky innocence was an affectation, as much as Father Forest's Santa Claus image.

The aspen shrieked. Her leaves spiked, her eyes rolled, and her mouth widened into a gash across her bark face. "He must come see! Spruces crowd my aspens back into the valleys. My aspens lose mountain exposure. My aspens starve for sunlight!" Her stick body shook. "You must let me see him!" Launching herself at the window, she clawed at the shutters.

Cassie retreated fast. "I'll tell him you're here," she said.

The aspen beamed, again a green child. "Goody."

Cassie escaped into the living room. Phosphorescent moss lit the walls in a faint green glow. Open flames, Father Forest had said, made his visitors nervous. Six visitors, birches, sickly green in the moss light, had planted themselves into the wood floor.

Stepping over their roots, Cassie whispered to Father Forest about the aspen. Father Forest grimaced—an odd expression on a Santa Claus. "Can you tell her 'not now'?"

"You know how she is," Cassie said.

"Oh, dear," Father Forest said. "I should go—"

"This is not acceptable." One of the birch-men flopped

the leaves on his head. Another birch frowned and said, "We have traveled a long way." A third spoke up: "We have important decisions to make."

"Oh, dearie dear," Father Forest said. "Cassie, my child, can't you pacify her?"

Cassie began to refuse, and then she stopped. Maybe this was her chance. If she could use the crazy tree-girl . . . Cassie's heart thudded, and she tried to sound nonchalant as she said, "I could convince her to show me the spruces. Tell her that I will report back to you."

He frowned. "Surely, she can wait a few—"

"She is seconds away from bursting in here," Cassie said. "As you can imagine, I would prefer not to walk so far." She patted her round stomach for emphasis. "But if it would help you . . ."

"Let the human go," one of the birch-women said. Another birch said, "Yes, let's get on with it." Another added, "Please, we have limited time."

Father Forest surrendered. "Very well. Go, then." He waved his hand to dismiss her as one of the birches tapped Father Forest's knee and said, "About that shade of yellow . . ."

"Golden tones are better, don't you agree?" Father Forest replied.

Cassie backed into the kitchen, certain he'd change his mind. Any second now, he'd realize his mistake. Her hand shook as she laid it on the door latch. Always before, it had behaved like solid wood.

She squeezed the latch and pulled—the door swung

open, and Cassie fell outside. Her knees shook. She leaned against the door frame. She sucked in oxygen. It smelled of spruce and soil. It smelled of shadows and sunlight.

"Little mother, is he with you?"

Cassie barely heard the aspen. She walked to the gate. Brown and brittle ferns brushed her skirt. She felt the warm crunch of spruce needles under her bare feet.

Run, her mind whispered, *run*.

"Little mother?" The aspen's voice held a dangerous note. She stomped her twig foot, and Cassie focused on her. She had to keep the aspen pacified if her escape was to work.

"He asked me to observe in his place," Cassie said. "I am to report back to him."

"All we want is our due," the aspen said, sweet again. "It is not fair. Other trees have much better exposure." Cassie opened the gate. Legs shaking, she walked out as the aspen continued, "Some trees have such good exposure that they can speak to the winds. Never aspens, though. It is not fair at all. It is injustice."

Just beyond the picket fence, the dark of the forest was primeval. Shriveled ferns shrouded the forest floor. Above, leaves and branches were knit so tightly that they choked light. She could lose herself in that darkness. She could disappear.

Cassie glanced back at the cottage. Innocent as a gingerbread house, the cottage glowed in the warm pink of morning. She could hear the rise and fall of the birch voices through the shutters. She expected Father Forest to tear out after her any second. Her heart beat as fast as mosquito wings. Forcing herself not to run, in case he watched from the window, Cassie walked into the forest, and the shadows swallowed her.

The aspen bounced beside her, again childlike. "What do you think?"

She knew it was her imagination, but it felt as if the trees were leaning in on her, suffocating her. As she squeezed between shrubs, she missed the openness of the pack ice. Out on the ice, her soul expanded—but here, she felt boxed in, claustrophobic even. Filtered through the canopy of ever-green branches, the light in the forest was an underwater green. Ferns and horsetails filled the spaces between the spruces. She stepped over roots and brown-leafed bushes.

"Are you listening to me?" the aspen demanded.

Cassie hadn't been. "You want exposure?"

"Yes!" The aspen's yellow eyes flashed. "Some trees on mountainsides can speak to the winds. Is that too much to ask? Some space to be heard?"

Cassie looked back over her shoulder. She couldn't see the cottage anymore. Now it was time to run. She didn't know how much time she had before Father Forest realized his mistake, but she had to be well beyond the reach of his vines when he did. She broke into a jog, cradling her over-size stomach. Rocks jabbed at her bare feet.

"Slow down, little mother."

"We have to reach the spruces!" Cassie said. "You want

me to see them quickly, don't you?" As soon as she had enough distance, she'd distract the aspen and lose her. Her skirt snagged on bushes and wrapped around her ankles. Reaching down, she hiked it up to her hips. She ran faster.

The aspen loped after Cassie. "But you're going the wrong way. My aspens are east! Little mother, stop!" Her shrill voice pierced the wind. She let out a screech.

Needles quivered overhead.

Holding her stomach protectively, Cassie ducked under a low-hanging branch. It slapped her forehead. She pressed her hand on her stinging head. Blood or sweat, it felt wet.

Ahead of her, bark melted like molten metal.

Cassie veered to the left, and a second wall of bark blocked her. She looked behind her. Bark sealed all the gaps. Caught! Cassie stumbled to a stop. All around her, wood ringed her in a solid circle. She spun.

Perched up in the branches, the tree-girl peered down at her. "I said *east!*"

Cassie heard a horrible cracking noise as the wall of trees split. It fell open as if lightning had struck it. Father Forest stood where the wall had been.

Cassie retreated until her back hit the wall of bark.

"You disappoint me," he said softly. "I thought we had an understanding. After all, it is your own interest that I am protecting."

"I wasn't . . . I mean, I didn't . . ." Cassie wanted to weep. Months, wasted!

"Oh, my child, you have to know it is pointless. You

cannot run from the forest when you are in the forest, any more than you can escape the sea from within the sea."

"I wasn't trying to escape," Cassie lied. "I was confused, and then the trees began to move and I was scared. That's why I ran."

Father Forest tsked with his tongue. "Come, come, now . . ."

Dropping from the branches, the aspen landed on the soft needles. "It is my fault. She was hurrying to help me, and she went the wrong way."

Cassie stared at her. The crazy aspen was unintentionally saving Cassie.

"Truly?" Father Forest said.

The tree-girl shrugged. Disgust colored her voice. "She's a foolish child."

Please believe it, Cassie thought at him. She said out loud, "She was upset. I wanted to hurry. I only wanted to help you. You've been like a real father to me." She nearly choked on the words.

Lines eased on his face. He nodded. He knew how insistent the tree-girl could be, didn't he? He could understand how it could make someone run, couldn't he? Cassie did not breathe. "Forgive me, child, for doubting you," he said. "Come back to the cottage." Smiling at her, he looped his gnarled arm around her waist. She tried not to tense.

The tree-girl bristled. "But my aspens!"

He put his other arm around the aspen. "Come too. We can discuss it." Arm around each of them, Father Forest propelled Cassie and the tree-girl forward through the rift in the wood wall that he'd created. Cassie glanced over her shoulder and saw the spruces slowly reverting to individual trees. She shivered. "Cold?" he asked.

"I'm fine," Cassie said. "I'll make her some tea to calm her." As soon as she saw the cottage, she strode forward, breaking out of his circling arm, and walked down the singing stones. The stones chimed cheerfully at her. She entered the cottage, and the latch clicked shut behind her. She did not let herself look back.

Inside, the birches were gone. Stepping over their root stains, she carried the kettle to the sink. Hands shaking, she filled it with water. Her mind ran in circles. She had not known he could control trees from a distance. Outside his home, Bear hadn't been able to affect molecules he wasn't touching. *But Sedna could*, Cassie thought. The mermaid had saved Cassie without touching her, and Father Forest was an overseer like Sedna.

How would she ever escape if he had that kind of power? How could she run from the forest within the forest? What part of the forest was not forest? The kettle overflowed. Water poured down the drain.

"Cassie, the water?" Father Forest said, entering the cottage. "It is not an endless well." Mechanically, she turned off the faucet. She stared at it without moving her hand.

Water was not part of the forest. She remembered: *The rivers are not my region.* Suddenly, she knew how to escape. She needed a river, a stream, a bog. Yes, a bog

would be perfect. He could not watch the whole circum-
ference at once. She could lose him in the middle and
come out on an unexpected side. But how would she ever
get to one? Father Forest would never let her outside
again, much less near water. What excuse did she have
to get near water?

The aspen let out a screech.

"Tea here, please," Father Forest said.

Cassie put the kettle on the stove, and after a few minutes, it whistled. She poured the steaming water into his
cup. She thought she sensed an idea forming as she poured.
He needed water for his special tea.

She brought the cup to Father Forest for the aspen.
Father Forest concentrated on the tea for a moment and
then encouraged the aspen to drink. After a few sips, the
tree-girl was calmer. Father Forest gave Cassie a grateful
look. "Thank you."

Cassie smiled sweetly.

❄ ❄ ❄ ❄ ❄

The next morning, as soon as Father Forest secluded himself in the living room, Cassie completed her preparations.
Checking over her shoulder to make sure she was alone, she
shoved a wad of mud, sticks, and stones into the kitchen
faucet. She jammed it farther in with the broom handle and
then added more, mixing it so it was as thick as mortar. All
the while, she listened for the telltale xylophone chime of
the stones outside the cottage.

She was certain the tree-girl would return. She'd listened

ICE

to Father Forest the day before. He'd only soothed her; he hadn't solved her problem. The aspen would be back.

Cassie finished plugging the faucet, and then she straightened. Her stomach sank. "Whoa, kiddo, what's going on in there?" She clasped her hands over her abdomen. It felt lower. What did that mean? Her heart thudded faster. She had time left, didn't she?

She could not give birth here. No doctors, no nurses, no hospitals. No Max to airlift her to Fairbanks. Just Father Forest and his crazy trees. She closed her eyes; the world spun. *Oh, God, not now. Not here.*

She could not let this child be born here with Father Forest. It would grow up a prisoner. She couldn't let that happen.

"Hellooo, little mother!" she heard.

"Work with me," Cassie whispered to her stomach, and then she called through the shutter slats, "So sorry to hear about the spruces."

Several octaves too high, the tree-girl squeaked, "Hear what?"

"Father Forest awarded the foothills of the Mackenzies to the spruces," Cassie said. "He decided last night. Didn't he tell you?"

As she'd hoped, her words were a match to kindling. The aspen exploded. Shrieking, the tree-girl slammed her stick body into the door. With a mighty crack, the cottage door burst open.

Father Forest ran into the kitchen.

The aspen was screeching loud enough to fell trees.

"Cassie, tea!" Father Forest shouted. "She's hysterical!"

Cassie ran to the kettle. Conveniently (and intentionally), it was empty. She brought it to the sink. She glanced over her shoulder. With his back to her, Father Forest wrung his hands over the tree-girl. The aspen whirled around the room, scratching gashes into the wood walls and tearing at leaves. Cassie turned the sink handle. "Plumbing's clogged!"

"Fix it!" Father Forest cried.

Cassie opened the cabinet under the sink. She squatted. She'd inserted the clog in the faucet to prevent drips, but the real problem with the plumbing was down here. She knew she could not fix it—not after all the trouble she had gone through to break it. This was one time when Father Forest's dependence on man-made things instead of magic worked to her advantage. She patted the Spic and Span fondly. "Doesn't look good," she said out loud. Pulling herself up by the counter, she said, "I'll try the bathroom."

"Hurry!" She could barely hear him over the aspen. For a tree, she had quite a set of lungs. Ears ringing, Cassie waddled to the bathroom.

"No luck," she called. "The well must be dry!" She returned to the kitchen.

He was near tears. "She needs tea!"

Cassie went for a pitcher on a shelf. Now here was the final step. She uttered a silent prayer. Heart beating in her throat, she said, "I could fetch some. Where's a stream?"

"Quarter mile north." He pointed. "Go!"

Cassie went.

The trees did not stop her.

TWENTY-SIX

Latitude 63° 55' 02" N
Longitude 125° 24' 08" W
Altitude 1296 ft.

CASSIE RAN, SOFT STEPS ON THE NEEDLES. She clutched the pitcher to her chest. Her breath roared in her ears. She felt the baby kick as if running with her. "Hang in there," she told it. "We'll make it. Just hang in there." Ligaments tugged as her stomach bounced.

She heard the stream gurgling like a drowning man.

She jumped over a root and landed on feather moss. Her feet slid, and she flailed for a branch. Catching one, she steadied herself before remembering it could be an enemy. She let go fast, and the branch snapped back.

The ground softened as she neared the stream, and Cassie sank into it like it was a sponge. Mud sucked at her feet, slowing her. She spotted the stream. Oh, no. It wasn't wide enough! It wasn't safe. The narrow stream was still within

Father Forest's reach. Balsam poplars and alders leaned over it. Horsetails and ferns draped in it. Cassie plowed through them and splashed into the water.

Bare feet on the wet rocks, she ran through the stream. She clenched her teeth as the rocks pinched. Miniature rapids swirled around her toes. *Please, let it lead to a river,* she thought.

Cassie saw a fern unfurl. Her gut tightened. *He knows.* Bushes rustled, and horsetails whipped her ankles. Branches stretched to scrape her skin. How could he know so quickly?

She heard the red squirrels chittering from the treetops— spies.

Branches waved like octopus tentacles. She kicked through them. She jammed her toe on a rock, and winced, slowing. Branches snagged her hair. She wouldn't get another chance at this. She had to make it *now.* She yanked. She felt strands rip from her head as she splashed down-stream.

Shadows fell across the stream. Cassie glanced up to see branches weaving and bending into a net. She chucked the pitcher at the tree. It recoiled. She ran under it. Shrub willow seized her skirt. She heard it tear.

"Little mother, wait!" Waving her arms, the tree-girl sprinted through the spruces. Father Forest could not be far behind.

Holding her bouncing stomach, Cassie bolted down miniature waterfalls. Rocks and twigs flew under her feet.

She had to run faster—for Bear, for Dad, for Gail, for the baby inside her.

"Stop!" Leaping over bushes, the aspen raced beside the stream. She stretched out her stick arms to Cassie. "It's too dangerous!"

Avoiding the aspen's arms, Cassie tripped over loose rocks. She fell, and her hands slapped the rocks. She clutched her stomach and propelled herself onto her feet.

In the distance, she heard a crashing.

"No, no, no," the aspen cried. "Danger! You must stop!" Her voice rose, approaching a shriek. "Stop!"

Cassie heard the sound of a waterfall. Suddenly, she saw it through the spruces: the river! Blue, beautiful, and wild, it rushed through the forest.

Branches slapped her. She shielded her face as she ran. Up ahead, the stream narrowed between boulders, spilled through them, and tumbled down ten feet into the stormy water below. Squatting on the boulders, Father Forest waited for her.

Cassie lowered her head like a bull. Father Forest was ten feet ahead of her. She barreled into the gap. As if scolding a toddler, he said, "No, Cassie, no. You'll hurt yourself. You'll hurt your baby."

Five feet ahead of her.

He held out his gnarled hand. "You must trust me. I promise you will be safe with me. I'll take care of you. I'll raise your child like my own."

Inches ahead of her.

"Think of your baby, its future," he said. "That's a good girl, take my hand. Come home with me."

She was there. "Like hell I will," she cried, and ducked under his hand and slid down the rock face. Scrambling, the aspen tried to stop her. "No, little mother!" Her fingers scratched Cassie's arm like claws.

Cassie spilled over the rocks. She hit the water feet first. Her bare feet slammed down on the sharp rocks of the river floor, and she doubled over, hissing. The stream crashed down onto her back. She heard the aspen scream.

Cassie straightened, and water tumbled over her shoulders and down her stomach. Her feet throbbed. Blood tinted the water and then swirled with the fast-moving current.

"Oh, please, come back!" the aspen called, again a little girl's voice.

Cassie fought the churning water. She lifted her foot, and the current grabbed it. She forced it down and wormed it between stones. She lifted her other foot. Wet, her skirt pulled with a weight that smacked against her legs. She raised her arms as the water deepened, and she gasped when the wet coolness licked her stomach.

Reaching the middle of the river, she forded downstream. Pleading with her, the aspen and Father Forest followed onshore. Mouth pressed into a grim line, Cassie focused her eyes on her feet over the broad curve of her stomach. Blood stopped swirling around her toes after a few minutes. Salmon darted through the clear water as passing streaks of silver. She hoped Father Forest was not on speaking terms with their munaqsri. How soon until the river was also her enemy?

The shore was suddenly quiet. She spared a glance at it. Father Forest and the aspen were nowhere to be seen. Bracing herself between the stones as the current pushed against her back, Cassie scanned the trees. Was it paranoia if the trees really were watching? She managed a grim smile.

Cassie waded to a boulder midriver and pulled herself out of the water like a whale beaching. In protest, the baby in her writhed. She stroked her undulating stomach and leaned back on one elbow. "Rest first. Then stage two," she said to it.

She should not have difficulty finding a bog. In a boreal forest, it was harder to *not* find one. In fall, the woods were riddled with them. Cassie rubbed her aching thighs, chilled into gooseflesh in the wind. The trick would be after the bog.

She knew where she was going; the aspen had told her: *Some trees on mountainsides can speak to the winds.* She remembered seeing the Mackenzies back when she'd been in the tundra. But the journey there . . .

First things first: Find the bog, lose her pursuers. Cassie slid off the rock. The water felt almost warm after the chilling air. She waded downstream of the boulder, then lowered herself in up to her shoulders. She lifted her legs. Her stomach buoyed with her torso. Floating, she was swept downstream.

❅ ❅ ❅ ❅ ❅

ICE

"Charming," Cassie said, half to herself and half to the bog. Steam rose around her from the rotting ferns and logs. Hell could not have more humidity. Or smell worse. She wrinkled her nose. The bog smelled cloying, the sweet-sour of decomposing vegetation. "Whose bright idea was this?" she asked aloud.

She waded across the muck. It squished between her toes and oozed over her bare feet like melted tar. Stepping into a patch of rotting leaves, Cassie sank to her knee. Mud slurped as she lifted her foot out. She grimaced. It was nearly impossible to distinguish depth. One false step, and she could drown in mud.

Cassie looked across the bog. Straggly spruces clung to the muck like sickly scarecrows stuck in an abandoned field. *Roots need ground,* she thought. *The mud will be shallow near the trees.* But were these trees in Father Forest's domain? She did not want to risk it. But she did not want to risk sinking into bottomless ooze either.

Mosquitoes descended en masse as she debated. In a cloud, they rained down on her unprotected skin. She swatted the air. "Bloodsucking vampires," she said. "This just gets better and better." She wondered if her slapping was attracting the attention of the mosquito munaqsri. *Anything could be an enemy,* she thought. She stopped slapping. Quickly compromising, she tugged a sapling out of the mud. Waving away mosquitoes and poking the ooze, she slogged forward.

She used her makeshift walking stick as a guide. If it sank

less than two feet, she waded forward; more than two feet, she went in another direction. She did not bother to test the pools of black water. Purple orchids and pitcher plants marked those bottomless pools. She steered wide around them, and worried she was doing figure eights through the bog. She missed her GPS.

By the time that sunset flared across the sky, she missed her water canteen even more. Cassie wet her lips, and she tasted mud. Her throat felt like sandpaper. The baby squirmed, and she felt an elbow in her rib. "Sorry," she said, patting her stomach. "It's not purified." The bog water looked like chocolate syrup in the fading light.

She had to stop—the growing shadows made it impossible to distinguish between the bottomless pits and the harmless puddles. Cassie curled up on a moss patch as Orion's belt poked through the deep blue. Hours later, she woke three inches deep in muck.

She extracted herself with the aid of her walking stick. Mud made her skin itch. Her hair was clotted. She stretched her back, and mossy mud slid off her shoulders.

Cassie eyed the muddy water. *Do you know how many bacteria are in that water?* her father's voice said in her head. *Could one sip hurt so much?* she argued with him. Her tongue felt swollen. It hurt to swallow. Indigestion was better than dehydration. Dehydration would kill her faster.

Kneeling, she swirled her hand in a pool of light brownish water. Water bugs scattered. Algae bobbed in the ripples.

ICE

She tried to think of it as iced tea. It had the same color and consistency. She scooped some into her hands and sipped. It spilled over her chin. "Oh, ew," she said. It tasted as vile as she imagined raw sewage would taste. She wiped her mouth with a muddy sleeve. Her stomach churned. But she needed the water. Her baby needed it.

Midway through the day, she drank again, and then she drank again in the evening. Thinking constantly of water, she had trouble concentrating. Jab the stick down, walk forward, jab the stick down, walk forward. She repeated it to herself as a litany.

During her second sunset in the bog, she found a patch of cloudberries. She fell to her knees in the muck. She tore the fat yellow berries from the bushes and shoved them into her mouth. Berries exploded like fireworks on her tongue, and the juices slid down her throat, as sharp as liquor. She tasted mud from her fingers, but she did not care. She ate until the bushes were bare, and then she slept beside them.

Her feet tingled, waking her near dawn. Reaching awkwardly around her stomach, she rubbed them. They were clammy to the touch. Skin that showed through the mud was red. She had to find dry land soon.

She combed through the patch of cloudberries. She found three uneaten berries, no more. The night before, she had been thorough. This morning, her stomach hurt. Taking up her walking stick again, she slogged on.

❊ ❊ ❊ ❊ ❊

Cassie saw a phalanx of spruces, shooting tall into the air. She leaned on her stick and hobbled on numb feet. Her stick sank five inches, then two, then one. The carpet changed from sphagnum moss to spruce needles. Ferns and club mosses replaced orchids. She hesitated five feet from the first white spruce. Dripping from her skirt in clumps, mud plopped irregularly to the ground. The forest could hold a thousand spies. Father Forest himself could be waiting for her.

She told herself he would not recognize her, caked with mud. Even if he did, he would keel over from the stench of her. Slowly, painfully, she climbed up a hill, out of the bog. Needles stuck to her feet, crackling softly.

At the top of the hill, Cassie stopped again and lowered herself onto a fallen log. Dark spruce green, broken by autumn leaves, stretched for miles and miles over the foothills of the mountains. The mountains, outlined in the sun, crowned the horizon. Honey golden and brushed with glacial white, the mountains were beyond beautiful, but it was hard to care when everything hurt.

Bending awkwardly around her stomach, Cassie wiped mud from the soles of her feet with ferns. Her feet were swollen and cold. As she wiped, she saw skin. It looked waxy and was mottled with burgundy splotches. She touched it, and it felt as spongy as moss. "Lovely," she said, swallowing back bile. She dried her feet as well as she could. She knew she should not walk on them, but the longer she stayed in one place, the more likely Father Forest was to find her.

ICE

She stood and winced. She felt the baby shove its knee (or elbow) outward. "Don't worry. I'm not giving up," she told it. "I'll keep you free."

Using her stick, she picked her way over rocks and roots down the hill. In spots, the hill was sheer. She had to snake down it, avoiding the drop-offs. Below her, she could see the reflected blue of a stream. If she had to, she told herself, she could move river to river, bog to bog, across the forested foothills. So long as she did not have to move faster than a shuffle.

She made it to the bottom. Her feet felt like blocks of wood, and she moved painfully slowly as the terrain went uphill again. Something rustled above her. Wind or munaqsri? Squirrel or spy? Heart thudding in her ears, she scanned the trees. She saw nothing.

Cassie sank against a spruce. "I hate this," she said to the tree. "I just want you to know that I hate this." She bent around her swollen stomach to examine her feet. Blistered now, they felt like they were burning. She picked off needles and dirt that had stuck to the blisters. There was nothing she could do for her feet, except hope that the trench foot did not worsen into gangrene. She felt her stomach skin ripple as the baby squirmed like a bird bashing its shell. It did not like her bending. "Just a little while longer," she said to it as she straightened. "We can do this."

Limping, she made it another mile on the strength of bravado before the rain began. On the slope of the next hill, she heard it before she felt it. Rain pelted the coniferous canopy. Aspens quivered. Rain burst through. She tilted her face up, and water spattered over her. Mud streaked down her neck as the bog muck sloughed off her. She caught drops in her hands and mouth and drank. Rain washed over the forest floor.

Needles underfoot became as slippery as soap. Cassie hurried to the shelter of a fallen spruce. She huddled under it as rain soaked the trees.

A steady trickle ran down her back, and Cassie shivered. She pressed against the cold bark. She imagined the baby inside her shivering too. She wondered if she was hurting it, being out here—and then she wondered when she'd begun to care what it felt. She couldn't remember a moment. It had sneaked up on her gradually with each kick, each hiccup, each shift she felt inside.

Cassie curled into a ball. Resting her head on a root, she wrapped her arms around her stomach as if she could cradle the baby within. Water pooled under her head. Her wet hair chilled her neck. In fits, she slept. She dreamed about Bear; she dreamed about Gram; she dreamed about a child with wide eyes and a distended stomach. The child stared at her without speaking until Cassie's eyes snapped open.

She was hot and shivering. Arms shaking, she struggled to sit. Water dripped onto her. Outside her makeshift shelter, it drizzled. She lurched out.

The world spun as she stood too fast, and she had to close her eyes. She put her hand on her forehead—hot to the touch. She knew she had a fever. Gram used to take care of her when she had a fever.

Opening her eyes, she looked for Gram.

She stumbled forward. "Gram, I don't feel well." It came out as mush. Her ears rang, and her vision blurred. She felt as if she were underwater. "Gram?"

Gram was a white bear. Then she was a starving child, eyes as wide as Father Forest's tea saucers. Cassie held her arms out.

The bear-child ran.

Cassie ran. Her head pounded and her feet throbbed. She saw fine white lines imposed over the forest. She saw a flash of darkness.

Cassie cradled her forehead in her hands. She wanted to outrun the throbbing in her head. She ran faster and, blind, burst through the trees.

She did not see the drop-off.

She did not see the rocks.

She fell. Sharp rocks hit as she somersaulted down the slope. Pain lanced through her. Screaming, she rolled.

She hit bottom. A stream gurgled beside her. Her hand dangled in it. *Wet*, she thought. She lost consciousness.

She had fever dreams: blood and heat and searing cold. As the dreams and the fever faded, the pain jolted her awake. She lay, twisted, on the rocks. Her skin felt tenderized. Her ears rang. Her head spun. Her stomach . . . She writhed and gasped for air. Her guts squeezed.

Oh, what have I done? Please, please, don't be dead.

Cassie tried to sit. She could not seem to get enough air. *Please, live. Live, damn you.*

Blackness swam up in her eyes as she moved. She vomited. Sharp pain sliced through her body as she heaved. She brought her hand, shaking, up to her mouth. And she saw the blood. She spread her fingers. Neon scarlet blood. It was all she could see. It consumed her world.

She was vomiting blood.

Cassie closed her eyes. Still saw red. She shuddered. She knew what it meant, alone and hurt. She had not only killed her baby. She had killed herself.

PART THREE

At the Back of the North Wind

TWENTY-SEVEN

**Latitude 63° 48' 11" N
Longitude 126° 02' 38" W
Altitude 1108 ft.**

CASSIE WAS DROWNING. She clawed at her throat. She was a beached fish, drowning in air. She saw a shadow cross over her. Fighting, she focused on it.

It looked like a young Inuit man.

But that didn't make any sense. She was alone, dying alone. Just her and her unborn, never-to-be-born child. "I'm sorry, sorry, sorry," she whispered. She squeezed her eyes shut.

When she opened them again, the man was waiting silently on the rocks above her. Suddenly, she understood: He was waiting for her to die. "Munaqsri," she rasped.

Startled, he lost his footing on the rocks. He skidded down a few feet before catching himself. Pebbles rolled into Cassie, and she flinched.

"You can see me! I thought you were . . . ," he said. "You know what I am?"

Yes, she knew. He was the human munaqsri. He was here to take her soul. Well, she wasn't going to let him. He was a munaqsri; he could manipulate molecules. He could save her! "Heal me," she demanded. She coughed. Blood speckled his pants leg.

He frowned at the blood and then at her. "If you know what I am, then you know I'm not here to heal you."

She batted his ankle with a weak hand. "You can," she said. He had the power. "Do it."

Gently, he said, "I'm sorry, but you're dying."

"Not dying." Not while he could save her. Straining to reach for him, she spat blood.

Leaning down, he touched her neck, feeling her pulse. "You must be especially determined." He released her. "You need to let go. Your body is too damaged to heal itself, and you must be in tremendous pain." He sounded almost kind. "I must take your soul now."

She closed her eyes for the briefest of instants and then opened them again. She concentrated on his words as if they were bubbles she had to catch. Her vision swam. "Can't have it."

"Hey, now, we don't want it drifting off beyond the ends of the earth."

She thought of the polar bears, their unclaimed souls drifting off beyond the ends of the earth unless—she remembered the owl and the hare—*unless another took them.*

Could she tempt the human munaqsri? "Know twenty-five thousand," Cassie said.

He squatted on the rocks beside her. "What was that?"

More strongly, she said, "Twenty-five thousand unclaimed souls." The effort made her gasp. She choked on air and started to shake.

Catching her shoulders, he steadied her. "Unclaimed? Did you say 'unclaimed'? As in without a munaqsri?" She could hear the excitement in his voice.

She closed her eyes. "Can't talk," she whispered. "Dying." *Please, let this work!*

"Twenty-five thousand souls." He was almost shouting. "You said twenty-five thousand! Where? Who?"

She took a breath as if to speak, but then shuddered— the shudder was not feigned. *Heal me!* she silently begged.

She heard him swear, and then pain shot through her as he pressed down on her rib cage. Her torso tightened and her ribs squeezed. She felt as if the ceiling of the sky were collapsing inward and the earth were ripping upward. She screamed. And then suddenly, the pain was gone.

Surprised, Cassie cut off midscream. She sat up on the blood-soaked rocks. She felt as light as helium. She practiced breathing. Her ribs expanded and contracted evenly. She prodded them. She did not even feel bruised. She looked at herself, bloody and healthy. She ran her hands over her stomach. "Is my baby . . ."

"Of course," he said, sounding offended. "I am a professional."

A wave of relief rolled over her with an intensity that shocked her. Tears flooded her eyes, and she examined her skin so he wouldn't notice. Thin pink lines showed where the rocks had pierced her. She flaked the dried blood off them. "Impressive work," she said, struggling to sound calm. "Thank you."

"We are not supposed to make exceptions, but for twenty-five thousand . . . With that many souls, I would never have another stillbirth." She heard wonder in his voice.

She looked up at him for the first time without the haze of pain. The munaqsri was a thin Inuit man with a caterpillar-fuzz mustache. He looked young—maybe Jeremy's age—but that didn't mean anything with munaqsri. He had shaved his hair so short that his scalp was visible. *He should have transplanted it to his upper lip instead,* she thought. His sparse mustache (plus the khakis, shirt, and tie) made him look more like a kid at his first job interview than a caretaker of the human race.

"The souls," he prompted. "Where are they?"

He had to be a new munaqsri. That would explain why he'd miscalculated and let her see him. She thought of stories of people who saw angels before they died. Perhaps more people saw munaqsri than anyone knew. "I can't promise the souls will be unclaimed forever," she cautioned. "Their munaqsri is out of his region, but he could come back at any time."

"Is it likely?" he asked.

She grinned. "I have been told it's impossible." It was as impossible as a talking bear, as impossible as running hundreds of miles in minutes, as impossible as her being alive, as impossible as birth. Cassie hugged her stomach. "Ever heard of a castle that's east of the sun and west of the moon?"

He shrugged. "If it were anyone's region, it would be mine. I'm assigned all the obscure locations."

Oh, wow, had she finally had a stroke of good luck? Cassie felt like singing.

"But it won't become my region until a human has been born or has died there." He scanned the trees. "Now that I think of it, this is the first time I have ever been here. Very nice."

"Mmm," she said noncommittally. If she had her way, she was never going to see another tree as long as she lived. "So you can't go east of the sun now?" It had been too much to hope for. Not being dead was enough of a gift. Besides, it didn't matter that he couldn't reach the troll castle. Her grandfather could. The munaqsri helped her stand, and she dusted herself off. Dirt stuck to the caking blood. She looked like she had been in a train wreck, but she felt like she could race up a mountain. "Do you know the North Wind?"

"What does he have to do with the souls?"

"Do you know him?" she pressed.

"Only in passing." He frowned, clearly unhappy with her change of subject.

"Could I get his attention from a mountain?"

"Twenty-five thousand souls, you said."

Cassie took a deep breath and said in a rush, "Take me to a mountain, and I'll tell you which species is missing its munaqsri." She knew she was asking a lot. After all, he had already saved her life.

He scowled. "You're trying to trick me."

Cassie shook her head vehemently. "I promise I'll tell you at the mountain."

"You promised before."

She glanced up at a gathering horde of chattering squirrels. Were they spies? "I've learned to be meticulous about promises to munaqsri. You assumed."

"You're going to destroy my reputation," he said.

"You don't have a reputation," she said. "No one knows munaqsri exist."

He shifted uncomfortably. "The other munaqsri . . . They talk. Most wouldn't have saved you. But I need those souls. . . . I hate being helpless at births."

Cassie thought of how Bear had reacted when a cub had been stillborn. She'd picked the best possible enticement for a munaqsri, she realized. "Think what it will do to your reputation if the other munaqsri find out you saved me *without* learning about the souls," she said. As if to emphasize her point, orange and gold leaves rustled. A lithe figure of twigs and leaves scurried across the branches. The human munaqsri glanced at the birchman, and Cassie's heart thumped in her throat. Quickly, she added, "But I wouldn't worry about them finding out. No one will know but you, me, and the entire boreal forest of North America."

"This is extortion," he said.

"Pretty much, yes," Cassie said. She tried to sound non-chalant. "Now, do you want those souls or not?" *Please, say yes.*

He laughed and held out his hand. "You are something," he said. "I'll warn you: I'm fast."

Cassie took his hand. Her heart sang. "Trust me. I can handle it." On healed feet, she climbed out of the streambed over her own bloodstains. Squirrels chittered insistently. She saw trees writhing up over the munaqsri's shoulder. Bark melted together. She had to go *now*. The human munaqsri turned to look, and Cassie leaned heavily onto his hand to distract him. She saw a blur between the spruces and said, "Come on. Impress me."

Flashing her a grin, the human munaqsri yanked her through the trees. Branches broke in rapid succession, sounding like a string of firecrackers. "Impressed?" he called back to her.

The trees were in motion behind them. "Not yet," she said.

He increased speed. Spruces flashed within inches. She yelped as a branch whipped her ankle. "Ow!" With the munaqsri touching her, the gash healed instantly.

"Trust me!" he said.

"Keep my limbs attached!"

ICE

Swerving like a fighter jet, he flew through the forest. She felt wind rush over her ears, and she wondered what happened when a munaqsri made Mach 1. Now would be a great time to test it. "Faster!" she said. She could not see distinct trees now—only dark shadow flashes. Fallen leaves showered in cyclones behind the munaqsri and Cassie. Only then, at impossible, dangerous speeds, did she begin to feel safe.

He stopped suddenly, and she shot forward, catching herself before she hit the rock slope. The munaqsri steadied her, and she saw the mountain rising up in front of her. "You did it," she breathed. She was on a mountainside above the tree line. She wanted to dance. Free of the forest!

"Twenty-five thousand," he reminded her.

"No promises about the souls' munaqsri," she said. "He could return." She wanted that clear. When Bear came back, she didn't want this man who had saved her life to feel cheated. She owed him that much at least.

He nodded hurriedly. "Tell me."

"Polar bears," she said.

"Arctic is my territory!" He turned to face north, as eager as a greyhound poised to run. "You're sure?"

Cassie smiled wryly. "I'd stake my life on it."

"I thank you. Newborns thank you," he said. "Good luck reaching the wind. What do you want with him anyway? He's reported to be . . . difficult."

"It's personal." Cassie shrugged as if it were a minor issue.

"Well, try not to kill yourself again. I won't save you twice."

"Understood," she said, and glanced up the slope. Snow speckled it, and the peak was shrouded in clouds. *Oh, my.*

He patted her stomach. "See you again soon." With a wink, he started across the mountain. She watched as each stride lengthened into ballerina leaps. She called after him, "Hey, do you have a name?"

He paused midstride. "I'm a munaqsri."

"Before then," she said. "Come on, I know you're new."

"It's not supposed to be obvious." His cheeks lit up in a blush. "It's Jamie. Jamison Ieuk."

"Very appropriate," she said. *Ieuk* meant "man" in Inupiaq. It was no different from Bear asking to be called Bear. "I'm Cassie."

He mimed tipping a hat. "Pleasure meeting you."

"Pleasure being saved by you," she said. She watched as he blurred into nothing. There was no trace of his passage. It was as if he had vanished. Cassie looked out across the vast forest of green, brown, and gold, and felt her heart soar. He had brought her hundreds of miles closer to Bear. Really, munaqsri were the only way to travel.

❆ ❆ ❆ ❆ ❆

With the sun on her back, she was soon sweating. She kicked her bare toes into the loose gravel to keep her footing. Above her, Dall sheep perched on rocks as they grazed on white heather and saxifrage. She watched them leap from rock to rock.

ICE

"Show-offs," she said. She waved her arms at them. "Clear the way!" Inside her, the baby punched as if in emphasis. She grinned and patted her stomach. It was odd—she felt like she had a teammate now. She wasn't doing this alone anymore. Her baby was going to rescue its father. "Out of the way, sheep! Baby on board!"

The sheep scattered.

As the slope steepened, Cassie used her hands. She felt as agile as a giant tortoise. She placed each foot carefully and then steadied herself with handholds. Her abdomen grazed the rocks.

She felt the baby squirm. "I promise I will never make you climb a mountain again, if you behave yourself this time," she said to her stomach. "Just stay in there awhile longer. Okay, kiddo?"

Grunting and panting, she clambered onto an outcropping. She rested on the ledge and cooled her face with crusted snow. Above the tree line, she could see across the valleys. Larches, leaves brilliant gold, shone like candles against the dark spruces. She wondered how high she'd have to climb for the North Wind to hear her. She held a hand out to feel the wind. "Wind munaqsri? Grandfather! Hello?"

No answer. She had to climb higher.

Cassie continued to inch up the mountainside. She repeated to herself with each step: *You may not be able to climb this mountain, but you can make it one more foot.* The sun passed behind the mountain, and she climbed, shivering, in shadows. She paused to call again with still no luck.

An hour later, the slope steepened. Continuing to climb, she jammed her fingers into a crack. Searching with her foot, she found a foothold. She pulled herself up. Feet braced, she reached for the outcropping. She stained the rocks with specks of blood from her scraped fingers. Swinging her leg up, she beached herself onto the ledge. Cassie leaned against the mountainside and panted. Below her, the trees were pick-up sticks and the wild sheep were dots on distant rocks.

High enough, she decided.

Back pressed against the mountain, Cassie got to her feet on the ledge. Wind whipped her hair into her face. She pushed it behind her ears, and she looked across the landscape. The height made her head spin. She could see hundreds of miles of forest. It stretched into the horizon. A flock of Canada geese flew beneath her. Pressing one hand on her stomach, she breathed deeply. She bet her baby would be born loving heights. Or with a deep-seated fear of them.

She closed her eyes to stop the dizziness. Time to see if it had been worth all the effort. Filling her lungs with wind, Cassie shouted, "North Wind! Grandfather!"

She felt wind on her face. It did not speak.

She shouted again: "I am Gail's daughter! I need to talk to you!"

He was out there somewhere, she was certain. But where? Was he all the wind, or only a piece of it? She wished she'd asked Gail about her family. She knew nothing about the wind munaqsri, except the fact that they were her family and they oversaw the munaqsri of the air. She hoped that was enough. It had to be. "I'm your granddaughter! Please, answer me! Grandfather! Uncles! Wind!"

Cassie shouted until her throat was raw. "Answer me! Please!" She could feel the wind—her hair and skirt flapped, and snow and gravel tumbled down the mountain—so why didn't he answer her? "Grandfather! Uncles! Munaqsri! I know you exist! Talk to me!"

Rock cracked. It split from the mountainside. She swallowed her scream as a chunk of rock collapsed inches from her outcropping. It tumbled, stirring other rocks. A mini-avalanche crashed down the side of the mountain. Shaken, she looked at where the rock had split.

A single eye stared at her.

It was an enormous eye. It looked like a curved, yellow mirror embedded in the rock. She saw her reflection, covered in dirt and blood, stomach bulging like a fun house distortion. She stared, transfixed. The eye blinked with an eyelid of granite that slid down like an avalanche and then up again. It was part of the mountain. Rocks were scales. Boulders were nostrils. She looked at the ledge behind her. She was clinging to its claws.

Open, the dragon's mouth was a cavern. If he yawned, peaks would crumble. Dirt plumed as he spoke. "You called for a munaqsri."

"I, uh, meant to call the wind munaqsri," Cassie said.

Judging from his six-foot eye, this munaqsri could have crushed the bowhead whale.

"You are wasting your breath shouting for my wind cousins," he said. "They will not hear you. You are too earthbound to catch their interest."

Now she learned this? After that climb? "What do I do?"

"Whatever you want." The dragon shrugged. Snow and rocks sloughed off the slope. With a thunderous sound, the mass slid down the mountain. Cassie watched it cascade beneath her in a billowing cloud. Below, trees snapped like toothpicks.

Cassie swallowed. "Can you help me?"

His rock eyelid slid over his eye. She waited, but it did not reopen. It looked indistinguishable from the other rock faces again. "Um, excuse me?" Cassie said politely.

He did not answer.

"Mr. Mountain?"

No answer. She pressed her lips together. She had not come this far to be intimidated by a bunch of rocks with eyes . . . even very large dragon eyes. She—correction, *they*: Cassie and her baby—were not going to be dissuaded. She wasn't alone in this. She drew courage from that. Steeling herself, Cassie thumped on his claw. "Answer me. Please. How do I get the winds' attention?"

He opened one eye and regarded her with his giant pupil. "There is one way."

"Tell me," she said.

ICE

The dragon laughed. Rocks danced off the mountain. She flattened herself against the slope and covered her ears as the rocks crashed. "You won't like it," he said.

"Tell me how! I am not afraid!" She pounded his claw with her fist. "Tell me, dammit!" He fixed his great eye on her and said one word:

"Fall."

TWENTY-EIGHT

Latitude 63° 26' 00" N
Longitude 130° 19' 53" W
Altitude 4325 ft.

CASSIE PEEKED OVER THE EDGE. FALL?

On the mountainside, the rocks looked like rows of serrated knives. Automatically, her hands cradled her stomach. She'd already tumbled down a cliff once. "It's not a vertical drop," Cassie protested. "I'd roll down the mountain, not fall through the air. It won't work."

"I can fix that," the dragon said. He shifted his weight. Beneath her ledge, the mountain crumbled. Avalanche! She clung to the dragon's claw and screamed. The grinding stopped. Irritably, he said, "Please don't scream."

She inched to the edge and peered over. Wind whipped her hair against her cheek. Below her, the slope was gone. The mountain went straight down for a quarter mile. Cassie scrambled back against his claw. Her heart pounded fast.

ICE

She was aware of how thin her skin felt and how breakable her bones were.

What's wrong with me? she asked herself. Only a few months ago, she had dived into the Arctic Ocean. How was this any different? Looking over the edge again, she swallowed hard. The dragon's tail, a string of granite, curled in the air. It was different. She wrapped her arms tighter around her stomach. Everything was different.

How far would she go for Bear? Where was the limit? *Was* there a limit? She wasn't risking just herself anymore.

The baby kicked against her hands, and she felt her skin roll like an ocean wave. "Are you up for this?" she asked her stomach. Another kick. It felt as if the baby were urging her onward. Cassie smiled. How far *would* she go to give her baby its daddy? East of the sun and west of the moon, of course. "C'mon, kiddo," she said. "Let's go find your daddy."

Cassie placed her toes on the lip of the ledge and looked out across the boreal forest. Wind whipped her hair so that it slapped her cheeks and forehead. She brushed it back. Her baby wouldn't grow up like she had, missing a parent she'd never known. "Can you call the wind munaqsri?" she asked the dragon.

"You truly intend to do this?" For once, he did not sound condescending. He sounded curious. "What possible reason could you have for hurling your soft, tiny body from me?"

She had a hundred reasons: because Bear had carved a statue of her in the center of the topiary garden, because

she could always make him laugh, because he'd let her
return to the station, because he won at chess and lost
at hockey, because he ran as fast as he could to polar
bear births, because he had seal breath even as a human,
because his hands were soft, because he was her Bear.
"Because I want my husband back," Cassie said. *And*, she
added silently, *because my baby deserves to know him.*
"Please call the winds."

"Very well," he said.

And then the dragon roared to the sky. Wind whipped
faster and faster around the mountain. Dust and rocks
tumbled down the slope. Cassie shielded her face.

"Now!" the dragon cried.

Holding her stomach, Cassie jumped. Sound tore from
her throat. "Grandfather! North Wind!" She plummeted
down, spiraling through the sky. The green and gold swath
of forest rushed toward her. "Wind munaqsri!" Air rushed
past her as loud as a scream.

Suddenly, wind slammed into her from two directions.
Squeezed, Cassie spurted up in the air. She arched over
the dragon's mountain and spun like a stray leaf, tossed by
wind. Snowcapped mountains spiraled below her. Oh, she
was going to vomit. "North Wind!" she cried.

"Poor child. She doesn't know her north from her south."
A voice swirled around her, sweeping under her and beside
her. It seemed to be coming from everywhere.

Streaks of cloud whipped past her. One of Gail's uncles?
"South Wind?" Cassie called.

"Let her fall." A second voice rushed past Cassie's ears. "She is nothing to us."

Suddenly, she sank. She tried to scramble, to grab anything solid. Clouds slipped through her fingers as cool mist on her skin. "I'm your niece! I'm Gail's daughter!" Below her, the Yukon River wound like a blue ribbon through the mountains—so tiny, so far down. "Please don't drop me!" A gust rolled her, and she screamed as she tumbled through the air. Wind rushed past her ears as loud as her own scream.

"We must keep her, East," the first voice—the South Wind—said.

Wind swept under her, and she was tossed up, up, up. "You can't keep me!" she shouted. "You have to help me!"

"We cannot keep her," the East Wind said, echoing her. "It was not right before; it is not right now." The air began to blacken. Rain splattered on Cassie's arm.

"But I want her!" the South Wind wailed like wind on the sea.

Cassie heard a crackle and saw a spark of white light jump from cloud to cloud. If they didn't stop, she could be electrocuted. "Please!" Cassie shouted. "Uncles!"

"See!" the South Wind said. "Listen to her. She's already family!"

"Yes, yes, I'm family! Gail's daughter!" Cassie cried into the rising storm. "Stop it! Don't storm! Please, stop!"

Instantly, the gray dispersed, and the breeze calmed to a whistle. "Did we hurt you?" the South Wind asked. "We don't wish to hurt you. Your mother was our favorite child. We adored her."

"She was a mistake," the East Wind said.

Cassie bristled. "Excuse me?"

The South Wind said soothingly, "It's an old argument. My brother did not approve of North's adopting your mother."

The East Wind growled like a rumble of thunder. "It was kidnapping."

"Adoption," the South Wind said.

"Kidnapping."

In a reasonable tone, the South Wind said, "If Abigail did not love us, she would not have sent her daughter to live with us."

Twisting in the air, Cassie tried to see the source of the voices. "I'm not here to live with you! I'm here to ask you to take me east of the sun and west of the moon!"

The air shuddered around her. "Oh, no, kitten. You cannot go there," the South Wind said. "It is not a nice place. Not a nice place at all."

"Not for living things," the East Wind agreed.

"Besides," the South Wind added, "it is too far. Much too far for us." He sounded pleased. Streaks of cloud zipped past Cassie like silver minnows in a river.

"But you're wind," Cassie said. "Wind goes everywhere."

"It's beyond the ends of the world," the East Wind said, and the sky darkened as he spoke. Deep gray stained the white clouds and spread.

ICE

Cassie felt a fat drop of rain hit her cheek. "The world is round. It doesn't have ends," she said. "Besides, Grandfather made it there. Can you take me to him?"

"Oh, kitten, you do not want to see him."

"He has a temper," the East Wind explained.

"Once, he was so angry he scattered us into hundreds of pieces all across the globe." The air trembled. "It took us weeks to reassemble."

He scattered his own brothers? She shivered. And these were the creatures that her mother had grown up with, that Gail had called family. "Just take me to him."

"Absolutely not," the South Wind said firmly. "He'll tear you to bits."

Cassie opened her mouth to argue, and her stomach squeezed. She clutched her stomach. Her baby! Not yet! She was so close to Bear! "For Gail's sake, take me to him!"

"But . . ."

Her stomach loosened, and she sucked in air. "Please! If you cared about Gail at all, take me to the North Wind!"

In answer, wind rushed around her. Her skirt whipped and twisted around her legs. As she went spinning through clouds, she cradled her stomach.

"You may want to close your eyes," the South Wind said to Cassie. "Some find this . . . distressing to their worldview."

"Don't worry about me," Cassie said. "I married a talking bear."

Enveloping her in empty air, the winds swept over the

forest. She felt her stomach contract again as the **two winds** sandwiched her. She spun through the air like a pinwheel.

❄ ❄ ❄ ❄ ❄

Clouds rocked underneath her, and she clenched her teeth, concentrating on not being sick. Faster and faster, she flew into the snow-toothed mountains. She slalomed between peaks. Veering close to one, the winds drove her toward the sheer face of the mountain glacier. "Watch it!" she yelled, and she sailed up the slope, bursting through clouds.

"We are here," the South Wind whispered. As the winds slowed, Cassie saw a massive mountainside. A jagged cave cut open the side of the ice-coated mountain like a wound.

Snow spewed from the mouth of the North Wind's cave as Cassie, carried by the two winds, flew toward it. Cold slammed into Cassie, and she catapulted backward through the air. She was caught in a sweep of wind as the North Wind roared: "BLAST YOU ALL. WHAT DO YOU WANT?"

Swirling around her, the South Wind whispered, "It is one of his bad days. Do you wish to leave now?" She felt the wind quivering. Tiny droplets of moisture beaded on Cassie's skin.

She wanted to say yes, to run as far from this new monster as she could. "No," she said. "This is what I came here to do. Bring me closer." As the winds lowered her to the cave, she called, "North Wind, I need to talk to you! I'm Gail's—"

"NEVER SPEAK HER NAME!" Howling, the North Wind tore out of his cave. He whipped around the peak at a

hundred miles per hour. *Mom called this monster "father"?*
Awed, Cassie watched boulders sail off the slope in showers
of hail and ice. One of her uncles whimpered as the debris
hit the mountainside in a mushroom cloud plume of dirt
and ice. The crash sparked other rockfalls.

Far below, she heard a dragon roar as the avalanches
cascaded. For an instant, hearing the dragon, the North
Wind slowed. This was her chance. She thought of her
mother rushing out of the station to protect her baby and
her husband. If Mom could confront him for the sake of her
family, then so could Cassie. She cupped her hands like a
megaphone. "You have to take me east of the sun and west
of the moon!"

"GO AWAY!"

"Now she's done it," she heard one of the winds whisper.

Hail hit her skin. Moaning, the winds huddled around
her, suspended beside the mountain. She shielded her face.
"Stop it!" Cassie cried.

"LEAVE ME ALONE!"

"Like hell I will!" she shouted back. "You have to help
me!"

"LEAVE ME TO MY MISERY!" Rattling the moun-
tain, the North Wind dove into his cave. A glacier cracked.
Thundering, it slid down the mountain.

"Push me closer," Cassie told the winds.

"I do not think that would be a good idea," the East
Wind said.

Clouds swaddled her and thickened into gray. "Oh, no,

kitten, no," the South Wind said. The mountain faded from view. "Don't ask this of us."

"As a favor to Gail," Cassie pleaded.

On the trembling breath of the winds, she rose to the opening of the cave. Closer, the resisting wind increased. She felt a contraction, as if the baby were protesting. Cassie shouted, "I'm your granddaughter!"

Abruptly, the North Wind deflated. Cassie barreled into the cave. She cycled for footing, and her toes brushed rocks. She landed like a shaky bird. Carefully, she straightened. In the corner of the cave, she saw a dark patch of swirling cloud. That was him—her breath quickened—her grandfather, Mom's kidnapper, the one who had been responsible for her mother's imprisonment and, indirectly, for Bear's fate. She began to feel an old anger build up inside her, and she latched on to it. "Hello, Grandfather."

The other winds bolted out of the cave.

"You come to torture me in my grief," he said.

"*Your* grief! For my whole life, I had no mother!"

Wind pooled around her feet and breathed through her hair. "Oh, my poor, sweet Gail. Lost to the world. Lost!"

He was so caught up in his own self-pity that he didn't even know his own daughter had been saved. "She's home."

"You lie!" He roared—air shot through the cave, and rocks tumbled. Pressing into a cleft in the cave wall, Cassie shielded her stomach from the wind. Her hair whipped her neck and her skirt pulled at her legs. She squeezed her eyes shut until the howling subsided into sobbing.

Her head throbbed, and her ears rang. She shook her head, and rocks rained out of her hair. "While you were busy feeling sorry for yourself, my husband sacrificed his freedom to save your daughter. He's trapped at the troll castle right now! And it's your fault. It all began with you. You are the worst parent—"

He moaned. "Cruel child. Leave me alone," he pleaded. "Please."

Gravel skittered, and cold air pricked her arms. "No, Grandfather," she said. "I won't." She felt her stomach contract again, and she doubled over. The North Wind howled, but this time, it was a short storm. Tucked in the rock cleft, Cassie waited until both the contraction and the winds abated. "For my whole life, I thought my mother was dead," she said. "My mother became a stranger to me because of you."

"Please," he begged. "Stop."

Cassie hugged her stomach. She'd be a good parent, better than the North Wind, better than the North Wind's daughter, better than Dad. She'd make sure her baby didn't grow up missing a parent. "Good thing I didn't learn about being family from you."

"I love my daughter!"

Again, she felt her stomach squeeze, sending shudders down her legs. Leaning against the wall of the cave, she caught her breath. "Did you love her enough to respect her wishes, or did you blast her off the face of the earth for leaving you? If you really loved her, you would have let her choose her own life."

He sobbed. "Why are you doing this to me?"

"You owe her," Cassie said flatly. "You owe *me*. Take me east of the sun and west of the moon."

"Granddaughter . . ."

More gently, Cassie said to the North Wind, "It's not too late to make it right. Please, Grandfather, take me there." She didn't add, *Before it* is *too late.*

He hit her with gale-force winds.

TWENTY-NINE

Latitude 63° 04' 01" N
Longitude 151° 00' 55" E
Altitude 16,573 ft.

SCREAMING, CASSIE TUMBLED like a rag doll out of the mouth of the North Wind's cave. She spun head over heels. The other winds shrieked, and she whipped into a tornado spiral: She faced the sky, the ground, the sky, the ground. Boulders and debris spun with her. She was going to be pulverized. "Grandfather!"

The North Wind shot through the whirlwind of rocks and ice. Scooping her inside his muscles of rain, he skimmed over a snow-crested peak with inches to spare. In his wake, the peak toppled and a dragon roared. Cassie hurtled through the air. Bones rattling, she burst out of the mountain range.

Tracts of forest were mowed flat.

She squeezed her eyes shut. When she opened them,

she was over the ocean. Her stomach seized. Waves were tossed forty feet into the air. Ships floundered. "Slow down! Please, slow down!" People were on those ships. He had to slow!

"Building momentum," he said like thunder. Cassie slammed her hands to her ears, but her whole body shook from the vibration of the sound. She felt her stomach tighten and release, another contraction. Bile rose in her throat. She choked it down. He tore on and on.

❆ ❆ ❆ ❆ ❆

The North Wind drooped, thinning into streaks. She slipped through the dissipating wind and clung to the empty air. Black water churned beneath Cassie, and she grasped for bits of cloud as they disintegrated around her. He sank so low that the crests of the waves dashed only inches below her.

"Are you afraid?" he whispered.

"No!" she said.

Her toes dipped into the ocean. She hissed, tucking her feet under her skirt. The torn hem trailed in the roiling waves. "How far?" she shouted. If he lost much more strength . . .

"There," he said in barely a whisper. She squinted through the roaring gray to see a massive shadow, a smudge on the horizon, then it was swallowed by the storm. Hungry waves licked her legs. She kicked at the water.

Without warning, her legs plunged into the ocean. "Grandfather!" He pushed in a burst, and she skimmed fast along the wild surface. When she looked up next from the churning depths, blackened rocks raced toward her, and the mountainous shadow blocked the sky. Waves broke around her, and he heaved her onto the shore.

She slammed down into the breakers, slicing her knees on the rocks. Waves crashed into her neck. Salt water in her face, she crawled, choking, up onto the rocky shore. She hoisted herself onto a boulder. Shivering and shaking, she stroked her stomach. "I'm sorry, kiddo. You all right in there?"

One wave crashed into her, knocking her sideways. She spat salt water as she clambered out of the swells. Slick seaweed coated the rocks, and another wave crashed into her legs before she managed to pull herself up to the first tree. Black and leafless as if burned, it did not seem to be alive. Shivering uncontrollably, she clung to it. "Grandfather, are you okay?"

The whole sky looked bruised. He stirred the sea, and she felt the wind. She took that to be a reply: He was alive. She pushed her hair out of her face. "Are we here?" she asked. Sea, wind-flung, sprayed her, as if in answer, and she flinched. "All right, all right." She turned.

Black as basalt, the troll castle loomed over the shore like a nightmare.

"Oh, God," she breathed. Suddenly, she was more afraid than she had been diving into the frigid ocean, hanging from Father Forest's ceiling, or falling from a dragon. She stared up at the monstrosity. It loomed over her, frighteningly silent.

Using the trees, she climbed toward the castle. Branches creaked and then cracked. Seaweed oozed between her toes. As she reached for the wall, her stomach tightened like a fist—hard. She doubled over, and for one terrible instant she thought, *The baby is coming* now.

Sweat popped out on her forehead as she strangled the nearest tree. She whispered to her stomach, "Be good, and I swear I will never again storm a castle while pregnant." For an instant, her eyes blurred, pricked with tears, as her insides squeezed.

Her breathing was as loud as the crashing waves. As the contraction passed, she realized that the waves and her breathing were the only sounds on the rock island. There were no gulls in the sky and no voices in the castle. It was as if the island were dead. "Please, Bear," she said. "Be all right." She put her hand on the damp wall. After all the miles, only a wall stood between them—the wall and the trolls, who were somewhere inside. She gulped. She could do this. She'd come so far. She wasn't going to be stopped now.

She tilted her head back. The wall rose incredibly high. She saw no windows or doors, only shadowed arrow slits. "Scaling the wall is out," she said, forcing lightness into her voice. She patted her stomach. "I know you wanted to." The crash of waves on the rocks swallowed her words and left her feeling even more small and alone. Holding the wall for balance, she started around the perimeter.

Storm clouds filled the sky, and it felt as if the world were hovering between day and night. She moved in and out of shadows as she made her way across the slippery rocks. In eerie semidarkness, she rounded the first corner.

Glistening with sea spray, the second wall could have been a mirror image of the first. It stretched unbroken to the end of the island. Black rocks led down to the sea. The same twisted, lifeless trees protruded from cracks between the rocks. Cassie felt her stomach tighten again—the contraction stealing her breath—and she waited it out, leaning against the chilled wall. Her skin cringed from her cold, wet clothes. When the pain subsided, she hurried across the rocks and turned the second corner. The third wall was also featureless stone. Three walls, no doors. She scrambled over the rocks and turned the third and final corner.

The castle had no door.

She leaned against the stone and wanted to cry. Cheek pressed to stone, she banged on the wall. "Hello? Let me in. Open up, damn you! Please, open."

Her stomach squeezed, and she bent over it with a groan. Bent, she saw the rock melt inward into the shape of a door. Surprise overwhelmed pain. She turned her head sideways. Instead of standing beside black basalt, she was standing beside a wooden door. How . . . *Magic*, she answered herself. She thought of Bear's castle.

She laid her hand flat on the door—warm and dry, it was untouched by sea spray—and pushed. She heard it clink, latched shut. She tried the latch. It rattled loosely in her hand.

Cassie examined the wood. It was half-rotted pine and

looked brittle. She wondered if she could break it down. She licked her lips. Throwing her body against a door, rotten or not . . . Did she have a better idea? If her contractions got much worse . . .

Cradling her stomach protectively, she rammed her shoulder into the door. It creaked. She backed up and bashed it again. She felt herself bruising, but the door did not break. She smashed into it again.

Cassie rubbed her shoulder. All she was doing was tenderizing her arm. After everything, to be stopped by a door . . . The thought made her feel ill. It couldn't end now, not like this.

She rattled the handle. Owen used to fix the station shed door all the time. She wished he were here with his tools. Squatting, she poked the wood around the handle. She bent sideways and felt for a rock. Rocks, unlike doors, were not in short supply. Finding a hand-size one, she held it like a mallet and hammered above the latch. It thudded dully, as if the air around the castle sucked sound. Behind her, in rhythm, waves pounded on the rocks. After pushing her hair behind her ears, she struck harder.

She felt the door weaken. She whacked it with all her strength, and the wood splintered. Cassie dropped the rock and pried pieces of wood away from the latch. She wormed her fingers through the widened hole, and her fingertips brushed the handle. She jiggled it. Wedging her hand in farther, she groped for the crosspiece of the latch itself.

"Yes," she exulted. She flicked it and heard it swing off

its hook. Scraping skin, she yanked her hand out of the hole and shoved the door open.

From the doorway, a rectangle of light fell onto the stone floor. Cassie stepped into it. She peered into the darkness. It was complete blackness—no contours, no shadows. Her heart thudded faster and she forced herself to stay calm. Wishing for her flashlight, she stepped out of the rectangle.

Behind her, the light dimmed, and a voice said, "No one ever tries to break *in*."

Cassie bolted for the door. Her hands slapped solid stone. She pounded on the wall, but the door had vanished. *Dammit, it's a trap.* She should have realized it. The materializing door had been too convenient. She pressed her back against the wall and strained to see or hear the troll. The room was as dark and as quiet as outer space. Her own breathing thundered. "Where are you?" she said. "Who are you?"

Without warning, the walls brightened like sheets of fluorescent bulbs. Sterile and white as a hospital, the room blazed. Cassie's eyes teared. She squinted, looking for the troll, but the room was blindingly empty. "You aren't a new one," the voice said from nowhere. "You're alive."

"And I intend to stay that way." Wishing she had some way to defend herself, she spun in a circle to see the whole room. "Show yourself."

In the center of the room, sparking out of nothing, a flame danced. Cassie had expected a Cro-Magnon man with horns and fangs. Somehow, this flame was worse. Pulsing red and orange, it ballooned into a writhing jellyfish. Red spread into pink, and the pink jellyfish sprouted tentacles. The tentacles thickened into arms and legs that stretched like rubber bands. It budded a head.

Cassie flattened against the wall. Oh, that was *not* human. "What are you?"

The thing appeared taller than Cassie because its . . . she hesitated to call them "feet" . . . did not touch the floor. It hovered six inches above. Translucent, it shone like the blinding walls. Still shifting shape, it began to look somewhat like a woman.

The pseudo-woman's skin rolled like water. Her face mushed into four noses, then smushed into one. Cassie swallowed, feeling queasy. "Can you . . . please pick a face?" She tried to sound casual, but her voice was shaking so hard that she half-squeaked the last word. She hoped the pseudo-woman hadn't noticed.

Blue spread over her skin, and the creature drooped. Purple tears poured from blank eyes. "Easy for you," she said. "You were born." Her tears ground valleys in her cheeks, and then were absorbed into her neck. Soon, her face was concave.

Cassie had to look away. "What are you?"

"You would call me a troll."

Cassie glanced back to see orange blooming on the troll's throat. The orange swirled like a giant kaleidoscope, and within seconds, the rash covered her entire body.

"What are you?" the troll asked.

"Uh, human," Cassie said.

ICE

The troll dismissed her. "We have no need for humans."
Spikes poked out of the troll's skin. They flashed as they
multiplied.

Wishing she felt braver in the face of this creature, Cassie
said, "I've come to free my husband."

"You are Cassie?" She softened her spikes like a deflat-
ing puffer fish. "You are the munaqsri's Cassie?"

Cassie shivered. "You know me?" How did a troll know
her name?

"Oh, yes." The troll smiled, and her mouth slid to her
ear. She looked like a garish Picasso woman, plus drooping
spikes. "He has mentioned you."

Bear had talked about her—to the troll? What did it
mean? It meant Bear was alive. She felt her heart thumping
like timpani. "He has? To you? Who are you?"

"I am the troll princess."

Cassie froze. "You married my husband."

"Of course." She sprouted feathers on her spikes. Blos-
soming over her body, translucent feathers clothed her in
seconds. "It was the bargain."

Cassie wanted to leap at her—she'd taken Bear!—but her
stomach seized. She doubled over, hissing. Dammit, they
were getting worse. She puffed until it passed. Straighten-
ing, she said, "Bargain's over. I'm bringing him home."

"Oh, no, we're not finished with him."

Cassie didn't like the sound of that. It sounded like . . .
Her heart pounded, and her hands shook. "You hurt one
inch of his fur . . ."

The troll princess laughed. "You are a funny thing. So lively."

"I want to see him. Now."

"We have no need for you to see him," the princess said. Cassie felt cool wind on her back and heard waves crash. She glanced behind her. The wooden door now stood open. "You can leave. We don't need you." The troll princess waved her feathered tentacles at the open door. "Go on, it is no trick. I promise you are free to leave. You can trust me—it is a magic promise."

"Not without Bear. Promise me he can leave."

"I told you, we need him."

"For what?"

Feathers combined into cilia. "He has to cooperate. The queen is disappointed in him. She had such high hopes for a munaqsri."

"You'd free him if he cooperated?" Could it be that simple? Meet their demands and then Bear could go free?

"You could convince him!" the troll said. Excited, the cilia waved. She shimmered in the white light. "Yes, he would listen to his Cassie."

Cassie didn't trust the troll. It couldn't be something good if Bear was refusing. She thought of the mermaid Sedna saying, *No one knows what trolls want.* "What won't he do?"

"He won't make me a baby."

For an instant, Cassie felt as if her heart had stopped.

THIRTY

Latitude indeterminate
Longitude indeterminate
Altitude indeterminate

THE TROLL PRINCESS MELTED THE WALLS. Retreating to the center of the room, Cassie tried to tell herself that this place was no different from Bear's ice castle and that the troll princess was no more inhuman than the winds, but it *felt* different. The troll pushed her jellied tentacles against another white wall, and it dissolved like a sugar cobweb. The castle itself was an illusion of earthliness.

Thick smoke poured into the room. "Do not be afraid," the troll princess said, and blinked with three eyes. A fourth blossomed on her forehead.

The smoke pressed on Cassie's skin like fabric, curling around her. She batted at her arms. Covered in clouds, the troll princess repeated, "Do not be afraid. We won't hurt you."

It wasn't smoke, Cassie realized, it was trolls. The air was thick with trolls. In the squirming cloud, she saw traces of eyes and teeth, fur and feathers, arms and tentacles. Strobe-like color flashed, like a surreal discotheque, and she panicked. "Don't touch me!" She slapped at them. It felt like pushing through rain. She realized she had felt this water-air before—when the trolls had taken Bear, back before the castle had melted.

Hundreds of trolls pressed their flimsy forms against her, only to dissipate like mist. She thought of her mother, imprisoned here for years, and knew it was hopeless to have come here without a clear plan. She wanted to screech like the aspen. Bear was almost in reach. She couldn't have come so far only to fail.

"Follow me," the troll princess said. Through the wispy shapes, she shone iridescent. She bobbed like a floating Japanese lantern.

Gritting her teeth, Cassie elbowed trolls out of her way. The trolls melted, as insubstantial as ghosts, as soundless as wisps of cloud. It was an eerie silence. The only sound was her own breathing. The trolls did not breathe. Shuddering, she hugged her stomach. Her uncles had been right: This was no place for living things. All her instincts were screaming at her to run away, but she kept going, deeper into the trolls.

Her heart sank as she followed the princess farther into the castle and through more and more trolls. Who was she to think she could go up against this—whatever "this" was?

ICE

She was just a human. She didn't have any magic.

Her stomach squeezed, and she had to stop. Clutching her stomach, she panted. Trolls swarmed her. She felt their light, damp touch on her neck and on her face. Colors teased the corners of her eyes.

Trolls thinned in front of her, and Cassie pushed sweat-streaked hair out of her eyes. She was standing before a dais of basalt. Filling the dais was the troll queen. Unlike the wisps all around her, the troll queen seemed as solid as a granite mountain. A thousand eyes coated her body like rivets.

Cassie straightened her shoulders and tried to stare back into the queen's splintered gaze. She hadn't let Father Forest or the winds see her fear; she wasn't going to let this queen see it either. Even if her rescue mission was doomed.

In unison, the eyes blinked. "We have no need for another human," the queen said in a voice like a hive of bees. "Why have you brought her to us?"

The troll princess floated to the dais. She was now a purple orb with a distorted humanesque face. She whispered to the queen.

With her thousand eyes, the queen scrutinized Cassie. "Interesting." She closed half her eyes, and those eyes hardened into silver plates.

Cassie lifted her chin and summoned her courage. This was what it had all been for—all for this moment. She would face down a troll queen. She would not take no for an answer. She would wring Bear out of her, if she had to.

"I'm here for my husband. And you cannot stop me."

"Very well," the queen said.

Cassie's jaw dropped open. "Excuse me?" She must have misheard, or at least misunderstood. "You'll let me . . . He's free to go?"

"Convince him to make my daughter a baby, and he is free."

Cassie opened and shut her mouth. "Can I talk to him?"

"Of course," the queen said.

Cassie's head spun. All he had to do was sleep with the troll princess, and he would be free? She bit her lip. Had he refused because he loved Cassie too much, or had he refused because he had not loved Cassie enough?

All around her, the trolls rustled. It sounded like wind in autumn leaves.

Out of the trolls, Bear came. Soundless, his paws padded on the stone. Cassie dug her fingernails into the palms of her hands. Her knees shook. Two feet in front of her, he stopped. His black eyes were unfathomable.

Cassie could not speak. She stretched her fingertips and touched his muzzle. His fur was as soft as she remembered. She buried her hand in his pelt. He nuzzled her hair. She threw her arms around his broad neck. "Good to see you, Your Royal Ursine Highness," she whispered.

"You came for me."

"Just in the area," she said. "Thought I'd say hello."

Bear dipped his head to Cassie's abdomen. He pressed his furry face to it. Cassie stroked his ears. "He . . . she . . .

is moving," Bear said. He looked at her. "Can you forgive me?"

Cassie swallowed a lump in her throat. "Yes. You?"

"Yes," he said.

She smiled, and then she hugged her stomach again as a contraction robbed her breath.

"My bears should have taken care of you," he said, concern in his voice. ·

When she could breathe again, she answered, "They did." It seemed like years ago that she'd been on the ice.

"Good," he said. They were silent for a moment. Cassie wished she could find words—there was so much she had wanted to say. As she'd crossed the ice, the tundra, and the forest, she'd imagined this moment over and over, but this wasn't how she'd pictured it, with thousands of trolls looking on.

"I missed you," he said simply.

She flushed and looked down at her pregnant self, speckled with blood and dirt. "Hardly the movie star rescuer."

"You are beautiful," he said.

She snorted.

"You have a beautiful soul."

"Nice euphemism."

"On an island of trolls, it is a compliment."

She glanced over at the troll queen. Spikes sprouted from her head and tail, outgrowths of the eye plates. "So," Cassie said conversationally, "is she going to skewer us?" Her voice cracked on the last word.

He touched her cheek with his wet nose and whispered in her ear, "Tell me the plan. I am ready."

She wanted to cry. So close! "Find the castle, find Bear. . . . That's as far as I got. You have any ideas?"

"I cannot do as they ask. It is not possible," he said. "They have no bodies. Otherwise, I would have been home to you in an instant." *Home to you*—the words sounded like music.

Of course, he couldn't impregnate a woman who had no body. He couldn't even magic her molecules—she had no molecules. "Besides, I'd be jealous." Her voice caught again.

"She cannot help us," the troll queen said. Cassie gripped his fur—no! She could not be losing him again. The troll princess drooped blue, and the queen stretched a tentacle to stroke her, as if to comfort her. It moved through the princess's body as if through water. She retracted the tentacle, and for an instant she was translucent. The queen, Cassie realized, was as shapeless as the other trolls. Bear was right—none of them had bodies. It was all an illusion. The queen's eyes fixed back on Cassie. Pulsing orange now, she said, "Remove the human. We have no need of her."

The trolls descended on them. "No!" Cassie shouted. Hundreds of trolls slid between Cassie and Bear and, crowbarlike, wedged them apart. She couldn't lose him a second time! "No, stop! Please!"

Bear was shouting too. She fought against the trolls. Each

ICE

one she pushed back was replaced by a dozen more. It was like fighting ocean waves. Trolls flowed into her.

Her stomach contracted, and for a second, Cassie lost ground. "No! Please, anything you want! Bargain with me! Anything!"

"No, Cassie! Save yourself!"

She shouted at the queen, "Tell me: What do you want?"

Surrounded by shadowy shapes, the queen writhed on the dais. "Life," she hissed. Instinctively, Cassie clutched her stomach.

"Do not do it!" Bear said.

"You have life?" Wingless, the queen rose into the air. "You have life in you?"

What did that have to do with anything? Cassie looked down at her stomach and thought of her long journey here—it had to do with everything.

"No, Cassie!" Bear snapped his teeth and swiped with his claws, but the trolls still blocked him.

She'd do what she had to do to save her Bear. That's what she'd done all along, all for him. Wasn't it? With her arms wrapped around her stomach, she looked at her love and wondered—had she done it for him, or for herself?

The troll queen, body spreading like ink, flew above her. "We will keep you, then, and we will have your child!" she exulted.

Cassie felt the damp touch of trolls on her stomach. She swung her hand out to ward them off and struck only empty air. "Your princess promised my freedom!"

The troll princess shrank into a ball. "I didn't know!" she wailed.

Growing like some mythical god, the queen filled the cavernous room. The trolls thickened around Cassie and Bear. Through wisps of gray, the queen throbbed orange and green. "Your baby for your king. It is our bargain."

Cassie looked down at her bulging stomach. Here was her chance for the two things she'd wanted when she'd begun this journey: her Bear and no baby. Except that it was not that simple. It hadn't been that simple for a while now. "There must be something else you want," she said.

"We make no other offer," the queen said.

Cassie stroked her stomach and almost felt déjà vu, though it wasn't her memory she was feeling. She knew this moment. This had been her mother's choice when she'd faced down the North Wind. This had been her father's choice when he'd honored Gail's sacrifice and stayed with the newborn Cassie. Cassie hadn't understood it before. She hadn't understood them. But she did now—the horrible frustration her father must have felt, having to make that choice, *this* choice. All at once, she forgave him; she forgave them both. How could she give up her baby? But how could she lose Bear? She needed him. She loved him.

"Do not do it, Cassie," he said. "Leave me. Please, I beg you." She heard the words: *If you love me, let me go.*

She loved him enough to leave all she had ever known, to turn her world upside down, to come to this place beyond all known places, to risk her life, to almost die.

ICE

Did she love him enough to let him go?

Yes, she did.

The queen pulsed brighter. "What is your answer?"

Bowing her head, Cassïe said a single word: "No."

THIRTY-ONE

Latitude indeterminate
Longitude indeterminate
Altitude indeterminate

HISSING, THE TROLLS ROLLED OVER THEM. One troll was a drop of water, but hundreds of thousands were a tidal wave. More trolls flooded between Cassie and Bear. No, wait! She wasn't ready yet! She hadn't said good-bye.

Bear blurred behind trolls as if underwater. Muscles straining, he pushed at the tide. Cassie skidded backward. "At least let me say good-bye! Please!" She heard him call her name, and the trolls hissed louder. "Bear, I love you!" she yelled. Could he hear her? Please, let him have heard her. He'd never heard her say it. "I'm sorry! I'm so sorry!" *For everything!* she wanted to say—for not trusting him, for endangering their baby, and most of all for failing to rescue him. She had proved to be her father's daughter to the end. She had found her limit, the line she would not cross, the cliff she would not leap off. Bear was now a white smudge behind the gray shadows. "Bear!"

Her stomach seized.

For an instant, she lost her breath, and the trolls swept her up. She sailed backward and rammed into a wall. Her face smushed sideways against stone. "You're crushing me!" Crushing the baby!

The walls melted, and Cassie spilled into the white room. Catching her balance, she ran toward the throne room, but the troll princess sealed the wall shut again with a word, separating Cassie from the other trolls and from Bear. Shouting, Cassie pounded on the wall until another contraction crushed the breath out of her. She felt wet run down her inner thighs. "Oh, no. God, no," she said. "Not now. Not here." Not without Bear. Not stranded on a troll island.

A pulsing orb, the troll princess said, "You truly have life in you?"

"Let me out of here," Cassie said. "Make the door appear." She had to get to her grandfather. He had to take her home.

The troll princess floated across the room and said, "Open," the magic word. The stone melted into the wooden door. Battered, it hung open, and Cassie heard the crash of waves. She bolted outside.

Sea air hit her face. "Grandfather!"

Black clouds swarmed.

"Grandfather, help me." She doubled over as another

contraction racked through her. Walking made the contractions worse. "Grandfather!" she screamed.

Fascinated, the troll princess oozed over the rocks. "Is this pain?"

Cassie slipped on seaweed as another contraction snatched her breath. She caught herself on a tree. Her arms and legs shook. "Please, Grandfather!"

He did not answer, or he did not hear. Wordless, the wind stirred the sea, and swells smashed into the shore.

The troll princess asked, "What is it like to feel pain?"

She had to keep calm. Calm. Calm. Cassie took deep breaths.

The princess sighed. "I wish I could feel pain."

Another contraction followed fast on the heels of the last. This was not a false alarm; she knew it. "Bear!" Breaking waves drowned her cry.

Contractions crashed on top of each other like a relentless sea storm. Cassie gasped for air. She flailed with pain. Her hands hit the rocks. She did not feel them. She yelled like an animal.

She didn't know how long it lasted—hours, minutes, days. Contractions came and went. She was caught inside them. The world outside her body ceased to exist. She couldn't think of a time before this and couldn't imagine a time after. It was just the pain, the rocks, and the sea. And then, like in the eye of a storm, the pain eased, and Cassie needed to push. She spread her skirt and squatted. *Push.* Veins jumped out on her neck, and sweat popped out on her forehead. Her lungs whooshed. *Push.* She was exploding. She wanted to climb out of her skin. It hurt to push, and it hurt not to push. She felt herself stretching. She would burst. More than anything, she wanted the baby out. She pushed.

A nervous-looking man perched on the rocks.

Cassie saw him. "Jamie! Help me!"

The troll princess darted behind him. He did not see her. "Are you all right?"

With clenched teeth, she said, "Catch the baby."

Jamie inched backward. "But . . ."

"Please!"

Gulping, Jamie knelt beside her on the rocks. "I can see the top of its head!" He looked up at Cassie. "It has hair."

She inhaled. "Soul ready?"

"No one has died today. I have no souls," he said. "I'm sorry, but it will be stillborn."

She had to push *now.* She resisted. "Like hell it will!"

"I told you, I am short on souls."

Pain hit. "Take mine!"

"Munaqsri don't kill."

She had to push! She howled. Her whole body wanted the baby out of her. But she would not let it. Not without a soul. "I want my baby!"

At Cassie's yell, the princess floated in closer.

"What is *that?*" Jamie scrambled back across the rocks.

Lifting her sweating head, Cassie looked at the troll princess. She was a troll from east of the sun and west of the

moon, which was, Cassie had been told again and again, beyond the ends of the earth, where no living thing ever went.

The phrase tickled a memory: *Is that what you want me to do? Let their souls drift beyond the ends of the earth? Beyond the ends of the earth?* Here?

Yes, here. On an island of trolls . . . *Trolls have no shape, no physical bodies,* Gail had said. *It's an island of wild spirits.* An island of wild spirits . . . an island of trolls . . . beyond the ends of the earth. *Not for living things. Nothing living ever goes there.* In a flash, Cassie understood: Trolls were souls. *He won't make me a baby,* the troll princess had said. *It is not possible,* Bear had said. *They have no bodies.* The troll princess didn't want to have a baby; she wanted to *be* a baby. "Here's your chance," she said to the troll princess. "You want to live?"

The princess flashed gold and silver. "You mean . . ."

What do you want? she'd asked the troll queen. *Life,* the queen had answered. "Yes or no," Cassie said. "Do you want to live?"

The troll princess brightened like an exploding star. "Yes!"

"Take her!" Cassie shouted, and pushed.

Jamie stared at her.

"She's a soul!" Cassie pointed at the troll princess.

The troll princess flew into Jamie's hands.

Cassie felt underneath her. She felt a head, as soft as a seal's, and she cradled it in the palms of her hands. Yelling,

she pushed one final time. She felt the baby slip into her hands, and she caught it, hands under its back.

"It's not breathing," the human munaqsri said. He hesitated for only a fraction of a second, and then he slid his fingers between the umbilical cord and the baby's tiny chest. He eased the cord over the baby's shoulder and then he produced a knife and cut the cord. The baby took its first breath. Pink spread from its chest outward.

Jamie helped her lift the baby, and she held her child close. Its skin was as slippery as egg yolk. She felt it squirm.

"It's a girl," Jamie said.

Cassie looked down, and beautiful blue eyes blinked up at her. "Oh, my," was all she could say. Transfixed, she stared at the miniature hands and the perfect round cheeks. The baby squinched up her little face and wailed as loud as the wind.

"She takes after her mother," Jamie noted.

Cassie laughed. Sweaty hair falling forward, she kissed her baby's head. The baby smelled as sweet as rain. "You came out of me," she whispered, cradling her baby girl.

She smiled down at her beautiful baby, cooing as the waves crashed onto the shore. She felt lighter than air. "You think you're magic," she said to Jamie. "Look at her. She's *real* magic."

"She's beautiful," Jamie said. Cassie glanced over at him and saw his cheeks were moist. "What are you going to name her?" he asked.

She didn't have to think about it. "Abigail." Her mother's

name. Above them, the sky swirled. Cassie wondered if the North Wind had heard her. "Abby for short." She gazed down at baby Abby, red and sticky and perfect in her arms. "Think she will remember?"

He shook his head. "Do you remember before you were born?"

"You got your wish," she said to the baby. "You are alive." Cassie's smile became beatific. She looked up at the human munaqsri. "Got another minute? I have an idea."

❄ ❄ ❄ ❄ ❄

Cassie cradled her baby against her chest as the trolls swarmed over them. "Munaqsri," she heard the trolls hiss as they encountered Jamie. He was, she guessed, the reason they were allowing her to return. He was new. "Munaqsri. Munaqsri."

Jamie peeled trolls from his skin. "They're everywhere!"

The walls melted around them. "Stay with me," she said. She marched through the horde of trolls with Jamie in her wake.

The troll queen hulked over her dais. Cassie stopped, trolls hovering in a semicircle around her, and cradled the baby against her. A thousand eyes blinked at her. This time, she was not afraid.

Jamie fell out of the press of trolls. He saw the queen. "Who is she?" Colors spread in a rainbow flare across the queen's broad back.

"She is a soul," Cassie said, not taking her eyes off the

queen. "Aren't you? You are the unclaimed souls, the ones munaqsri missed." The baby squirmed in her arms.

Tentacles sprouted on the troll queen. "New life!" She reached with a half-dozen writhing tentacles toward baby Abby.

Sounding nervous, Jamie murmured, "Uh, Cassie."

The tip of a tentacle brushed within inches of the baby's head. "We made no promise to the baby," the queen said. "We will keep it. Munaqsri and newborn both."

Cassie held her baby tight but didn't move. "I know why you kept my mother, why you bargained with my husband, why you want my baby. You want them to help you be alive, like you were supposed to be."

Trolls whispered like leaves.

"I'm right, aren't I," she said. "You want to be alive."

"Yes," the queen hissed.

Cassie smiled down at her baby. Her red hair brushed the baby's tiny hands. Baby Abby gurgled. "Her soul was the troll princess."

All color drained from the queen.

The trolls erupted.

Jamie ducked as the trolls whipped in a frenzied tornado around them. Cassie planted her feet on the ground, baby in her arms, and waited.

The queen shrieked, "Make us live!"

Startled, Abby cried. "Shh," Cassie said as she rocked the baby. "Don't shout," she said to the queen.

"Please," the queen whispered.

She took a deep breath. "Promise to release Bear."

"Promised!"

Her knees wobbled. She'd done it! But she wasn't finished yet. Cassie glanced at Jamie, who was on the floor with his arms over his head. "And promise to take no more prisoners."

The queen soared up to the ceiling. "Promised!"

Cassie's heart soared. Done, and done! She felt as if a bell had sounded deep within her, thrumming through her rib cage and over her skin. She'd done it. Mom was safe now. No more nightmares. Cassie felt giddy. "Anything else?" She asked Jamie.

"It would be nice if they would stop dive-bombing me." He batted away trolls as he stood.

Cassie laughed. "You take twenty-five thousand souls, in place of the polar bears. Go on. Take them."

Jamie obeyed, and the trolls who surrounded him now leaped onto him. They compressed like wisps of cotton in his arms. Thousands swarmed him, but the mass didn't thin. She wondered how many trolls there were. She may have found herself a lifetime task, she thought.

"And the remainder of us?" the queen asked, watching.

She thought of Fluffy the arctic fox and the mermaid Sedna. They'd helped, even if not quite in the way they'd meant to. "I owe a few favors. I'll find you homes." She smiled. What a way to save the whales. "I promise."

"Done and promised!" the queen sang.

And then Bear walked out of the chaos of swirling trolls,

and Cassie stepped forward. Bear paced toward her, and the mist of a thousand trolls melted around him. He halted in front of her, and his black eyes drank her in. The trolls whipped in iridescent spirals over their heads.

For a long moment, Cassie and Bear simply stared at each other. She felt as if every cell in her body were singing, as if she were going to burst out of her skin.

He touched the tiny head of their baby with his nose. "She is beautiful," he said.

All Cassie could do was nod.

Eyes shining, he looked at Cassie. "My Cassie, my *tuvaaqan.*"

Trolls whirled around them, thickening into a wind. "I told you I would find you," she said. "I said I'd free you."

"I will never doubt you again," he said. He leaned his cheek against hers, and she closed her eyes and felt the warm fur soft on her face. "Shall we go home, beloved?" he asked.

She smiled. "Yes," she said.

Cassie then looked at the queen, who signaled to the trolls. Swirling faster, the trolls rushed beneath Cassie and Bear and lifted them into the air. Below, Jamie waved as the castle melted around them. Gray clouds swept alongside them as they skimmed over the black rocks of the island and above the waves of the sea.

With her new daughter in her arms, Cassie curled against Bear. Gently, he wrapped his front paws around her and baby Abby.

Together, carried by lost souls, they flew home.